BUZZ AROUND THE TRACK

They Said It

"What does Brianna think she's doing, telling me how to handle my brothers? She just reminded me why I'd never want my wife involved in my team."
—Chad Matheson

"Chad hasn't budged on his views about mixing business and marriage. It would be dangerous for me to fantasize otherwise."
—Brianna Hudson

"Readers looking for gossip about the kidnapped Grosso baby, or about Brent Sanford's expulsion from NASCAR for allegedly sabotaging another competitor's race car, won't find it in my book."
—Tara Dalton

"If the Grossos are NASCAR royalty, then I'm the pretender to the throne. My team doesn't have their kind of money… but I want that championship."
—Garrett Clark

ROMANCE

ABBY GAINES

Like some of her favorite NASCAR drivers, Abby Gaines's first love was open-wheel dirt track racing. But the lure of NASCAR—the speed, the power, the awesome scale—proved irresistible, just as it did for those drivers. Now Abby is thrilled to be combining her love of NASCAR with her love of writing.

Checkered Past, Chad Matheson's story, is the second book Abby has written about the Matheson family, following *Back on Track.* Readers who've been asking for more of the Matheson brothers can also look forward to *The Comeback,* Zack Matheson's story, in November 2009.

When she's not writing romance novels for Harlequin's officially licensed NASCAR romance series and for Harlequin Superromance, Abby works as editor of a speedway magazine. She lives with her husband and three children just a short drive from her favorite dirt track.

Visit Abby at www.abbygaines.com, where you'll find an extra "After the End" scene for *Checkered Past,* or feel free to e-mail her, abby@abbygaines.com, and let her know if you enjoyed this story.

NASCAR

CHECKERED PAST

Abby Gaines

HARLEQUIN®

TORONTO • NEW YORK • LONDON
AMSTERDAM • PARIS • SYDNEY • HAMBURG
STOCKHOLM • ATHENS • TOKYO • MILAN • MADRID
PRAGUE • WARSAW • BUDAPEST • AUCKLAND

Recycling programs for this product may not exist in your area.

ISBN-13: 978-0-373-18521-4
ISBN-10:   0-373-18521-9

CHECKERED PAST

Copyright © 2009 by Harlequin Books S.A.

Abby Gaines is acknowledged as the author of this work.

NASCAR® and the NASCAR Library Collection® are registered trademarks of the National Association for Stock Car Auto Racing, Inc.

www.eHarlequin.com

Printed in U.S.A.

Acknowledgment

With love to Karina Bliss, who's been with me
from Day One of this wild writing adventure.
Thanks for the inspiration and the friendship.

NASCAR HIDDEN LEGACIES

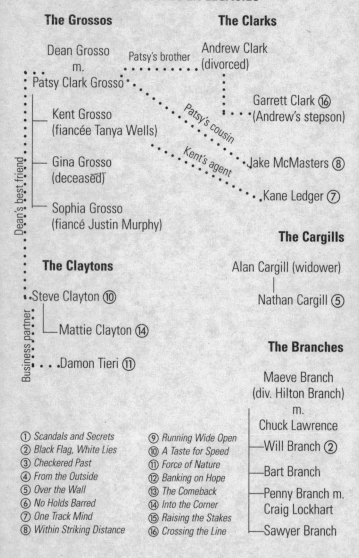

The Grossos

Dean Grosso
m.
Patsy Clark Grosso

— Kent Grosso
(fiancée Tanya Wells)

— Gina Grosso
(deceased)

— Sophia Grosso
(fiancé Justin Murphy)

Patsy's brother

Dean's best friend

Patsy's cousin

Kent's agent

The Clarks

Andrew Clark
(divorced)

Garrett Clark ⑯
(Andrew's stepson)

Jake McMasters ⑧

Kane Ledger ⑦

The Claytons

Steve Clayton ⑩

— Mattie Clayton ⑭

··· Damon Tieri ⑪

Business partner

The Cargills

Alan Cargill (widower)

Nathan Cargill ⑤

The Branches

Maeve Branch
(div. Hilton Branch)
m.
Chuck Lawrence

— Will Branch ②

— Bart Branch

— Penny Branch m.
Craig Lockhart

— Sawyer Branch

① *Scandals and Secrets*
② *Black Flag, White Lies*
③ *Checkered Past*
④ *From the Outside*
⑤ *Over the Wall*
⑥ *No Holds Barred*
⑦ *One Track Mind*
⑧ *Within Striking Distance*
⑨ *Running Wide Open*
⑩ *A Taste for Speed*
⑪ *Force of Nature*
⑫ *Banking on Hope*
⑬ *The Comeback*
⑭ *Into the Corner*
⑮ *Raising the Stakes*
⑯ *Crossing the Line*

THE FAMILIES AND THE CONNECTIONS

The Sanfords

Bobby Sanford
(deceased)
m.
Kath Sanford

— Adam Sanford ①

— Brent Sanford ⑫

— Trey Sanford ⑨

The Hunts

Dan Hunt
m.
Linda (Willard) Hunt
(deceased)

— Ethan Hunt ⑥

— Jared Hunt ⑮

— Hope Hunt ⑫

— Grace Hunt Winters ⑯
(widow of Todd Winters)

The Mathesons

Brady Matheson
(widower)
(fiancée Julie-Anne Blake)

— Chad Matheson ③

— Zack Matheson ⑬

— Trent Matheson
(fiancée Kelly Greenwood)

The Daltons

Buddy Dalton
m.
Shirley Dalton

— Mallory Dalton ④

— Tara Dalton ①

— Emma-Lea Dalton

CHAPTER ONE

March, nearly two years ago

CHAD MATHESON leaned back against the overstuffed pillows of the honeymoon suite's super-king-size bed. Mentally, he listed everything he knew about his bride.

Her name: Brianna Hudson. *Good start.* Except now, he supposed, she was Brianna Matheson. *Hell.*

Chad swallowed a mouthful of the coffee Brianna had poured him from the room-service trolley on her way to the bathroom. He'd pretended he was still asleep when she set the cup on the nightstand. He needed to think.

The shower had stopped a few minutes ago, and now he kept one ear on the sound of the hair dryer running behind the closed door.

He knew her date of birth, courtesy of their marriage license— and that had come as a surprise, because she looked older than twenty-three.

He knew she was from Atlanta; her Georgia accent, soft and smooth amid the late-night ruckus of NASCAR fans celebrating at the Vegas Getaway Hotel's casino, had attracted him the moment they'd met.

That moment had been three days—Chad glanced at the chunky steel watch on his wrist—eleven hours and twenty-six minutes ago.

What the hell had he done?

He didn't have a good track record in relationships, didn't run them as well as he ran a NASCAR team—and he'd just committed himself to the ultimate relationship challenge.

He took another slug of coffee. Next time his little brother won a NASCAR Sprint Cup Series race and started throwing around phrases like "Who dares wins" and "You never get what you want if you won't take a risk," Chad would turn around and walk away.

Concentrate—she'll be out any moment. He closed his eyes, pinched the bridge of his nose. Okay, he knew Brianna was smart and cute, and she had a way of catching him up in the moment, making him forget about the stress of running a race team. That was a good thing. Wasn't it?

He knew she was kind—when they'd found a puppy wandering at the outskirts of town yesterday, she'd delayed their trip into the desert until they got hold of the owner and returned the dog. He knew that when she drank a milk shake—her favorite beverage—she made loud, unashamed slurping sounds as she chased the last of the shake around the glass with her straw.

Irrelevant, the logical side of his brain chided. *The facts, just the facts.* Okay, he knew Brianna didn't work in NASCAR. She had a degree in hotel management. She was an only child, her parents had divorced when she was twelve, and her mom had remarried, to an Australian cattle baron. Brianna had been working in Spain the past year and was about to take a job at a hotel in Miami. At least, she was before Chad derailed her plans with his marriage proposal.

He thought some more. Then drew a blank. Nope, there weren't any other facts he knew about his wife.

Sudden silence told him Brianna had finished drying her hair. Soon she would emerge from the bathroom and join him for breakfast. Just as she would every day for the rest of their lives. For one second Chad couldn't remember what she looked like. His mind raced, flipping through mental snapshots of the past few days, trying to pin down her image. He broke out in a sweat. His family would think he was a certifiable lunatic, and dammit, they'd be right. He shoved aside the duvet, grabbed last night's polo shirt and pants—the clothes he'd got married in—and scrambled into them.

"Hey, there." Brianna stood in front of him, smiling shyly, chestnut hair catching the spring sunlight that filtered through the gauze curtains. She wore snug-fitting jeans and a lilac wrap sweater that emphasized her curves.

Any formal, first-day-of-married-life greeting Chad might have planned drifted away as his gaze absorbed the indent of her waist, the flare of her hips, her long legs. "Uh, hey, yourself."

She laughed at his dazed tone. Her laugh was one of the things he loved about her. It started off low, then ended a couple of notes higher, as if her delight grew by the moment.

Relief flooded him, even as his body tightened at the thought of last night. He loved her, so he'd married her.

So what if until now, his life had been all planning and calculated strategy?

"You look great." He moved toward her and took her in his arms. Man, this felt so right, the top of her head perfect for him to rest his chin on, her curves fitted against him as snug as a spark plug in a cylinder head. He inhaled the smell of her—clean, minty, flowery, like springtime—and pulled her harder against him.

"Wow," she said, "you really are insatiable." Her hands crept around to his butt.

"For you," he said. "Only for you." He drew back so he could read her face. "Are you okay?"

"I feel fantastic." No doubt, no hesitation. Brianna went up on tiptoe and planted a kiss on his mouth, bold and hungry.

Chad grinned as he responded. Last night he'd become her first lover. They'd spent the day out in the desert, the wide-open, empty spaces curiously intimate, making them feel as if they were the only two people on earth. The kisses they'd shared had kindled a heat that could only be assuaged in one way. When they'd stopped for a drink in the hotel lobby bar on their return, Chad had invited Brianna to his hotel room.

She'd said yes.

Then she'd told him she was a virgin.

"I always thought I'd wait until I got married," she said. "I know nobody does that these days, but sometimes it's hard to trust a guy when he says…things."

Chad was honored she'd chosen to abandon her caution with him, but he hadn't been about to pressure her. "We don't have to do this now," he assured her, though the thought killed him. "We can go out to dinner, maybe do some dancing…"

She pressed a finger to his lips. "I want to. It's crazy, since we've only known each other a few days, but…Chad, I love you."

Everything had come together in Chad's mind, like that moment you find the perfect groove on a race track and know you're going to win. *That* was the feeling that consumed him when he was with Brianna, kept her at the front of his thoughts when he wasn't.

Love.

"I love you, too," he'd said slowly, savoring the words.

Which called for another kiss. When it ended, Brianna nodded toward the elevators. "So now we can go upstairs?"

"No way." He'd grabbed her by the wrist, tugged her off her bar stool. "You wanted to wait until you're married, and that's exactly what you're going to be."

When she didn't move, just clutched the edges of her bar stool as if she was as dizzy as he felt, he said, "I love you, Brianna. I've never said that to another woman. I want to marry you." He laughed at the sensation that swirled through him. "I've never said that to a woman, either. Sweetheart, say you'll marry me."

Filled with heady optimism, along with a couple glasses of champagne—not enough, unfortunately, to blame for their impulsiveness—they'd headed out to the marriage-license bureau on Clark Avenue. From there, they'd gone around the corner to the Two Hearts Chapel. They'd had to wait for two other couples ahead of them, but neither of them changed their mind. Forty-five minutes later, they'd exchanged their vows.

Maybe their lovemaking had been so fantastic because it had

the legitimacy of marriage…or maybe, Chad thought, it was because he really did love Brianna, and the panic he'd felt on waking was because he'd forgotten that for just a moment.

"I DON'T KNOW about you, but I'm starving," Brianna said.

Chad—*my husband!*—pulled out a chair for her. When he smiled down at her, her heart kicked in her chest.

He's as wonderful as I remembered.

She'd delayed coming out of the bathroom, overwhelmed by the enormity of having married a man she hardly knew. She'd always been impulsive—her father never stopped lamenting the fact—but this…nothing compared to this.

Dad would be furious. For an instant, doubt flickered in Brianna's heart. Her father would demand to see the prenuptial agreement. She could imagine his reaction when she told him they didn't need one. *I hope.* She was as certain as she could be that Chad didn't know who her father was.

She peeked at him from beneath lowered lids as he served her breakfast from the oversized trolley. He dished up far too much…or did he have activities in mind for which she'd need to recoup her strength? In which case… She accepted the laden plate. "Thanks."

She smirked when he piled his own plate twice as high.

As Chad ground pepper over his eggs and bacon, he said, "You realize we went a little crazy last night."

The doubt flickered again. "The good kind of crazy," Brianna replied.

Was there a moment's hesitation before he nodded? "I'll be lucky if your dad doesn't take a shotgun to me."

"Uh, Chad, there's something I should have told you."

"I already figured you can't cook." His blue eyes teased her, calmed her anxiety.

She feigned outrage. "For all you know, I'm a Cordon Bleu chef."

"You gave that one away last night when I filled out the room-service order."

She remembered saying something about boiled eggs being the limit of her culinary capabilities. "Cooking's not everything." She took a mouthful of scrambled eggs. "Mmm, yep, best left to the professionals."

"Absolutely," he agreed. "Housekeeping isn't everything, either."

"What makes you think…?" She stopped, aware of her clothes and belongings strewn around the room, while Chad's were neatly folded on top of his suitcase. Who was she trying to kid? Besides, she could afford a cook and a housekeeper.

He quirked an eyebrow. "Any other dark secrets?"

"Just one." She drew a deep breath and exhaled a rush of words. "My family is pretty rich."

He didn't look surprised.

"Really rich."

He shrugged. "I noticed the fancy labels on your clothes last night…"

She blushed. "One of the reasons I never slept with anyone before was because I never knew if a guy liked me for myself or because of who my father is."

Now he looked interested. "You do mean seriously rich."

"My father is Brian Hudson." She buttered her toast and waited for the other shoe to drop.

"Brian—the hotel guy?"

She laughed. No one had ever called her father "the hotel guy" before. At least, not to her. "That's him—majority owner and driving force of Getaway Resorts. I'm named after him." Her father's desire that she be just like him had shadowed her from the moment of her birth.

"Your *father* owns this place?" With a sweep of his hand, Chad indicated their room.

She nodded. "That's why I ducked into the bathroom while you checked us into this suite. I don't know any of the staff here, but there's always a chance someone might recognize me."

"You should have told me." He frowned, and she guessed he was remembering how she'd given the briefest of answers to his questions about her family. Before she'd suggested they get to know each other without "all that baggage."

She put down her knife. "Men are often more interested in my dad's money than they are in me—" his snort was gratifying and she smiled "—which is why I didn't say anything at first. Later, I didn't think about it. All I could think about was you."

"Huh," was all he said. But she caught the gleam of satisfaction in his eyes.

"I'm sorry I kept it a secret, but this doesn't change anything?" Her statement came out a question.

Chad ran a hand around his jaw. She remembered the rough prickle of the new day's beard against her skin in the small hours of the morning.

"It complicates matters." He leaned back, folded his arms across his powerful chest. "I understand why you didn't say anything, because I did exactly the same."

Now *that* she didn't expect. Apprehension quivered in her stomach as she recalled how readily he'd agreed—too readily?—to her suggestion that they leave the family baggage out of their conversation. She said with forced lightness, "Is your dad rich, too?"

"Not as rich as yours. But my family spends more time in the public eye."

Matheson. Brianna played the name in her mind, tried to associate it with anyone she'd heard of. "I can't think…"

"I told you I hope to take over my father's engineering business, and that's true." Chad paused. "His business is Matheson Performance Industries."

She looked blankly at him.

"Dad and I are joint owners of Matheson Racing," Chad said.

"Oh. Right." Matheson…did they own last year's Kentucky Derby winner?

"The NASCAR team." His voice showed a hint of impatience.

Brianna knew a little about NASCAR: stock cars, hugely popular, races all over the country. You couldn't grow up in the

South without learning at least that much about the sport that consumed the lives of so many people. But though her father watched the occasional race on TV, she'd never seen it. "You own a NASCAR team?" She digested the news. "I guess that makes you a big guy?"

He waggled his eyebrows; warmth curled through her. She relaxed into a chuckle. "I meant a big guy in NASCAR."

"Our team is one of the best." Pride, not arrogance, colored the words. "My younger brother Trent is a previous NASCAR Nationwide Series champion. He won the NASCAR Sprint Cup Series race here on Sunday."

Sunday. Right before they'd met. No wonder Chad had been so expansive that night.

She'd been standing outside the hotel's piano bar, taking a break from the bachelorette party she'd flown into Las Vegas to attend. She'd come all the way from Spain, where her job on the Costa del Sol had recently finished. During the party, her father had phoned. Not so much for a chat as to harangue her.

Chad had seen her glum expression, the sag of her shoulders as she ended the call, and asked if she was okay. When he suggested they have a drink, she couldn't resist the pull of his apparent concern for her. They'd talked…and talked. Brianna hadn't censored herself; she'd shared all her thoughts and feelings. He'd been just as open, which was why the chemistry between them had been so powerful.

Brianna couldn't wait to spend her life with a man who didn't push her away.

But now, she admitted reluctantly, they had to unpack the family baggage. Feeling her way, she said, "A NASCAR team sounds like a big commitment."

"Huge," Chad agreed. "It's not just the cars and the races—it's a significant business in its own right, and every year it grows a new dimension. These days, to run a NASCAR team, you have to be part investment banker, part technician, part strategist and a whole lot of marketing expert." He topped up her coffee, then his. "I'm good on the numbers and the strategy, and Dad's the greatest technician I know. Neither of us is too hot on the marketing."

In the world he described, it didn't sound as if he had much free time. Brianna ventured warily, "You said, when you asked me to marry you, we could go anywhere, do anything. Did you mean that?"

CHAD SHIFTED in his seat. "I meant..." What *had* he meant? Anywhere in North Carolina? It didn't sound like a generous offer. "I meant, we get to travel a lot."

When they'd met, Brianna had been excited about the change of scene her new job in Miami offered. Knowing she would be living several states away had been a factor in his hasty marriage proposal.

"To be honest—" he wished he *had* been more honest, less carried away by his emotions "—I'm pretty much tied to the team during the NASCAR season. But we can vacation anywhere you like." Anywhere with cell phone coverage.

"So, we'll live in Charlotte?" she said.

"I have a place out at Mountain Island Lake. That's about fifteen, twenty minutes from uptown." It was quiet out there, and Brianna was apparently used to cosmopolitan living.

Her chestnut hair swung forward as she busied herself spreading jelly on her sourdough toast. "I guess I have a lot to learn about NASCAR."

"Once you start coming to races, you'll pick it up in no time." Chad was back on familiar ground, and his confidence rose. "Hopefully you'll love it."

She grinned that wide, delighted smile he'd fallen in love with. "I will, I know it. So, is the rest of your family involved in the team? You said you had two brothers. One of them is...Trent, right?"

"Uh-huh. Zack, who's between me and Trent, used to race for the team. He quit a couple of years back—he has a stake in a race-track-simulation software company in Atlanta."

"Did you used to race, too?" she asked.

He downed half his orange juice. "I drove in the NASCAR Camping World Truck Series for a couple of years. I won a few races—not enough."

"I'll bet you were great," she said loyally.

Chad's heart lifted. "I was good, not great," he corrected her. "There's often a moment in a race that your gut tells you is the moment where you'll win or lose. Great drivers throw everything they have into that moment. No hesitation, even if it looks—" he shook his head "—insane. I'm not that kind of guy."

"And Trent is?"

"Oh, yeah." Chad laughed, remembering the many occasions when Trent had just about given him a heart attack with his full-throttle, no-holds-barred ducking and diving on the track. "That's Trent, through and through. He's brilliant. He just needs to get a bit more responsible so he has more control over his results."

"I can't wait to meet him and Zack," she said. "And your dad."

Chad could definitely wait to make that particular introduction. "Do you think you'll get a job at the Getaway in Charlotte?"

Brianna shook her head. "I can't work for Getaway." The finality in her voice raised a question. Before he could ask it, she stuck a finger in the air, as if she'd had a lightbulb moment. "But you know what? I have those marketing skills you and your father are missing. Maybe I can join you in running the team."

Chad froze, then consciously relaxed. He tried to sound regretful as he said, "You don't have the knowledge of the sport."

She waved her piece of toast at him, dismissing his argument. "Like you said, I'll get the hang of it fast. And you can give me after-hours tutoring." Her saucy smile told him some of that tutoring would take place in bed, and even while his brain warned him to close down this line of conversation, his body was tempted.

"Seriously, Chad, I'm good at what I do—sponsorship, media relations, corporate communications, image-building. You need all that, right? It would be so cool to work together."

Cool. The word reminded Chad she was eleven years younger than his thirty-four. Which made her idealistic, romantic. Appealing qualities—lovable qualities—but there was no place for them when it came to running a NASCAR team.

"I'm not a big fan of mixing business and marriage," he said. "Too much scope for disagreement." He knew that firsthand.

Her smile faltered. "Surely we can weather a few disagreements."

"Why ask for trouble?"

As she pushed her plate away, her fork clattered onto the table, then fell to the floor. Chad leaned down to pick it up; he wiped at the grease mark on the carpet with a napkin. Giving her time to forget the idea.

"Maybe I could start working with you," Brianna said when he sat up again, "then quit if you're not happy with how it's going."

Dammit, this was their honeymoon, not a job interview. "I don't want my wife working with me," he said. Even *he* could hear that sounded harsh; Brianna's expression turned tense. He reached across the table for her hand. With his thumb, he traced the narrow gold band on her ring finger. He'd bought it at the wedding chapel; he wasn't even sure it was real gold. He'd buy her a much better ring when they got home.

"Sweetheart," he said, "this isn't about you, it's about the nature of running a team. I get so busy, I wouldn't have time to enjoy your being there. I'd probably snap at you." His fingers brushed her wrist, circled her pulse. "I'd rather you worked somewhere else, and I could look forward to cozy evenings with you at the end of each day."

Her expression softened. "I like the sound of the cozy evenings."

"Me, too. On race weekends we'll have those evenings in my motor home at the track," he said.

"Cool!" She entwined her fingers with his. "Chad, it doesn't matter where we are, as long as we're together."

"You're right." He paused. "Though I should warn you, I work long hours during the season."

"Oh?" she said cautiously.

"But the minute I walk in the door, I'm all yours," he promised. "No shoptalk."

"But if NASCAR's such a big part of your family's life, I'll want to hear about it," she objected.

"Obviously there'll be *some* NASCAR talk," he improvised. "But I won't bore you with all the petty frustrations and problems."

"But, sweetheart—" her smile turned perplexed "—that's what I'm there for. You and I are a team."

"I already have a team," he joked. "You and I are a marriage."

She flinched. What the heck was that about? Chad felt as if he was standing in the middle of a race track, dodging cars.

"Brianna, that doesn't mean I don't want to hear all *your* frustrations and problems," he said. "It's just that I get enough of mine during the day."

"You don't think I can help you deal with them?" Brianna asked. Her voice sounded damp.

This was exactly what he hated about mixing business with his personal life: the constant danger of causing offense through some innocuous comment. "Of course I don't think that. I'm sure you're great at…dealing with stuff. But I'm good at it, too, so, you know, I don't really need…" He trailed off.

Brianna was rubbing her cheeks with the palms of her hands, as if anticipating that they would soon be wet. Chad felt in his pocket for his handkerchief.

"I think of marriage as being an equal partnership," she said.

"Me, too." He hadn't thought about it before, but it made sense. "We'll have a great partnership," he promised. "We'll be partners at home, in bed…" His voice dropped at the thought of making love with her.

"But I won't be part of your work."

"Exactly." He grinned, relieved. "And when you're ready, we'll have kids, and we'll be partners looking after them."

"I do want kids," she said, and it occurred to Chad that this was a conversation they should have had before they got married.

Luckily they felt the same way. "But I'd like to have you to myself a few years first."

"Ditto." He lifted her fingers to his lips, kissed her knuckles. "I'm not looking forward to spending weekends apart from you. I want you coming to the races as long as possible."

Brianna frowned. Uh-oh, had he just stuck a spade back in that hole he'd managed to fill in?

"Can't our children come to the races?" she asked.

It was such a wildly hypothetical question on the first day of their marriage…they might not even have kids…*we might not even stay married*…. He closed down that line of thought. "Some people do take their kids," he admitted. "I've always thought it seems pretty disruptive."

She pulled her hand back. "But if the kids and I don't mind that, we can come, right? Even if we need a bigger motor home."

Chad's motor home was the biggest you could buy. "We'll talk about that when it happens," he said. Firmly.

"We'll talk about it, or you'll decide?" Definite annoyance in her voice now. Her chin went up in the air, challenging him.

He decided it was a rhetorical question.

When he didn't say anything, her eyes widened. Her mouth formed a slow O of shock.

"What do you want to get out of this marriage?" she asked.

Brianna spoke so hesitantly, Chad didn't hear the first word of her question. He thought she'd asked, *Do you want to get out of this marriage?* His instinctive, internal response was a horrified *No.* Then *Yes.*

"Of course I don't want to get out of it." But still grappling with his conflicting reactions, he didn't sound convincing. Then he realized, from her horrified gasp, what she'd really said—and that she'd seen the uncertainty, the betrayal, in his face.

His stomach lurched. *Do something! Fix this!* He might know squat about marriage, but he knew how to fix things.

"We don't know each other very well. It'll take time to settle into life together, maybe a long time." He was babbling, hardly aware of what he said. "Brianna…sweetheart, I've always thought of marriage as a kind of haven from the rest of my life."

She opened her mouth, but he hurried on. "A partnership, like you said—absolutely. But also…separate. It's not easy running Matheson Racing, and it's taken a long time to get the place operating smoothly. Marriage and family—" he glanced down at his enormous breakfast and realized he'd lost his appetite "—with their high emotional component—"

"Their *what?*" she said, incredulous.

Chad realized that the glitter in her brown eyes was anger, not tears. "Bad choice of words," he said hastily. He drew a long breath. Dammit, he was trying to explain something serious, and she was pulling him up for being *unromantic.* "Marriage and family are complicated. Mixing you—*us*—with the running of the team will make everything harder."

"But you already have family involved in the team—your brother, your dad."

"Believe me, that's more than enough." He shoved a hand through his hair. "Between them, they can be impossible. Often as not, I'm struggling to keep it together."

"And you think having me around will make it harder to keep it together, not easier."

He wasn't stupid enough to answer that.

"Let me tell you what I want out of this marriage," she said. Her face was somber; she sounded older than she had a few minutes ago. "I want a partnership that will last through thick and thin."

"So do I," he said promptly.

"A true partnership, where you and I are an integral part of every aspect of each other's lives, for better or for worse. Where we make decisions together, and when we mess up, our love for each other doesn't suffer. Where we share our thoughts, our hopes, our disappointments. All in, nothing held back. That's a healthy marriage."

She sounded as if she wanted to fuse herself to him. Chad stared at her, his mind scrambling to find the words that would say enough, but not promise something he couldn't deliver.

Brianna swiped at her lips with her napkin and stood up. She moved to stand behind her chair, putting it between them. "Is that what you're offering, Chad?" Her voice wobbled, and he had the sense of something precious slipping from his grasp, about to shatter…yet he couldn't will himself to grab hold of it.

"Not in those words," he said cautiously. "Brianna, can't we find a compromise?" Though he was pretty sure he didn't have much room to move within her ideal-marriage picture. Which meant she'd be doing most of the compromising.

But, heck, one of them had to budge. He got up, walked over to her; she took a step backward.

"When we met, you were so *into* me, so intense," she said. "What you're saying now seems so different."

"I didn't lie to you," he said. "We're on vacation, the whole getting-to-know-each-other was on fast-forward. Of course it was intense. Then, neither of us admitted the full truth about our families. There were bound to be some bumps when we hit the real world."

She nodded, acknowledging his point. But she gripped the back of her chair so hard, her knuckles whitened. "Chad, I can't compromise on what I see as the fundamental building block for a marriage. I want a close, loving relationship with a man who needs me as much as I need him."

"I need you." Then, truthfully, "Hell, Brianna, I don't even know what you're talking about."

She gave a half sob, half laugh. "I'm starting to realize that."

He reached out, ran his thumb across the satin skin of her cheek. "I want to tell you I'll do whatever it is you want…but I'm not sure I can." He'd never felt so helpless in his life.

"And you're not sure you want to," she suggested.

A denial sprang to his lips, then fell away. Truth was, he didn't like the sound of what she was asking, didn't think it should be necessary for them to have a good marriage. He swallowed—his throat was so parched it was like being out there in the desert under a scorching sun.

"I think," she said, "we might have made a mistake." She clapped both hands to her mouth as if she could push the words back in.

Too late.

Chad had thought the same thing a hundred times in the past half hour. Yet hearing it from her now, he felt as if all the oxygen in the room had disappeared.

Then came a sense of relief, like the valve being opened on an overinflated tire.

He heard himself say, "What are you suggesting? You want a divorce?"

She gulped. "I…yes…if you think so."

What the hell did that mean? Yes or no? Of course he didn't want a divorce, they'd only just got married. But she might want one—he'd rushed her into this, worried he might lose her. Sure, she'd told him she was impulsive…but he should have known better. She was so much younger, but he hadn't even considered that her expectations might differ from his.

It was clear from the conversation they'd just had that she would be miserable married to him.

If she wanted out, did he have any right to stop her? Did he *want* to stop her?

"If we decide that's the best course of action—" he sounded more like her lawyer than her husband "—I can take care of the process." Oh, yeah, now he was willing to step up to the plate. Still, he'd started this mess by proposing, so it was only fitting that he should clean it up.

He tried to gauge what Brianna was thinking. Her lips were pressed together, but she wasn't crying. He supposed it wasn't possible to be *heartbroken* over someone you'd known just a few days. He rubbed at the ache in his chest. Hell, he hoped it wasn't.

"I, uh, I guess this kind of thing happens a lot in Vegas," he said, the words stilted. "Mistakes. People making them."

She didn't reply.

He ran a hand around the back of his neck. "If we split up now, you'll go to Florida?" He slapped away the urge to tell her they could work this out. He'd never been one for self-delusion.

She nodded. "And you'll be back with Matheson Racing." Her voice was high and distant, as if she was holding her breath.

"Yeah." He looked at her, held her gaze. *Stay. It's not too late.* But that was the crazy part of him talking, the one that had started this. It wasn't the real him. "I can apply for a divorce in North Carolina."

Brianna looked away. "It'll be as if this never happened."

CHAPTER TWO

New Year's Day, twenty-two months later

BRIANNA'S FATHER'S house was a glowing testament to Brian Hudson's indomitable will to succeed and to the lofty standards he set himself and others.

As Brianna swung her Mustang into the parking bay adjacent to the marble front steps, illuminated by impressive outdoor lighting, she couldn't help but acknowledge what her dad had achieved.

He'd parlayed his own father's legacy of a half-dozen three-star hotels into a nationwide chain of five-star hotels and resorts. Before she was born, he'd torn down the family home in Buckhead, Atlanta's wealthiest suburb, and replaced it with this ten-thousand-square-foot neo-Georgian mansion.

After Brianna's mom left, he and Brianna had rattled around the place, disappointing each other, until she went away to college.

She climbed out of the car. She shivered, not at the sharp needles of sleet that hit her face, but because this was the nearest she'd been to Charlotte—where Chad lived his well-ordered life without her—since Vegas.

He was 240 miles away; if she got back in her car now, she could—

Margaret, her father's housekeeper, opened the front door. "Happy New Year!" she called.

Brianna's New Year's resolution, made at a friend's party in the small hours of this morning, had been to stop thinking about Chad.

It had taken a long time, after Las Vegas—even in the privacy of her own thoughts she avoided using the phrase *since the wedding*—to piece together her shattered heart. Then anger had flooded it, testing its newly healed cracks to the limit. Anger with herself for marrying Chad on the false assumption that he loved her, valued her, just as she was. Anger with Chad for his refusal to share his life with her in a meaningful way.

He'd phoned her a few days after she left Las Vegas to see how she was doing. He'd sounded so aloof that Brianna had ended the call as fast as she could. Maybe that was a mistake. Because now, she had days when she wanted to jump on the next plane and tell him…what? That she was over him, that leaving was the smartest decision she'd ever made? Or that she missed him, that she couldn't forget him.

She preferred the days when all she felt at the thought of Chad was numbness, when she could almost ignore the nagging sense that they'd left things unfinished. On those days, she never wanted to see him again—the spirit in which she'd forged her New Year's resolution.

Which she'd just broken. *Pathetic,* she scolded herself as she climbed the steps to the porch. She hugged Margaret. "Happy New Year to you, too."

"Your father's in his office," the older woman said. "Go on through—I'll bring you a shake. Strawberry?"

"Better make it tea," Brianna said with regret. Her father considered milk shakes childish. She remembered Chad teasing her about her fondness for them, but in a nice way. Once, she'd offered to share her shake with him, and they'd made it a race to finish, seeing who could slurp the loudest. Chad had managed an impressive volume, but Brianna was the expert.

As she walked down the wide hallway, she straightened her slim, chocolate-brown wool skirt, the waistband of which had become twisted during the ten-hour drive from Miami. Although the central heating kept the house warm, she buttoned her suit jacket.

She didn't normally dress this conservatively…but she would have no chance of making peace with her father once he started criticizing her appearance, along with goodness knew what else.

He might have mellowed since the news. Outside the study she tucked her hair behind her ears, then rapped once, sharply, on the paneled oak door before she turned the handle.

Her father looked up as she entered. His face broke into one of his rare smiles, filling her with hope.

"Dad, it's great to see you." She moved swiftly across the room to hug and kiss him as he rose from his seat.

He returned the embrace with his usual perfunctory peck on the cheek, then ran an assessing gaze over her. "You look good, Brianna." A hint of surprise in his voice.

She'd passed the first test. Brianna felt her smile widen. For once in her life, she was going to play everything her father's way.

She sat down in the wing chair Brian indicated. He sank back into his leather swivel chair a little more heavily than usual.

"I didn't expect you until well after New Year's," he said. In the past, she'd been reluctant to respond to his summonses. It usually took a couple of weeks to pull herself into a state that wouldn't attract his censure. "If I'd known all I had to do to get you to come home was get cancer, I'd have done it years ago." He laughed at his black humor.

"Dad…please." Just like that, she lost the battle to be as strong as he was, the only kind of strength he would respect. She laced her fingers in her lap so she wouldn't fidget. "I'm worried about you."

He frowned. "If you're here because you think I don't have much time left, you shouldn't have bothered. Plenty of life in me yet."

Three months, max, according to the doctor, to whom Brian had grudgingly given permission to talk to Brianna. The medic had insisted someone be informed, in case Brian became too ill to make decisions on his treatment.

"You look well," Brianna admitted.

That made her father smile, but it faded as he ran a hand over his hair. "I won't have this much longer. I start chemo next week."

She heard the pang of loss in his voice. Her dad's hair had turned silver a decade ago, but he'd always been proud of his thick locks.

"Whatever support you need, Dad, I'll give it. My contract in Miami is up, so I'm a free agent." She'd actually pulled out of the contract a month early so she could come here. But her father wouldn't approve of that.

"Why didn't they renew? Didn't that football sponsorship deliver the returns you predicted? I told you it was risky."

Brian couldn't help himself—nosing out failure came as naturally to him as breathing.

"If you must know, the sponsorship exceeded expectations." Brianna heard herself getting defensive and pulled back. "Peppers—" the hotel chain she worked for "—planned to renew my contract, but I wanted to be with you."

"Because you think I'm dying?" he said, appalled. "Even if I was, I wouldn't need someone holding my hand."

He didn't need anyone, least of all his daughter.

"It's taken me forty years to build this business to what it is today," he said. "Forty years of damned hard work that I'm not about to give up on because a bunch of medical tests say I'm sick. Whatever those doctors think, I'm not ready to go."

Typical of her father to believe his iron will could hold back disease. The doctor had been clear that the chemotherapy was palliative, to reduce the symptoms. Her father's pancreatic cancer was too far advanced to hope for a remission.

Margaret came in with the tea; Brian gave Brianna a nod that approved her choice of beverage.

When his longtime housekeeper left, he said, "I'd hoped you were coming back because you're ready to take an interest in the business that's made this family great." Brian was the majority shareholder, but several Hudson cousins also had a stake in the company, and family members held some of the top jobs.

"I am interested in it, Dad."

"Don't you think it's time you grew out of this childish rebellion?"

Brianna's refusal to work at Getaway wasn't so much a rebellion as avoidance. As a child, she found that her attempts to engage her dad had at best failed, at worst irritated him. When she left for college she'd decided that, rather than continue trying to connect with him, she'd keep contact to a minimum so she wouldn't jeopardize what little affection he had for her.

"I don't want us to argue," she said. Not when this was her last chance to make that connection.

"Good, because I have just the job for you."

"Dad, I didn't come for a job." Her father was the opposite of Chad; he liked to hire family. Unlike Chad, he wasn't fazed by the emotional ramifications—he simply ignored them.

"You came because you don't want any regrets when I die." Her father's shrewd mind missed nothing.

"Yes," she said.

He drew his chin back in surprise at her directness, but recovered quickly. "A couple of weeks ago, before the doctors got this bee in their bonnet, I kicked off a special project, something I wanted to handle myself. Now it seems the chemo might slow me down."

It *might.*

"The project can't wait," her father continued. "I want you working on it for the next few weeks."

Don't argue, she reminded herself. She could figure out a way to refuse politely. "What is it?"

"You remember last October I told you I wanted to sponsor a NASCAR team?"

As always, Brianna didn't like talking about NASCAR. Unfortunately her father's interest in the sport had grown over the past year from watching the occasional race to serious fandom, so the topic came up more often than she liked. "I remember."

"I've decided to go ahead," her father said. "It's in the budget for this year. All I need to do—all *you* need to do—is choose the right driver to spend the money on."

"I'm not a NASCAR expert," Brianna said hedging.

"You're a sponsorship expert, or so you claim, and you knew enough about NASCAR last time we talked." They'd spoken soon after the final race in last year's NASCAR Sprint Cup Series at Miami. Unlike her father, Brianna hadn't gone to the race, though she lived just a few miles from the track and had been offered corporate hospitality. She couldn't risk running into Chad. She'd watched it on TV and met up with her dad afterward.

Her father closed his eyes and let out a slow, careful breath that suggested he was in pain.

"Can I get you something?" Brianna half rose.

His eyes snapped open. "You can get me a NASCAR deal. I've made some initial contacts, I need you to assess the opportunity and report back with a recommendation on sponsorship."

Brianna gripped the arms of her chair as she sat back down. "Dad, you're sick. This can't be a priority."

"I'm having treatment, which I expect to be successful," he said. "The NASCAR season starts next month. I don't want to miss out because of a glitch in my health. I want this set up in time for the race at Daytona." He glanced at the calendar on his desk planner. "That gives you around six weeks."

He sounded so confident of his recovery, she could almost believe him. Brianna rubbed her eyes, the long drive from Miami catching up with her. If there was even the remotest chance that her father could beat the cancer, having the immediate goal of sponsoring a NASCAR driver might help him.

But what if there was no chance?

He wouldn't admit that, and he would fret about the lost opportunity, which couldn't be good for his health. She could spend six weeks on the project, then still have a few weeks with her father.

No, no, no. I don't want to get involved in NASCAR.

But this wasn't just about her. "What team are you looking at?" She held her breath.

"FastMax. Driver named Garrett Clark. He seems to be the next big thing."

She exhaled. If the work had to be done before the season started, she probably wouldn't even run into Chad. "What would the assessment involve?"

Her father talked through what he had in mind, and it sounded well within her capabilities. Which was important, because if she committed to the project, she couldn't risk failing.

"I'll expect progress reports," Brian said. "But day-to-day you'll have sole responsibility."

Despite herself, Brianna was flattered. Her father's previous offers of work would have put her under his close scrutiny or that of one of his trusted senior managers. This project offered a level of independence.

"What you've described won't take six weeks," she said. "Two, maybe three at the most."

"You forget," Brian said dryly, "I always do business using the contention system."

Her dad believed people tried harder if they had to fight for what they wanted. He'd never handed anyone anything, and he wasn't about to start with FastMax Racing.

"You need to evaluate an alternative team, too," her father said. "I like FastMax, but at this stage the field's wide open. Either of the prospective drivers could win our sponsorship."

"Is the other team Cargill Racing?" she guessed. Her father admired Cargill's new driver, Kent Grosso.

He shook his head regretfully. "Grosso's all sewn up. I want you to take a look at Zack Matheson."

Her heart stopped beating; the plaid pattern of the carpet blurred beneath her feet. "Matheson?"

Her dad frowned. "You know the team—it was you who got me interested in them." She remembered talking with her father about Matheson Racing last year, in an attempt to find some common ground. She'd had no idea it had worked. "I've been following their progress since then," Brian said. "You were right, Trent Matheson is a great driver. His brother Zack is back on the team this year—he's likely to be hot stuff, and he doesn't have a sponsor."

She knew that; she'd been following the team's fortunes ever since Las Vegas.

"Chad Matheson, the team owner, seems a competent man." High praise from her father. "The media call him the Boss. He's earned a lot of respect."

She knew that, too—but unlike her father, she didn't consider the nickname something to be admired.

It would be impossible for her to evaluate Matheson Racing!

"Dad, I'm honored to be asked—" she began.

"That's quitting talk," her father said sharply. "The next word out of your mouth will be *but*."

"*However…*" she said carefully.

He wasn't buying it; he slammed his hand down on his desk with a force that suggested he was fighting fit. "Don't give me *however*. If you believe those doctors, this will be the last thing I ever ask of you."

She shot out of her seat. "That's blackmail."

He waved her back down. "Do you have a good reason for refusing this project?"

Not one she could tell him.

"Zack Matheson is testing this weekend at Halesboro," he said. "I told them I'd go up there, but I canceled. You can go in my place." He tipped his head back against his chair, and regarded her through half-closed eyes. "Do this job for me, Brianna," he ordered. Then, "Please."

There were so many things wrong with the scheme she didn't know where to start. No matter what her disobedient instincts sometimes told her, she didn't want to see Chad. She didn't want to leave Atlanta while her dad was sick.

And she didn't want to mess with her successful strategy of

not exposing herself to her father's criticism. Things might not have got any better between them over the years, but at least they hadn't got worse.

But she was here to make a last-ditch effort to secure his love. And he'd asked for her help. Contrary to her earlier thoughts, he did need her, in his own way.

She swallowed to moisten her dry throat. "I'll do it."

Because in the big picture, her reluctance to confront Chad meant nothing.

Her father was dying, but her marriage was dead.

"YOU KNOW WHO she is, right?"

Chad's head snapped around at the question so fast he almost collided with the shelf that hung at eye level in the lounge of the No. 429 car's hauler. His youngest brother, Trent, continued autographing the stack of photos he'd brought with him to the track at Halesboro. He didn't *look* as if he suspected anything.

Chad glanced back at his computer screen, at the lap times Trent and Zack had recorded during this morning's testing. As soon as the lunch break was over, they'd head out of the hauler and both NASCAR Sprint Cup Series drivers would be put through their paces again. Chad forced unconcern into his voice. "You mean Brianna Hudson?"

Trent put down his pen, shook his wrist to loosen it up. "She's Brian Hudson's daughter."

Relief had Chad chuckling, though humor was the furthest thing from his mind. "With a name like that, who'd have guessed?"

Chad hadn't.

Trent rolled his eyes. "I'm saying, wise guy, that her dad can afford to sponsor ten NASCAR Sprint Cup cars. If we impress this woman, it could solve our sponsorship problems for life." He resumed autographing. "Though, really, I guess it's you who has to impress her."

Maybe Trent *was* toying with him, after all. "How do you figure that?" Chad asked.

Trent shrugged. "Zack's an unknown quantity—his track record is too out-of-date to tell a sponsor much. Brianna Hudson will have to buy into you as team owner and manager, into your confidence in Zack and your ability to manage his comeback." Trent grinned. "But, hey, no pressure."

When Brian Hudson had called a couple of weeks ago, Chad's first thought was that something had happened to Brianna. He'd clutched the phone convulsively to his ear—but of course Hudson wouldn't have called him about that. Then he'd wondered if the man had discovered what happened in Las Vegas and was calling to tear a strip off him. The news that Getaway Resorts might sponsor Zack had been both a relief and an anticlimax.

Chad had considered turning Hudson down on the grounds he was already in discussions with two other potential sponsors.

But that would be stupid, with the NASCAR Sprint Cup Series season looming and nothing signed with either of the other companies.

So he'd expunged Brianna from his mind—it was never easy—and given Brian's overture a guarded welcome. They'd agreed Hudson would come to Halesboro. A week ago, his secretary had canceled the visit without giving a reason.

Yesterday morning, she'd called to say Getaway Resorts' new NASCAR sponsorship manager, Brianna Hudson, would attend the practice.

Chad glanced at his watch for the thousandth time. She should be here by now. He didn't like to think of her driving in the bad weather that had hit Atlanta over New Year's.

"Maybe she's had an accident." The thought chilled him to the bone.

"Maybe she's one of those women who are always late," Trent said prosaically.

Chad realized he had no idea if that was the case. Maybe Brianna simply had cold feet. He hoped so. Hoped her feet were so cold she'd send someone else in her place.

Was it her idea to take on the job of evaluating Matheson

Racing? She'd told Chad she couldn't work for her dad, but he'd never got to the bottom of that.

Chad's gut told him she'd be as unhappy with this situation as he was. So there was only one way to handle it. Separate the business from the personal.

To do that, he'd have to stop remembering how she'd looked asleep in his arms.

He cursed, tried to focus on the numbers on his computer screen.

"Kelly showed me a photo of her in a magazine, at some society party in Miami," Trent said. "She's quite a looker."

"If you flirt with her, you'll be spitting teeth out the other side of your head," Chad said. He'd intended a mock threat, but the words came out with unexpected violence.

Trent held up a hand. "Whoa, I'm an engaged man. Why would I flirt with anyone, let alone a sponsor, when I have Kelly?"

Chad snorted. Trent might not flirt exactly, but engaged or not, he couldn't *not* charm women, any more than he could not breathe. Wasn't that one of the reasons Chad hadn't told Brianna who his brother was when they first met? He hadn't wanted her asking for an introduction to Trent, falling for Trent…

The same Trent who right now was looking at Chad speculatively.

Chad said, "We don't want—" he wasn't sure he could say her name without giving himself away "—the sponsor to think you're harassing her."

That was unfair and they both knew it.

"I get that you're stressed, bro," Trent said, "so I'll let that go."

"Thanks," Chad muttered. Maybe he should step outside and try Brianna's cell phone again—he'd left her a message earlier, but her phone had been switched off. He needed to tell her that no one in his family knew about their…previous acquaintance.

"Hello?" A voice—*her* voice—came from the doorway of the hauler.

Too late. Relief that she wasn't lying mangled at the side of the interstate and panic—he'd failed dismally to prepare himself for her arrival—surged through Chad. The saliva drained from his mouth; sweat broke out on his palms. He maneuvered out from the table's built-in seating, bumping his knee as he went.

Trent stood, too.

"Stay here," Chad barked.

His brother raised his eyebrows, but for once in his life, did as he was told.

Brushing his hands against his jeans, Chad moved out into the galley-style body of the hauler.

And saw his wife.

CHAPTER THREE

CHAD HAD THOUGHT he knew every detail of her face. But she was more beautiful than he remembered. He'd underestimated the sleek sheen of her chestnut hair, forgotten how her hair framed her face and heightened the delicacy of her features, the slimness of her neck. He'd sold short the tempting fullness of her lips.

The avoid-thinking-about-Brianna strategy he'd adopted the past two years meant he hadn't considered the possibility of her seeing other men. One look at her, and he was convinced she was here because she was getting married again and wanted that divorce. Dammit, he should have thought about it! Stupid! If he ever had to sell Matheson Racing, he could join North Carolina Zoo as an ostrich.

He tugged at his collar as he started forward; three steps narrowed the distance between them to nothing. He wanted to confront her about the guy she planned to marry, tell her she couldn't...

Get a grip. This is about the team, not about me.

"Brianna." Croaky—he sounded like a schoolboy whose voice was breaking. Chad cleared his throat, tried again. "Hi, I'm Chad Matheson."

With that, he told her how he planned to play this. He stuck out a hand, invited her cooperation.

"Pleased to meet you, Chad," she said slowly. She put her hand in his. The feel of her fingers...his memory hadn't lied about this, about the way her touch could reach to his core.

She glanced down, and he realized he'd forgotten to shake. He got it over with, reclaimed his hand, and with it his senses.

"Glad you could make it up here today," he said briskly. "The team is looking forward to meeting you."

"Me first." Trent spoke from behind him. Chad was thankful neither he nor Brianna had said anything incriminating.

Trent introduced himself and shook Brianna's hand. He made a real effort, Chad saw, to tone down his megawatt charm, but with limited success.

Chad said, "Trent, I need to brief Brianna on a couple of things. Why don't you go tell the team to start up, and we'll be out shortly."

Trent proved extraordinarily cooperative once again, managing to leave with only one killer grin at Brianna, which she barely returned. Chad didn't want to think about how relieved he was at that. He ushered her into the office and closed the door firmly behind them.

They were alone.

BRIANNA COULD hardly reconcile the man who stood before her, his face all harsh planes, his eyes hooded and cool, with the tender, almost playful man who had loved her so well in Las Vegas.

This Chad's mouth didn't appear to be made for kissing, for exploring her, for murmuring words of love with a kind of surprised, hesitant pleasure that told her he wasn't used to saying such things.

This Chad's broad shoulders and powerful physique intimidated rather than protected. And the voice that could thrill her senses merely by reading the weather forecast…today, it held no more inflection than if he'd been talking to a stranger.

"Chad," she said helplessly.

The stiffness of his stance eased, made him look more familiar.

"Thanks for not giving anything away," he said. "No one around here knows we're married."

"So…we still are?" She'd wondered if he'd applied for the

divorce and somehow the notification hadn't caught up with her. She hadn't wanted to contact him and ask.

He made a dashing movement with his hand. "I know I said I'd organize the divorce," he said defensively. "I've been busy."

Their marriage had never been at the top of his priority list. His excuse—*busy*—confirmed all the suspicions she'd had that horrible morning after their wedding. That she, that they as a couple, were not his priority.

Unfortunately the reminder didn't stop her from noticing the blue of his eyes or the little lines at the corners of his mouth that hadn't been there two years ago. She tore her gaze away, glanced around the cramped office—couldn't they have built it bigger so she wouldn't have to stand so close to him?

"It was quite a shock to hear you were coming."

"For me, too." Brianna's knees shook with the strain of keeping her upright; she slid uninvited into the seat that wrapped around the table.

"Your hair's a little shorter," he said.

It was, a very little.

"Haircut," she murmured inanely. One of the reasons she'd fallen in love with Chad was that he paid close attention to everything about her. It had made her feel she mattered.

"It looks nice." He shoved his hands into his pockets.

Brianna always thought of him as being in complete control of himself and his situation. The realization he felt as awkward as she did cheered her.

She rubbed her neck—it was getting sore from looking up at him. "You seem…taller."

He huffed a tense laugh and sat down on the other side of the table. "I'm still the same." After a moment he added, "Height."

Did that mean he'd changed in some other way?

"Chad," she said, "I know we need to talk about work. But can I just say…I didn't choose to get involved in Getaway's sponsorship, but now that I'm here, I hope we can talk about what happened."

His face blanked. "I can't see how that will help us get our jobs done."

"I need closure," she said.

His eyebrows lifted at her tone, more demanding than before. She'd known what she wanted back then, but had been unsure of whether her desire for an open, sharing relationship was reasonable. Now she knew for certain she wouldn't accept less. And she wouldn't let Chad off the hook about helping her find closure. She had to move on.

He drummed his fingers on the tabletop. "Maybe we can talk after you've completed your assessment. Things are frantic around here just now."

As if to prove his words, someone rapped on the office door. A man stuck his head around. He nodded at Brianna and said, "We're ready to roll, Chad."

"Be right out," Chad replied. When the man left, he said to Brianna, "That's Dave Harmon, Zack's crew chief." He straightened the papers on the desk into a neat stack. "Brianna, this isn't an easy situation. I think it's important to keep it strictly business."

Of course he did!

"Fine," she said coolly. "I won't push it for now. There's plenty of time—for the next little while, I'm not going anywhere." She wondered if things would have turned out differently if she'd said that—*I'm not going anywhere*—two years ago, when he'd given her all the reasons he couldn't be the husband she wanted.

He eyed her warily, uncertain, apparently, of her mood. Then he leaned back, relaxed a little. "How about I tell you about the team and about Zack's plans for the season?"

By the time they made it outside twenty minutes later, the two Matheson Racing cars were heading out along pit road. Chad introduced Brianna to Dave Harmon, an enormous man with hands the size of hubcaps, and to Trent's crew chief, the relatively slight—though probably still a good two hundred pounds—Rod Sutton. Both men got right back to work after a quick greeting.

"And this is Lori Garland—" Chad beckoned to the only other woman in the pits "—who owns this race track."

Lori Garland was a bit shorter than Brianna. Her hair was a similar color, though more reddish, but her eyes were green. She shook Brianna's hand. "Welcome to Halesboro. If there's anything you need that you can't find, let me know." She turned a dazzling smile on Chad. "That goes for you, too. Your wish is my command." Her tone was joking, but Brianna sensed she meant it. Had Chad already found closure by seeing other women?

"Thanks, Lori," Chad said.

The woman touched her hair, as if to make sure she was looking her best for him, then excused herself to go check on the pit crew.

"She seems anxious to please." Brianna didn't quite manage to leach the acid from her tone.

He sent her a puzzled look.

"She was flirting with you." *And my palm is itching to slap her.* She clasped her hands behind her back.

Chad blinked. "No, she wasn't."

"'Your wish is my command,'" Brianna simpered.

His puzzlement gave way to a slow smile that reminded her so forcibly of Las Vegas that a lump formed in her throat.

"This track has had some financial troubles," he said, his smile getting wider by the second. "Lori's desperate for teams to use it as a practice venue, so she takes a very personal interest in making sure there are no problems."

"Oh." Brianna sucked in her cheeks. "I see. Poor woman." *Could we do that again without me acting like a jealous wife?*

Speculation glinted in Chad's eyes. "Would you mind if she flirted with me?"

"Not at all," she lied. "Uh, is your father here today?"

His smile faded. "Dad had a heart attack back in November—he's not supposed to travel too far."

"Chad, that's awful." She reached out a hand to touch him…and found herself holding a pair of binoculars he'd passed to her.

"He had bypass surgery. He'll be fine. Use these to watch the cars," he said, closing down any discussion of his father's health.

Brianna pressed her lips together as she trained the binoculars on the object of her visit, Zack's No. 548 car. Unlike Trent's No. 429, which had every available inch covered in sponsor logos, the electric-blue No. 548 was bare in the most important places—the hood and the rear panels.

A few seconds later, the cars roared past the pits. Brianna had only ever watched NASCAR on TV. Obviously you got a different perspective at the track, but it seemed to her the two brothers were driving closer to each other than necessary. Since Trent was out in front, Zack had to be the aggressor.

Chad thought so, too, because his voice had a grim edge when he said into his headset, "Pull back, Zack."

No. 548 might have pulled back a tiny bit, but Brianna didn't think so.

"Would you describe Zack as a disciplined driver?" she asked. Her father's instructions had been quite clear: no loose cannons. For once, she agreed with him. A NASCAR sponsorship was a huge financial commitment, and Getaway should make it as safe a bet as possible. They needed a driver who could be trusted to do the right thing at the right time, whether it was driving responsibly or talking up his sponsor in a media interview.

"The guys get excited being out in their new cars for the first time," Chad said. She noticed he hadn't answered her question.

Ten minutes later, on a clear stretch of track, Zack crashed his car into the wall. It spun around twice, hit the wall again, then flipped tail over tip before landing back on four wheels, with some interesting dents in the panelwork.

Zack's crew chief cursed. Several team members climbed aboard a golf cart and headed across the infield toward the No. 548 car.

"What happened there?" Brianna asked.

A muscle jumped in Chad's jaw. "That's what I want to know." He peered through his binoculars. "Zack's out of the car, he's fine." His tone suggested that unless the car's brakes had failed, making the crash unavoidable, Zack wouldn't be fine for long.

Trent rolled into the pits, his car still intact. He clambered out the window and pulled off his helmet. "That guy is crazy, Chad. He won't let go of his stupid grudge." He saw Brianna and shut up.

Before she could say, "Don't mind me," the golf cart arrived back with Zack aboard.

Ignoring Chad and Brianna, he went straight for Trent.

"You idiot." Zack grabbed his brother's shoulder. "You nearly lost control going too fast into Turn Four. You could have knocked me out."

Trent shrugged him off. "I didn't need to knock you out— you're more than able to wreck your own car."

"That happened because I was busy avoiding you." Zack stepped so close to Trent he gave the phrase "in your face" new meaning. "Watch it, little brother."

Trent's chin jutted forward. "I'll be watching, all right. I'll watch you lose every race this season."

Zack's hand formed a fist.

"Enough!" Chad roared the single word. His brothers broke apart, but there was still a solid wall of anger between them. "Trent, I want you back out in that car for another fifty laps, and if you don't fix that fishtail you've got going into the corners, you'll have me to answer to." He turned to Zack. "As for you, get yourself to the doctor and have him check you out. Assuming he says there's still a brain somewhere in that head of yours, you'll be pulling shifts at the workshop until we have another car ready. There's a price to pay when you hit the wall."

Brianna observed the rigidity in Chad's spine, the tightness of his jaw. This must be the kind of team-related pressure he'd talked about when they split up. She said lightly, "I thought hitting the wall was an occupational hazard in NASCAR."

"Not if you're doing it right," he growled.

Zack started to argue, but Chad spoke over him, his voice now controlled. "Zack, I'd like to introduce you to Brianna Hudson, head of NASCAR sponsorship at Getaway Resorts."

Zack's dawning horror as he computed the impression he'd made on his potential sponsor was almost funny. He groaned, closed his eyes. Brianna felt sorry for him, even though the crash and the ensuing argument had been his fault.

Zack opened his eyes and stuck out a hand. "I apologize that you had to see me at my worst. Can we start over?"

She shook his hand. "You promise that's your worst?"

He broke into a grin that transformed his face, made him look more like Chad. "Promise."

"What about him?" Brianna glanced at Chad. "Have I seen Chad at his worst?"

She heard Chad's indrawn breath.

Zack's lips twitched. "Chad's all bark—at least, he doesn't bite often."

At the thought of Chad biting…or nipping…Brianna lost her cool. She felt color creeping over her collarbones, and up her neck.

CHAD COULD HAVE strangled his bratty brothers. Zack and Trent couldn't have made a worse impression—how the heck was Getaway Resorts supposed to see them as a unified team if the two drivers were at each other's throats?

And what was with Brianna's sudden blush? How come Zack was smiling wider than he had since he'd come back to Charlotte?

When Brianna had walked into the hauler at lunchtime, Chad had thought she was the same as before, only more beautiful. Now he realized she was more outspoken, her wit sharper. She was harder to read.

A man could like those things, could find them a challenge.

Finding a sponsor for Zack was all the challenge he could handle, he reminded himself. Brianna was questioning Zack now about his decision to return to NASCAR Sprint Cup Series racing, and Zack appeared to be handling it okay. He was still smiling at her.

Chad took a step closer to Brianna. If Trent's smile was a potent weapon, Zack's was even more so, simply because it was rarely bestowed and somehow the recipient always sensed that.

Zack's more reticent nature might have meant he didn't have as many women after him as Chad and Trent had had in the past, but those who did pursue him stuck like glue.

Something shifted in Chad's chest, like tectonic plates grinding together beneath the earth's surface.

"Time you got going, Zack." The words came out like the kind of peremptory command he could see Brianna didn't care for. Her eyebrows lowered in a frown. It made her look cute, dammit, and at the same time made him feel he had to explain himself to Zack, or to her.

This was exactly why he hadn't wanted his wife working with him. You couldn't be the boss of a team like Matheson Racing, of two drivers as strong-willed as Trent and Zack, without being willing and able to bruise egos and run over sensitivities.

Zack said, "I'm just telling Brianna about—"

"Now," Chad said.

Zack gave a mock salute—which ordinarily would have made Chad laugh—and went to join his team in the garage.

"You'll have to excuse my brothers," Chad said to Brianna. "They're both extremely competitive, which helps make them great drivers. But it doesn't always make them easy to get along with."

She nodded. He wished she'd say something.

Like *I missed you.*

With an inward groan, he canceled the thought. He should have known he'd feel an instant attraction to Brianna again; he should have had his defenses in place.

Thankfully it was never too late to get a grip.

"Let's head back to the hauler and discuss how you plan to do your evaluation." *Let's not discuss our marriage.* Then he remembered how claustrophobic the hauler had been, the two of them in that office. "On second thought, let's walk." He glanced at her long-sleeved, mint-green top, at the light jacket she'd pulled over it. Chad dragged off his Matheson Racing polar fleece, draped it over her shoulders. "You'll need this out there."

Brianna clutched at the fleece to stop it from slipping and murmured her thanks. They walked across the track and onto the infield.

But walking seemed a bad idea, too. Because in Las Vegas, they'd walked everywhere hand in hand. Chad had to fight the instinct to grab hold of her.

"Tell me how this assessment will work," he said brusquely.

"I need to complete my evaluation before Daytona," she said. The race in February was a huge media opportunity—Getaway would want its name on a car by then. "I'll need a full briefing about the team's finances, plus a copy of the latest audited accounts."

"Tony Winters, our accountant, has all that. He'll also supply the contract terms we like to use with sponsors."

"And I'll supply the terms Getaway likes to use," she said. The standard terms were merely a place to start negotiating—they both knew that.

The breeze picked up. Chad said, "Maybe you should wear that fleece."

To his surprise, she did as he suggested. She handed him her folder while she scrambled into the sweater. Chad could only take about two seconds of seeing the lift of her curves, the way her top pulled away from the waistband of her pants, revealing a sliver of midriff, before he had to turn away.

"That's better." Brianna smiled slightly. "I'll also need return on investment reports for previous sponsors—Trent's sponsors, I guess, since you won't have anything recent for Zack. And your proposals for how we can get the most out of a sponsorship this season."

Chad nodded. He prided himself on being measurable and accountable when it came to giving sponsors a return for their money. "These are the easy things," he said. "What about the intangibles?"

"I'll be looking at personality, ethos, whether the team and driver are a good fit for Getaway," she said. "Whether this feels right."

Trent zoomed past them on the track. Chad watched him take Turn Two with more control than he'd shown earlier.

"Those touchy-feelies, as my dad calls them, aren't so easy to measure," he said. He hated that they were so important, but he couldn't deny that a NASCAR sponsorship was about much more than money. When a team and a sponsor gelled, the results could be spectacular. "Have you done this kind of assessment before?"

"Assessing and managing sponsorships was my responsibility in my last job. I haven't worked in NASCAR, but I'm a huge fan and I—"

"Since when are you a fan?" he said, surprised.

"I, uh…" She faltered, and her cheeks reddened. She fixed her gaze on Trent's car, a distant red blur. "My point is, I have a passion for the sport and for finding a sponsorship that will work for Getaway."

"So you became a fan after we got married?" Maybe not only after they got married, but *because* they got married? Chad stopped walking, so he could process the information. He imagined Brianna seeing him on TV over the past couple of years, wondered how she'd felt.

"It doesn't matter how long I've been a fan," she said shortly. "I like to immerse myself in what I do, whether it's watching NASCAR races or developing sponsorships. I intend to throw myself into this task 24/7."

It sounded a lot like her views on marriage.

A lot like his views, too. On the team, at least, and on NASCAR. He could respect that kind of dedication.

"You know I'm evaluating FastMax Racing, too?" she asked.

"Yep. Garrett Clark is an exciting driver," Chad said fairly. "But Matheson Racing has a proven track record of wins in the NASCAR Sprint Cup Series and the NASCAR Nationwide Series. My father is widely respected throughout the sport—the Matheson name carries cachet. One of those intangibles you were talking about."

She nodded.

"So long as we're being open," he said, "you should know I'm talking to two other potential sponsors."

"Country Bread," she guessed. She or someone at Getaway obviously had an ear to the ground.

"That's one of them. The other company's interest is confidential at this stage." Delacord Theaters certainly seemed serious about a sponsorship. If he could firm up them or Country Bread in the next week, he could tell Getaway thanks, but no thanks, and Brianna could leave.

They'd reached the infield care center, where drivers were treated on race day after a crash. They stopped in the shelter of the concrete block structure. He said carefully, "You mentioned earlier that you didn't choose to do this project. Will our past history affect your ability to be objective?"

Her eyes sparked. "You mean, you can keep your business and personal lives separate, but you don't believe I can?"

"Brianna," he said, "that's why we split up."

Damn, what happened to not talking about that?

There was a charged silence. Then she turned away.

"My assessment will be made on a purely professional basis," she said. "I'm looking for a driver who'll deliver the media impressions we want, and a team that's closely aligned with Getaway's values. Nothing else matters."

"Loyalty, teamwork, service." He'd read the values on the company's Web site; he pounced on the chance to return the conversation to a business footing. "Matheson Racing believes in those things, too."

He touched her elbow to indicate a change of direction back toward the hauler. They were walking into the wind now; Brianna hunched her shoulders.

"Chad," she said, "if Getaway were to sponsor Matheson Racing, I'd be looking for better teamwork than I saw today."

Chad bristled. "NASCAR's an emotional sport. My brothers yell when things get tense, but they get along just fine."

"The problem," Brianna said delicately, "wasn't your brothers."

Chad frowned…and then it hit him. "Me? *I'm* the problem?"

She sidestepped away from him. "To me, control is the opposite of teamwork. What I saw today was a dictatorship, and not a benign one."

"Teams need leadership," he said tightly, "and that's what I give. To survive the long haul in NASCAR, you need discipline. If I don't clamp down on those guys, they're out of—" He broke off.

"Control?" she suggested. Her tone said *I told you so*. She walked on ahead, leaving Chad fuming. Then she turned and said, "If we're talking about why we split up, maybe it was because I didn't believe you meant your offer to compromise. What I've seen today says I was right to doubt you. Here in your world, it's your way or no way."

The blood roared in Chad's ears. "This teamwork garbage isn't about how I run Matheson Racing," he accused her. "It's about us, our marriage." He caught up to her. "In case you've forgotten, you were the one who said you couldn't compromise."

"Not on that one, fundamental issue," she said. "On anything else…try me."

He picked up his pace. "I suggest we end this discussion now."

"Because it's getting too personal?" she taunted, slightly breathless from hurrying to keep up. "Just like our marriage?"

How had a conversation that had started with audited accounts and contract terms ended up with a dissection of his faults? Would every conversation do the same?

Not if he could help it.

They'd almost reached the pits; Chad could see the hauler beyond. Deliberately he flexed his fingers at his sides, stretched them apart. "Okay, you want to talk? You want closure? We'll have dinner next Tuesday back in Charlotte." Too bad if he sounded every inch the tyrant she'd accused him of being. "I'll pick you up at your hotel at seven, and we'll hash this out so it doesn't get in the way of our work."

And if she thought that his deciding when and where they would have dinner was in any way dictatorial, she should never have married him in the first place.

As they climbed over the pit wall, tension, confusion and anger milled inside Chad, obliterating the calm he strove to bring to his job.

This meeting wasn't *professional,* it wasn't *strictly business.* Everything about Brianna was painfully, perilously personal.

CHAPTER FOUR

BRIANNA CONSIDERED standing Chad up for their dinner on Tuesday night, to show him the error of his high-handed approach. But she'd asked him to talk and finally managed to goad him into it. So if she went to dinner, she might have a hope of doing her job without being assailed by emotions—and an instinctive attraction that was purely the result of a lack of closure.

She applied lipstick in a bolder shade than usual, checking her reflection in the mirror of her suite at the Charlotte Getaway. She looked her best in the slim-fitting, green wool dress, and her best was pretty good. So why did her hand tremble so much that she had to wipe off the lipstick and start over?

She and Chad had been together as husband and wife for a whole sixteen hours—it couldn't be that difficult to hash it out, as Chad put it.

The room phone rang—it was reception, telling her Chad was waiting.

"I'll come down." She didn't want him in a hotel room with her. That would bring back way too many memories.

Downstairs she saw Chad before he saw her. He wore a sports jacket, dark gray, with a black polo shirt and black pants. His brows were drawn together in a frown; he looked about as communicative as a concrete wall.

Then he said mildly, "You look nice. Is there anywhere in particular you'd like to eat?"

Brianna burst out laughing and felt an immediate lifting of the strain that had dogged her preparations for tonight.

"What?" he demanded, those brows knitting more tightly.

"You can't tell me you haven't already made a reservation," she said. "Admit it—it just occurred to you that you could score a point by asking me where I want to eat."

The severe line of his mouth yielded to a reluctant smile. "It's hard to get into the best places without a reservation."

"I don't mind where we go," she said, "so why don't we follow your original plan."

"You promise you won't call me a dictator?" he asked as they headed through the automatic doors and out into the cold evening.

He sounded almost as if she'd hurt his feelings—but even the media had nicknamed him the Boss. No way could Brianna's words have come as a surprise.

"I promise," she said. And that sounded so weirdly like a marriage vow, even though the words were different, that she shivered.

"Would you like my jacket?" Chad was already shrugging it off.

At her insistence, he kept the jacket on. The valet had his Viper Coupe waiting, so they hit the road.

They drove maybe ten blocks, into the heart of uptown, before Chad began to look for a parking space on the busy streets. Obviously the Boss vibes were in full working order, because the second he murmured, "Here would be good," a car in front of them vacated its space.

"How did you do that?" She watched the taillights of the receding car. "How did you make that car leave?"

"Mind over matter." He grinned as he slipped into the almost too-small parking space with ease.

As she unclipped her seat belt, Chad said, "Damn! There's my dad."

She glanced around. "Where?"

Before she could figure out which of the male pedestrians on the sidewalk might be Brady Matheson, Chad had pushed her head down below the level of the door.

"What are you doing?" She struggled under his grip.

"I don't want Dad to see you." Perhaps aware he was pressing on the sensitive skin at her nape, he loosened his hand.

Her head still on her knees, Brianna said, "This is crazy. I'm going to sit up."

"Don't!" Chad said sharply. "Remember, Dad had a heart attack recently."

She twisted her head to face him. "And seeing me in your car will give him another one?"

"He's worried about me, and—" Chad broke off. "I haven't told him Getaway is a sponsor prospect. I don't want to get his hopes up, then have him upset if it doesn't work out."

His words kept Brianna in her place. Was there something wrong with Chad that made his dad worry about him? Or was this just Chad deciding what was best for his father, the way he did for his brothers, the way he'd wanted to do for her?

"Ah, heck," Chad said, "he's seen me." He let go of Brianna, buzzed down his window and called, "Hi, Dad."

"Son." Brady Matheson's voice was gruff, but pleased.

Brianna sat up slowly, certain her face was red from the blood that had rushed to her head. Her hair must be a mess. She ran her fingers through it.

"What are you doing out at this time of night?" Chad asked.

"I'm not an invalid." Brady sounded annoyed now. "I had a drink with a friend. Club soda," he said in a resigned tone that suggested he was getting the information in before the inevitable question was asked.

Her hair more or less restored, Brianna turned to look at him. The man outside the car was Chad twenty years on. Brady Matheson's hair was almost entirely gray, and his blue eyes had more laugh lines around them than Chad's—a lot more—but the resemblance was amazing.

"Who's this?" Brady asked.

"Dad, meet Brianna Hudson," Chad said.

"I, uh, dropped my earring." Brianna fingered the pearl stud in her left ear. "I found it on the floor."

Brady Matheson was all smiles as he leaned in the window to talk past his son. "Nice to meet you, Brianna. I didn't know Chad was seeing someone."

Get yourself out of this one, Chad.

He looked torn, as if he couldn't decide which was the lesser of two evils—letting his father think they were dating or admitting a working relationship. With a sigh, he said, "Dad, Brianna's a colleague. She works for Getaway Resorts."

Brady processed that. "You're Brian Hudson's girl?"

She nodded. He sent his son an inquiring glance.

"Getaway is possibly interested in a NASCAR sponsorship," Chad said. "Brianna and I are having dinner to talk about what that might involve."

Brady didn't look as if the news was about to trigger a coronary. His eyes, so like Chad's, gleamed. "Maybe I should join you. I know more than anyone about what this team can do for a sponsor."

"It's just a casual chat," Chad said firmly. "Besides, don't you have to meet Julie-Anne?"

Brady had been scowling at Chad's dismissal, but now his face brightened and he glanced at his watch. "You're right, I'm late. We're eating at Chez Pierre. How about you?"

"I have a reservation at BamBam," Chad said with evident relief.

"Nice to meet you, Brianna." Brady reached across and shook her hand.

This is my father-in-law. The thought was unexpected—she hadn't thought of Zack and Trent as her brothers-in-law when she'd met them. Briefly she tightened her grip on his hand. "You, too," she said.

"If you want a team to sponsor, you can't do better than Matheson Racing," Brady said. "There's not a tighter-run ship in NASCAR. They call Chad 'the Boss,' you know."

The Boss groaned softly, and Brianna almost felt sorry for him. "I've heard," she said.

BamBam, Chad's chosen restaurant, was very hip, white-on-white decor, with a circular, neon-lit glass bar in the middle of the room. Tables surrounded it like satellites.

Brianna's seat gave her a view of the entire place, and she smiled her thanks at the maître d' as he handed her a menu.

"Your dad seems nice," she said after the man had gone.

"He's a good guy," Chad said.

"Who's Julie-Anne? He looked excited at the thought of seeing her."

His mouth tightened. "She's Dad's secretary—and his fiancée."

CHAD KEPT his face neutral as he talked about one of his least favorite topics. "They got engaged right after his heart attack."

"You don't approve," Brianna guessed.

"Let's just say I don't think it's a good idea to rush into marriage."

That probably fell into the category of inflammatory remarks, given their circumstances.

But Brianna didn't rise to it. "Your parents are divorced, right?"

"That happened years ago," he said. "Mom married a diplomat who was posted to Eastern Europe back in the Cold War days. She wasn't able to keep us boys with her."

Her eyes warmed. "You must have missed her."

"I was too young to remember her well. Dad married Rosie, his second wife, right after. They got along much better than he and Mom ever did."

Her answering murmur sounded suspiciously like sympathy, which he didn't need. Then she dropped her gaze to her menu, giving him a chance to observe her. He hadn't let himself peruse that figure-hugging green dress earlier.

He kept his inspection to a minimum, just enough to note that she looked great. Because even though tonight was personal, not business, he didn't want her to stir his interest. He wanted to wave the checkered flag on their marriage once and for all, and if Brianna preferred to use a New Age term like *closure* for it, then she was welcome.

She closed her menu.

"You've chosen already?" he asked. It was a long menu.

"I saw the scallops right at the top."

Did she always jump into things without weighing all the options?

Chad read the menu thoroughly before settling on the beef daube—if they'd called it a stew they couldn't have charged such an extravagant price—with candied parsnips. The waiter took their orders, and Chad requested a bottle of cabernet. Brianna liked red wine.

"Let's talk about *your* dad, instead of mine," he said. "How did you end up coming here in his place?"

She bit her lip. "Dad's not well. With the NASCAR season starting so soon, he asked me to step in for him."

"Is it anything serious?" Chad asked.

She lifted one shoulder. "He assures me he'll be okay."

"I had the impression you two aren't close," Chad said. "I guess it's good that he asked you to get involved in the sponsorship."

"Mmm," she said.

For someone who was so keen to share everything, she wasn't saying much. "How did Matheson Racing end up on his shopping list?" he persisted.

"There aren't many top-flight drivers without a sponsor," she said.

"There are enough to give your father some choice."

She took a bread roll from the basket and toyed with it. Even in the candlelight, Chad could see that her color was high.

"I mentioned Matheson Racing to him last year. It seemed a way to connect with him, what with his newfound passion for NASCAR."

It struck Chad she'd been looking for a connection with *him*, too, one he hadn't been prepared to offer. Which, considering he was her husband, she had every right to be unhappy about.

We should never have got married.

"Why do you find it so hard to connect with your father?" he asked.

She sipped her wine, then set her glass down. "I can't measure up to Dad's standards. It's mostly easier just to avoid him."

Her tone was pragmatic, but she blinked rapidly. Chad wished he'd asked the question two years ago. Though what good that would have done... "Hard to avoid him now that you're working for him," he observed.

She grimaced. "With this project, I'm doing things his way."

"You think that's how to measure up?" Then he saw the hope in her eyes, and realized this was about much more than work. "Brianna, you don't earn people's love by doing things their way."

Brady Matheson's sons got a clap on the back when things went the way he wanted, and his vocal disapproval when they didn't. Despite the lack of emotional display, Chad always knew his dad loved him.

Nothing complicated about it.

She lifted her chin. "You can make it easier for them to love you."

Was she thinking about their marriage? That if one of them had been prepared to do things the other's way, it might have worked out?

The waiter brought their meals, and there was a brief flurry of activity as they sampled their food, adjusted the seasoning, replenished wineglasses. Chad welcomed the break—but knew it couldn't last.

When they were settled into their meal, he said, "How do we go about finding closure?"

Brianna smiled. "You sound about as excited as if you were asking how do we go about do-it-yourself root-canal surgery."

"Sorry," he said, meaning it. "Believe it or not, I'm thinking closure isn't such a dumb idea." His whole life had been out of whack since he'd met Brianna, and that had to stop. Now was a good time. "I just don't know where to start."

"I think," she said, "we discuss how we feel about what went wrong."

"Uh-huh. You go first," he encouraged her, and dug into his stew.

She put down her knife and fork. "You said you loved me."

Chad choked on a piece of carrot and just about had it coming out his nose. Brianna packed a mighty punch when she chose to. "Can't we start somewhere else?" he said, indignant, when he'd finished coughing.

"Was it a lie?" Her brown gaze was clear, searching.

Dammit, she wasn't going to drop it. He wiped his mouth with his napkin, stalling for time. The easiest thing would be to say he'd gotten carried away, mistaken infatuation, or lust, for love. He willed himself to take the easy way out.

"It wasn't a lie," he said. For Pete's sake, what happened to his willpower when she was around?

She nodded slowly. "Then…?"

That was the one-word, sixty-four-thousand-dollar question.

"You said the same thing," he reminded her.

Brianna rubbed her arms as if she was cold. "I wasn't lying, either."

A part of Chad wanted to whoop for joy. But it wasn't the mature, together part of him that he relied on to get through life.

"I didn't realize then that love is about more than talking about your feelings," she said. "Love is something you do. Or not."

"I did love you," he said. "It wasn't just words." If he could just forget the need to prove himself, this would be a lot easier.

She twirled the stem of her wineglass between her fingers; the red liquid swayed and sloshed. "I don't think a guy who loved his wife would let her leave so easily."

"You mean, it was all my fault?"

"Not all," she said. Unconvincingly.

"Maybe a woman who loved her husband wouldn't give up on him just because he didn't automatically want her in every part of his life." He took a swig of his wine. "Maybe she'd take a chance they could work things out."

Her eyes widened as if she'd never considered the possibility. Whereas Chad had second-guessed that morning so many times…

"I couldn't," she said. "I've never mattered to anyone, Chad. I told you a little about my dad, and my mom's so busy with her charitable foundations in Australia… I'm not saying my parents don't care about me, but I've never been an essential part of their lives. Or anyone's life."

Chad couldn't imagine that. Everyone in his family was an integral part of the team, even Zack.

Brianna pressed against the edge of the table with her fingertips. "Are you surprised I wanted more from my marriage?"

He dodged a stab of guilt. "Are you surprised I wasn't ready to share every breath I take with someone I'd known only three days?"

"Then why did you ask me to marry you?"

Their voices had risen, and people at the surrounding tables were staring. This was crazy, Chad thought. No wonder he hadn't gotten married before; it was like walking through a minefield in hobnail boots.

He took a deep breath. "You and I are two totally different people, and if we'd spent five minutes together in our normal environment, we would have realized that."

"You're right," she said. "Our marriage was all wrong."

"So—" ignoring the heaviness in his chest, he took his argument to its logical conclusion "—it's probably a good idea if we get that divorce started." *And stop talking about things that are only going to hurt us.*

She swallowed. "Have we been separated long enough? Legally, I mean?"

"We've been separated at least a year and one of us has lived in North Carolina through that time, so we're okay." He forked a mouthful of the stew, his appetite returning now that they were off the personal questions. "I don't know how long it takes for the divorce to come through once we lodge an application. Are you in a rush for it?" Even though he'd brought up the subject, his food turned dry in his mouth as he considered the reasons she might what a divorce fast.

"No rush," she said. Which, suddenly, was nowhere near enough information.

"You're not…seeing anyone?" Pressure built, as if his heart

was being squeezed by a fist inside his chest. It was a natural pos-sessiveness, Chad assured himself, a caveman instinct any red-blooded guy would feel toward his wife.

"I'm not seeing anyone." She paused. "I haven't seen anyone."

The grip on his heart loosened and his blood resumed pumping. He watched her chase a scallop around her plate with her fork.

The conversation felt one-sided. "Aren't you going to ask if I'm seeing someone?" he said.

"I'm not sure I want to know."

"I haven't dated since we got married," he said.

Something hung in the air between them—a promise, a memory, a confirmation of fidelity that was in no way justified. Chad was profoundly grateful for it.

"Are you happy?" Brianna asked.

Breath whooshed out of him. "Do you have to keep asking those questions?"

"I don't think any marriage breakup is entirely painless," she said, "so I'm asking if you're happy."

Now she wanted to know? She'd been gone almost two years without contact and now she wanted to know if he was over her? "Damn right I'm happy," he said. It came out angry, not at all happy.

This was exactly the kind of conversation he hated. Why couldn't people just get on with life, rather than analyzing every emotion that came their way? And if they had to analyze it, surely they didn't have to share it.

"How about you?" he heard himself say. "Are you happy?"

Unlike him, she didn't jump into a reply.

"I enjoyed Florida and I've had a wonderful couple of years work-wise," she said at last. "I'm worried about Dad, and yet I'm happy to be doing something for him."

Chad wondered how sick her father was.

"I still want to find someone who really loves me, who I love back," she said. "So while I don't like that we split up, I guess I'm happy I didn't settle for something less with you."

He refused to consider the insult implicit in that. Time to put an end to these questions. "Given that you're happy and I'm happy, does that mean we have closure?"

"Maybe we do." She sounded surprised.

Chad lifted his wineglass before she could think of something else to ask. "To closure."

"Closure," she echoed as she clinked her glass against his.

He said hopefully, "Now we can just be two colleagues having dinner."

A giggle erupted from Brianna as she set her wineglass back on the table.

"What's so funny?" He'd always loved—*liked*—her laugh, the way her eyes warmed and her lips parted.

"I just realized this is your worst nightmare," she said.

"How do you figure that?"

"We split up because you didn't want to work with me, and look at us now. You're working with your wife."

He could have made some comment about the fact that she wouldn't be his wife much longer, but she looked cute with the light of triumph in her eyes. "I guess I'll have to handle it."

The mood continued to lighten as they talked about NASCAR and the forthcoming season while they finished their meals. Brianna didn't order dessert—like Chad, she probably didn't want to push their luck.

It was only nine o'clock when they pulled up outside the main entrance of the Charlotte Getaway.

Chad cut the engine. Brianna put a hand on her door. "Don't get out—I'll be fine. Thank you for dinner."

"Thanks for the closure," Chad said.

"The closure was great," she agreed.

An awkward silence filled the car. Chad thought about shaking her hand, but that seemed stupid after the conversation they'd had. A kiss on the cheek…yes, that was surely the appropriate farewell gesture between two mature, amicably divorcing adults.

The light from the hotel lobby spilled into the car, forming a halo behind Brianna, throwing her face into shadow. He leaned across; she presented her left cheek.

As he moved in, he caught the scent of lilies and lemons—the same perfume she'd worn in Las Vegas.

He touched his lips to her smooth skin…and the taste of her flooded his memory, a wave pounding so hard he couldn't pull back.

Brianna moved against him, questioning…yet not drawing away. Then she turned her face toward him.

Before he could think, Chad's mouth was on hers. He fastened his lips to hers and kissed her with a fervent, ravenous hunger.

After a shocked fraction of a second, her response rose beneath his kiss. Their tongues met, clashed, melded—pressed together by a last-time urgency.

Chad touched a hand to Brianna's waist, and she shivered against him. She was sensitive there, he remembered, so sensitive… Her arms came around his neck, tugging him closer. He moved, maneuvering over the hand brake, and claimed her mouth.

She was warm and welcoming and tasted incredible. He groaned against her…and she stiffened, then pulled away.

"That wasn't supposed to happen." Her breath came fast; her eyes were wide.

He touched a finger to her throat, felt the frantic pulse. "There was nothing wrong with the physical side of our marriage."

He wanted to make love to her right now. He glanced at the hotel—she had a room up there, a bed.

She interpreted his glance. "Wanting each other physically is what got us into this mess in the first place."

It was a denial of the *love* side of the equation, but right now that seemed like a good way to play it. Reluctantly Chad abandoned the fantasy of ending up in bed with her. "You're right," he said. "That was a bad idea, given we just did that whole closure thing."

Because now, with one touch of his lips to hers, he'd blown the whole damned thing wide open.

CHAPTER FIVE

THE RECEPTIONIST at FastMax Racing smiled at Brianna. "Mr. Clark will be here directly."

"Thank you." Brianna liked this place already. The welcome was friendly, and a couple of staff members who'd passed by had also spoken a word of greeting. An air of suppressed excitement created a sense of purposeful activity—even the receptionist was stuffing envelopes with photos of Garrett Clark when she wasn't picking up calls from her switchboard.

Pictures of Garrett and his No. 402 car dominated the walls. The adjoining souvenir store—more Garrett paraphernalia—was already crowded.

This was the perfect place to take Brianna's mind off Chad and last night's kiss. Why did he have to do that, just when they'd attained some kind of peace?

Like I fought him off, she thought in disgust. She couldn't deny she'd been curious to reacquaint herself with his mouth. Over the past two years, she'd convinced herself their wedding night couldn't have been as amazing as she remembered. But with one kiss, he'd stripped away that pretense and left her…wanting.

She blew out a cooling breath. She couldn't go into her meeting all steamed up. And she shouldn't be thinking about Matheson Racing during her visit to FastMax. Who was she trying to kid? She was thinking about Chad, not his team!

"Brianna?" A warm, male voice spoke from behind her.

Brianna turned…and every female receptor in her body screamed *Hot!* The man smiling at her—way too young to be

FastMax Racing owner, Andrew Clark—had dark hair and warm brown eyes that made her think of melting chocolate.

"You're Garrett Clark," she said. FastMax's NASCAR Sprint Cup Series driver was famous for his good looks and charm, and she could see why.

"Yes, ma'am." He shook her hand, held on to it with unashamed interest as he looked her over. His smile widened.

Okay, the guy was an inveterate flirt. But Brianna would have to be made of stone not to be flattered. *He can press my starter any time,* she told herself. *Yessir.*

Except…when Garrett cupped her elbow to steer her around the reception toward the offices in back, she didn't have the slightest urge to lean in closer, the way she had with Chad, despite her struggle against it.

"My lucky day." Garrett grinned down at her as he held the door for her to precede him. *Nice manners, too.* "I get first dibs on the beautiful girl."

Brianna rolled her eyes. "Does flattery work with your other sponsors? Because it doesn't do a lot for Getaway Resorts."

He waved his free hand carelessly. "As if I could think about money with you around."

The man was outrageous…but she found herself smiling—as, she'd bet, had every woman he'd tried that line on this week.

"I do hope you get serious when our meeting starts," she said.

"I'm always serious about my racing," he said, and beneath the laughing face she caught a hint of steel.

"I'm pleased to hear it."

"But I'm never serious at dinnertime," he said hopefully.

She laughed, even though talking about dinner sent the memory of Chad's kiss firing through her mind. "Thanks, but I'm busy."

Dinner with Garrett Clark was probably just what she needed. His expert attentions would surely put Chad in the shade.

They climbed a wide staircase to a mezzanine floor.

"The head honcho's office is up here," Garrett said, "along with a couple of meeting rooms."

"The head honcho being your stepfather, right?"

"Uh-huh." He grinned. "It drives him nuts when I call him that."

Andrew Clark was, thankfully, not as charming as his stepson—being in the same room with two men of that ilk would be exhausting. Instead, he was friendly, courteous, unassuming.

"You've met Garrett," he said with a resigned pride that appealed to Brianna. "Let me assure you we take our racing very seriously."

Over the next two hours, he showed her exactly that. Andrew was the brother of Patsy Grosso, wife of current NASCAR Sprint Cup Series champion Dean Grosso and co-owner of Cargill-Grosso Racing. The Grossos were NASCAR royalty—the contrast between FastMax's public profile and his sister's team couldn't be greater. FastMax was one of the smaller teams in NASCAR.

Perhaps because of that, it seemed as if everyone here had a stake in every aspect of the business, and the answers to Brianna's questions were simple and direct, no matter who they came from.

She could imagine doing business with Andrew Clark. She could see Garrett Clark as being an asset to the Getaway brand.

Immediately she felt disloyal to Chad. *I don't owe him any loyalty. My loyalty is to Dad. I need to do what's best for him.*

On first impressions, FastMax shaped up nicely on the numbers, too—the team was efficiently run, with no signs of excess fat that Getaway would be forced to subsidize.

"We're looking for at least a ten-million-dollar commitment, for a minimum of two years," Andrew Clark told Brianna as he ran through the budget for this year's NASCAR Sprint Cup Series season. "I don't mind telling you, we've been running close to the wind, budget-wise. To tide us over we just signed a short-term sponsorship for next month's races at Daytona. Rokutsu is launching a new gaming console and wants to make a splash. They're paying a premium for a one-off sponsorship."

"That's a heck of a splash," Brianna said. The electronics giant obviously had money to burn.

"That means the No. 402 car won't be available to Getaway— or to anyone else—until after Daytona," Andrew said.

"I believe you're also talking to Country Bread," she said.

"Yep, but I know Country Bread is talking to another team, as well as us and Matheson Racing. We want to get the right partner."

Given that her overwhelming impression of FastMax was that this team was enthusiastic, honest and determined to kick butt on the track, Brianna didn't think they would have much trouble finding a sponsor.

"We're testing in Kentucky in a couple of weeks' time," Andrew said as they went for lunch in the team cafeteria—all part of giving Brianna a feel for what made this place tick. "I hope you'll join us there. Garrett behind the wheel of a stock car is something else. He's good on TV, but he's incredible live."

"I'd love to come." She watched Garrett, who'd stopped at another table to talk to a couple of mechanics. He was well liked and respected by everyone. She hadn't had the same impression of Zack Matheson. Of Trent, maybe, but not Zack.

"Is it hard, working with family?" she asked Andrew.

"It's not always easy," he said. "But there's more good than bad." He glanced fondly at his stepson. "When there's family involved, there's more meaning to it, know what I mean?"

"I think I do," Brianna said.

CHAD'S SECRETARY came to find him in the workshop on Thursday with the news that Jay Nicholson from Delacord Theaters was on the line.

Chad took the stairs two at a time—Delacord had been thorough in its assessment of Matheson Racing, which they'd completed a couple of days ago. He had the impression they liked what they saw. If they made a sponsorship offer now, it would solve all his problems—business *and* personal.

"I presented our findings at yesterday's board meeting." Jay didn't bother with small talk, one of many things Chad liked about the man. "We agreed unanimously it'd be hard to find a better-run outfit than Matheson Racing."

"Thanks," Chad said. *Take that, Brianna.*

"But the dollars are a real problem," Jay said.

Chad sat down behind his desk, clicked to open the budget file on his laptop. "Tell me your concerns, and we'll see what we can do." This was a negotiation, after all.

Jay laughed shortly. "Not much, Chad, I'm sorry. The reality is starting to hit home with the board about how much money we'll be up for."

Zack appeared in the doorway of Chad's office, alerted to the fact that his future might be decided in this phone call. Chad hated the thought of letting his brother down. He ran a hand over his face, held the phone tighter.

"It didn't help," Jay said, "that Zack wrecked the car at Halesboro." Delacord hadn't been at the track, but Jay had asked Chad how the practice had gone. "If we were sponsoring Zack now, we'd be paying to fix up a car the fans haven't even seen yet. We wouldn't want to start the season spending, say, ten million dollars, only to have you coming to us for more money later on."

"One wreck isn't a good indicator of how much money you'll spend over time," Chad said.

Zack grimaced an apology, obviously getting the gist. He sat down at Chad's meeting table.

"Your case isn't helped by the fact that your driver is an unknown quantity," Jay said. "The world loves Trent, but that doesn't mean they'll love Zack."

Knowing his brothers were polar opposites, Chad had to agree. Zack wouldn't win any popularity contests.

"What's the bottom line here, Jay?"

The other man's sigh was the confirmation he didn't need. "We've decided our budget, and to some extent our marketing demographic, will be better served by a NASCAR Nationwide Series sponsorship."

Chad shifted his reality, marshaled his thoughts. "Our NASCAR Nationwide driver Ryan Thorne shows a lot of promise." Maybe he could put Delacord on Thorne's car, and convince Thorne's sponsor to move up to the NASCAR Sprint Cup Series car…

"A couple of the board members mentioned an interest in Roberto Castillo," Jay said apologetically.

It was hardly surprising, Chad thought. Ex-Formula One driver Castillo was new to NASCAR, but he had an incredibly high profile. "So, as far as Matheson is concerned, Delacord's money is off the table?"

Zack's face set in harsh, tense lines.

"Afraid so," Jay said.

They ended the call on good terms—not only was NASCAR too small a world to start slanging matches, but Chad genuinely liked Jay. Still, when he hung up the phone, he uttered a couple of curses.

"You can say that again," Zack said. So Chad did.

But there was no time to wallow in disappointment. When he was done cursing, he said briskly, "We need to start putting some pressure on Country Bread, see if they're ready to open their wallet yet."

"They might be our last hope." Zack's voice was calm, but he kicked unconsciously at the table leg. "Garrett Clark has a sponsorship deal with Getaway all but signed on the dotted line."

Brianna chose FastMax over Matheson? Over me?

Chad put down his pen before he stabbed something. "You sure about that?"

"His crew chief told Dave over drinks last night."

Surely Brianna hadn't been so spooked by that kiss that she went and handed the sponsorship to FastMax. Hurt and frustration churned in his gut.

He pulled up his runaway imagination. He knew Brianna—not as well as he should have before he married her maybe, but he knew she wasn't malicious. Gorgeous, sexy, sweet, vulnerable…yes. Malicious, no.

But Garrett Clark was famed for his ability to charm. Could he charm ten or twelve million dollars out of a woman? Brianna had shown herself capable of making impulsive decisions on the romantic front. Chad ignored the fact that he'd made the same impulsive decision.

"Clark's trying to psych us out," he told Zack, hoping it was true. "And you and Dave are letting him."

Zack let out a frustrated breath. "You're right. But just the thought that we might not even start the season if I don't sign a sponsor…"

"We're a better team than FastMax, and on a good day you're a better driver than Clark." Chad ignored his brother's scowl. "If Getaway signs Clark, that leaves less competition for Country Bread's money."

"Country Bread doesn't have as much to spend as Getaway." *Yeah, but at least I'm not married to anyone there.*

The flatness in Zack's eyes betrayed his stress. He was a loner—the unhappier he got, the more he clammed up. If things got any worse around here, Chad thought, his brother might disappear to Atlanta again, and they'd face more years of silence. The past couple of years, before Brady's heart attack brought Zack back to Charlotte, had been tough on everyone.

"I'll get you a sponsor," Chad said.

Zack's face loosened up, his eyes flickered. "Thanks."

One word was better than none on the scale of his brother's emotional health, Chad supposed.

He sighed; he sounded like Brianna, with her insistence that communication—sharing, as she called it—was a sign of a healthy relationship. He shook his head, shook off the overanalysis bug.

After Zack left, Chad sat for a long time staring out the window over the parking lot where performance cars way outnumbered regular sedans and SUVs.

If he put his analysis where it mattered—into the sponsorship—he had to agree Zack was right. Getaway Resorts was, in every respect other than the personal, a better sponsor for them than Country Bread, which was spreading its attentions around. The situation with Delacord showed how quickly a prospective sponsorship could disappear. They couldn't afford to rely on Country Bread.

And what was he doing about it? Nothing. Since Brianna's

reappearance, he'd thought more about her than about securing the best outcome for the team.

Chad made a sound of disgust and spun his chair back to his desk. He'd never in his life waited to see how the chips would fall. When he wanted something, he went out and got it.

He would call the guys at Country Bread, see what else they needed in order to choose Matheson Racing. And he would call Brianna and do whatever it took to secure the sponsorship.

She'd said she would throw herself into her assessment 24/7. Chad was damned if she'd spend that 24/7 with Garrett Clark. He picked up the phone.

THERE WAS ONLY so much FastMax Racing material Brianna could read in one sitting. When the financial printouts started to blur, she left her hotel room and headed to the park across the road.

She sat down on a bench, making the most of the limited winter sunshine. The wooden seat held some lingering dampness—she'd probably end up with a mark on her skirt.

The buzz of her cell phone distracted her from that minor worry. The caller was Chad.

He started with an apology for not being in touch with her sooner. Then he admitted he'd put off talking to her because the situation still felt awkward. Which she considered surprisingly honest of him.

"Maybe we're coming at this the wrong way," Chad said. "Thinking we can shut out our personal history. You can assure me all you like that our past won't affect your decision, and I can say that our marriage is irrelevant, but it's not true."

"You're right," she murmured. She could hardly deny it when she'd spent more time talking to FastMax than to Matheson Racing this week purely because no one at FastMax had seen her naked!

"I think about you," Chad said. His voice turned husky. "Since that kiss, I can't help remembering—"

"Don't." The word came out a squeak. Brianna fanned her

face. She needed to stop thinking *naked* when Chad was in the vicinity, even on the other end of a phone line. She should never have kissed him back. She should have consigned the question *Is Chad as good a kisser as I remember?* to the annals of Great Unanswered Questions of All Time.

He cleared his throat. "So let's admit this is difficult. Admit we don't know how the heck to deal with the situation."

"You'll admit that?" she teased, suddenly feeling lighter. She stretched her legs out in front of her, tipped her head back to see the pale sky.

"I will if you will."

Electric silence. As if he was talking about something else entirely.

Brianna's stomach quivered. *Don't think naked thoughts!*

"Okay," she said. "This is difficult, and I don't know how the heck to deal with the situation."

"This is difficult," Chad repeated solemnly. "And I don't know how the heck to deal with the situation."

Silence. Then Brianna snorted a laugh. "I feel like I just joined AA, or a convent or something."

"Hmm. I can't see you in a convent." The huskiness was back. *Nakednakednaked.* Brianna slapped her own face. *Cut it out!*

"Are you beating up your phone?" Chad's voice was low, sexy.

"So, dealing with this difficult situation…" she said, returning to the subject clumsily. She stood, started to walk—best not to be too relaxed at a time like this.

"No more avoiding the issue or each other," he ordered, switching into the Boss mode. "We both have a job to do. We both need to put our best into it. My usual practice with interested sponsors is to invite them to spend a solid chunk of time at Matheson Racing headquarters to get a real feel for what we do. So that's what I'm inviting you to do."

"Uh, how much time?" Sure, the theory was good, but in practice…

"A week," he said.

One week with Chad. Good grief, that was longer than Brianna had known him before she married him.

"The team headquarters is about as unromantic a place as you can imagine," he said. "I guarantee it'll cool things down."

She could definitely do with cooling down.

"A week of your time learning about the team," he elaborated. "A week of my time, giving this deal my best shot. All in, nothing held back."

Now that was downright manipulative—and quite impressive, Brianna acknowledged, that he'd remembered her exact words from their breakup. Before she knew what had happened, she'd agreed to spend a whole week at Matheson Racing.

Kind of like *Before she knew what had happened, she'd agreed to spend her whole life with Chad.*

Look how well that had turned out.

TUESDAY MORNING—Matheson Racing's week generally started on Tuesday, because during the season, Monday was most people's only day off—Brianna sat in her Mustang convertible outside the concrete-and-glass team headquarters and gave herself a pep talk. She could do this, she could spend a week with Chad.

She checked her hair one last time in the mirror on her visor. "Get out of this car and walk into that building," she told herself sternly.

Her feet stayed stuck to the floor.

There was one sure way to put herself in the right frame of mind for her sojourn at Matheson Racing. Brianna pulled out her cell phone and dialed her father.

"What's wrong?" Brian Hudson demanded.

"Just wanted to see how you are," she said cheerfully. She'd phoned him a few times since she'd arrived in Charlotte, so her call couldn't be a surprise. Yet still, he assumed she was calling because she'd screwed up.

No wonder she'd never dared tell him about the mess that had been her marriage. Of course, Chad hadn't told his family, either—the thought made her feel marginally more competent.

"I'm all right," her father said. "Damn chemo's taking it out of me. Can't swallow much."

"If you need me to come down—"

"I'll be fine. I need you to do your job."

She sighed. "Okay, then, how about a progress report?" She gave him a rundown on her meetings with FastMax and Matheson Racing. "I'm about to spend a week at Matheson, getting a feeling for how the team operates."

"Make sure you give their accountant a proper grilling."

Will that make you love me? If I do a good job of grilling the accountant?

"I get the impression," Brianna said, "that Country Bread is very interested in Garrett Clark."

Her dad made a dismissive sound. "If we want Clark, we'll outbid them. Are they sniffing around Matheson?"

"Some. Nowhere near as enthusiastically as they are around Clark," she admitted. Which was a worry. Why wasn't Country Bread as interested in Zack? "They're talking to another team, too, I'm not sure which one."

They talked for a few more minutes. Brianna ended the call suitably fired up not to take any garbage from anyone, and headed into the Matheson Racing headquarters. The moment the automatic door swished closed behind her, she knew Chad was right. The cool, quiet atmosphere was a much better place for them to meet than in the adrenaline-fueled chaos of a racetrack or the seductive environs of a restaurant or hotel room.

She could practically feel her seesawing emotions being taken over by businesslike pragmatism. She'd bet she wouldn't even think about kissing Chad in this environment.

"Brianna Hudson to see Chad Matheson," she said crisply to the receptionist.

He came out to meet her, casual but handsome in dark pants with his striped shirt untucked. He shook her hand. And proved she'd been overconfident about not wanting to kiss him here. She whipped her hand back, fingers curled around the lingering sensation of his touch.

"I've set you up in my office," he said as they walked upstairs.

She faltered, grabbed hold of the balustrade. "Doesn't Zack have an office? Shouldn't I be with him?"

He steadied her with a hand on her arm, then released her, fast. "He's sharing with Trent right now, and that's enough friction—adding a third person to the space would cause a riot."

"These are your brothers who get on, and I quote, 'just fine'?"

A small smile acknowledged her hit. "Plus, Zack's spending a lot of time in the gym, and running ten miles a day. His fitness probably isn't what you want to evaluate."

"No," she admitted.

"If you want to see how Zack's doing and how the team works, a week in my office will give you access to his crew-chief briefings and strategy planning. You'll get a good feel for his strengths and weaknesses."

"For a guy who used to be determined to keep me out of his business, you're offering plenty of information."

He held open a door and ushered her in. "Since our personal relationship is on its way out, I don't expect it to be a problem."

Silly me.

The large, sunlit office had plush gray carpet and a wooden desk, maybe mahogany, positioned to give Chad a view of the outdoors. A second desk had been set up at right angles to it. Brianna wouldn't be obliged to look him in the eye constantly; that was something.

"Let me know if you have areas of specific interest for this week," Chad said. "But I'm thinking mainly you'll do whatever I'm doing."

"If only you'd said that two years ago," Brianna murmured.

CHAPTER SIX

CHAD'S EYES NARROWED, but he didn't rise to the provocation. "This morning, like every Tuesday, I'll meet with all the crew chiefs together. If necessary, I'll talk privately to one or two of them afterward. Trent and Zack will come in this afternoon for separate briefings, again with their crew chiefs."

He'd barely finished speaking when the four crew chiefs—Zack's and Trent's, plus those of Ryan Thorne, the team's NASCAR Nationwide Series driver, and Kyle Samson, the NASCAR Camping World Truck Series driver, entered.

The meeting that followed ran with the precision of a finely tuned race car. Each crew chief shared his agenda for the week and any particular challenges—personnel or mechanical—facing his team. The group discussed everything, for the most part without acrimony. When someone did take things personally, Chad smoothed it over.

It was, Brianna felt, an impressive performance. She said little during the meeting, interjecting a question occasionally. By the time the meeting ended at one o'clock, she was filled with appreciation for the complexities of getting a race car on the track for a season of NASCAR Sprint Cup Series racing.

"Let's grab a sandwich downstairs," Chad told her after his office emptied out.

The small cafeteria was crowded, so Chad suggested they take their bagged lunches outside—although it was chilly, the sun shone brightly and the sky was clear.

They sat on the front steps of the building. Brianna unwrapped her egg-salad sandwich.

"Looks good," she said.

"Uh-huh."

As she bit into the sandwich, she turned to look at Chad and found his eyes on her. Their gazes connected. And stayed that way.

The building behind them receded, and Brianna felt pelted by sensory impressions: Chad's strong fingers, tanned against the white sandwich sack; Chad's elbows propped casually on his knees, a position of relaxed strength; the rustle of paper as she put down her sandwich; the distant slam of a car door in the parking lot and the call of a bird overhead. Being here, a place she'd imagined so many times, felt unreal.

Chad cleared his throat. "Any questions about what you saw this morning?"

"Just one," she said. "What's so complicated that you couldn't share this with your wife?"

Chad pulled out his steak sandwich and crumpled the paper bag. The sensual atmosphere evaporated; his voice was clipped. "Today was a walk in the park compared with a typical day during the season. It's not until we're racing every weekend that the pressure hits."

He took a quick bite of his sandwich. As he chewed, he seemed to relax a little, maybe to think about her question.

"The job is harder when my brothers are around," he admitted. "When it's just Dave and Rod and the other crew chiefs, there's none of that emotional claptrap, no one taking things personally."

Brianna feigned shock. "You mean Dave Harmon isn't in touch with his emotions?"

A smile curved Chad's lips and moved on up to his eyes. "Surprised, huh?"

"Of course," she said fairly, "I shouldn't judge by appearances. He may be an incredibly sensitive guy."

Chad pursed his lips. "I think," he said, "in Dave's case it's safe to judge by appearances."

Brianna chuckled.

His expression sobered. "I know I hurt you two years ago

when I said I didn't want to work with you. But I stand by that. I wouldn't want to burden someone else with my own pressure."

"Or," she said, "you could share those pressures with someone, so that you don't go home each night ready to tear your hair out."

He was shaking his head before she finished her sentence. "This business can be hard," he said. "Marriage is just as hard. Heck, breaking up after a three-day marriage was more difficult than I'd ever have dreamed it could be. Business plus marriage… no way. Not for me."

ON WEDNESDAY Brianna got to meet Steve Parr, Matheson Racing's sponsor liaison. While Chad took responsibility for finding new sponsors, once the deal was signed, Steve worked with them day to day.

Steve and Chad met Wednesdays to discuss the week's sponsor-related activities—it was Chad's way of keeping track of potential dissatisfaction among sponsors, and also helped balance out the drivers' time. While they had contractual commitments to their sponsors, there was still some give-and-take about what specific events the driver would attend.

Chad asked Steve to brief Brianna about the kinds of activities that he believed delivered the best return on a sponsor's investment.

"I'm keen to hear that," Brianna admitted. Her final recommendation would come down to where the dollars would be best spent. For Brian Hudson, everything had a measure.

Acceptable, or not good enough.

Halfway through Steve's discourse, Trent came in without knocking.

"Dad alert," he said. "Julie-Anne just called—he'll be here in five."

Chad groaned. Brianna could sympathize; she'd feel exactly the same to be told her father was five minutes away.

"Did Julie-Anne say what he wants?" Chad asked.

Trent shook his head. "She said he's fretting about the sponsor search."

Both men glanced at Brianna.

"Do you want me to leave?" she asked.

"That might be best," Chad said.

At the same time Trent said, "No way."

Chad scowled at his brother. "I don't want Dad hassling Brianna."

That wasn't the reason she expected. Brianna scanned his face, wondering if his concern was genuine, or if he just didn't want his wife and his family in the same place at the same time.

"Brianna looks as if she can take care of herself." Trent winked at her. She smiled back—no one could ignore his easy charm.

Chad's scowl deepened.

Trent continued, "You know Dad will feel happier if he can see progress. And if he's happier, he's healthier."

"How ill is he, exactly?" Brianna asked Chad. "I thought you said the surgery was successful."

"A quadruple bypass has a minimum three-month recovery period," Chad said. "Which means Dad's not supposed to be working...but I can't stop him from worrying about this place."

Chad's brow furrowed; she wanted to touch that furrow, smooth it away.

"Let me guess," she said. She switched to a gruff tone. "He's worked too hard to build his empire, so he's not about to let a little heart attack slow him down."

Chad blinked. "Pretty much his exact words."

"And his doctors don't know anything."

"Morons, all of them." He smiled.

"People just don't understand that if your dad doesn't keep on top of everything at work, the place will fall apart."

"It's a wonder we haven't declared bankruptcy," Chad said solemnly.

"And the fact that you're worried about him?"

He spread his hands. "Just me being girly."

"I knew it."

Chad said, "No offense to girls."

"None taken," Brianna said. Electricity arced between them.

Trent waved. "Uh, you two? There are other people in the room, and Dad's about to be one of them."

Right on cue, they heard Brady's gravelly voice in the reception below. Steve Parr excused himself on the grounds he needed to get back to work, and a minute later, Brady walked in. He looked surprised, then pleased to see Brianna. He shook her hand first, then Chad's, then Trent's.

"Where's that daughter-in-law of mine?" he demanded.

Brianna froze. Chad did, too. Then Trent said, "Your daughter-in-law-*to-be* is spending a couple of days with her mom figuring out the wedding arrangements."

"Dad's talking about Kelly, Trent's fiancée," Chad told Brianna, his voice too loud.

"How exciting!" Briana said, her voice too bright. "When's the wedding?"

Chad glanced at the calendar on the wall. "The thirty-first."

"That's less than three weeks away," Brianna said.

"Can't come soon enough for me." Trent sat down, she guessed to encourage his dad to take the weight off his feet, too. "Speaking of weddings…Dad, have you and Julie-Anne set a date yet?"

Brady's mouth tightened. "We'll get to it. I'd like to have you and Kelly out of the way first." He sat down heavily in the leather chair opposite Chad's desk. "I'm not here to talk about weddings—I get enough of that with Julie-Anne. Next thing you'll be asking me about dresses."

For a guy who'd recently got engaged, Brady didn't sound too thrilled with the concept of weddings.

"I agree, Dad," Chad said. "There's no need for you and Julie-Anne to rush into this wedding."

Like we did, said the look he gave Brianna.

"I didn't say I don't want to rush," Brady snapped. "I love Julie-Anne."

Brianna gave Chad a look of her own. One that said, *Your dad's better at this than you are.*

"If we could have a decent NASCAR conversation for once," Brady said, "you can tell me how Zack's sponsorship is shaping up. Does the fact that Brianna's here mean good news?"

"No," Chad said.

"Chad suggested I spend a week here seeing how the team works," Brianna elaborated.

Brady nodded his approval. "Matheson Racing is all about family. Apart from our superior drivers, that's our big advantage over FastMax."

"FastMax is a family team, too," Chad pointed out.

"Stepfather, stepson. It's not the same." Brady dismissed the Clark-family dynamic with a snort. He obviously didn't consider their link to the Grossos worthy of mention. "You and your brothers are part of a dynasty, part of what NASCAR's all about."

Chad rolled his eyes.

"So far, NASCAR seems to be mainly about meetings," Brianna joked to Brady. "I've seen more of the meeting rooms here than I have of the cars."

The older man's face lit up. "Then it's a good thing I came by. Have you taken a look around the workshop?"

"Briefly," she said.

Brady harrumphed. "That's where the blood is on the floor— not literally," he assured her, "but that's where the race starts. Why has Chad got you cooped up here with him?"

"Dad, Brianna's trying to understand the business side of the team."

Chad's protest was ignored.

"I imagine all you've heard about me from my boys is that I had a heart attack and I'm marrying my secretary," Brady said.

Brianna made a sound of demurral, but she felt telltale color in her cheeks.

Brady threw his "boys" a fulminating look. "Or should I say, I'm marrying my secretary *again*."

"Uh, I hadn't heard the *again* part," she said.

"You mean Chad hasn't got on to that yet?" Brady marveled.

"He hasn't told you his and Zack's mom was my secretary when we met?"

Trent had a different mother from Brady's other sons? What else hadn't he told her? She shot a querying glance at Chad. He shrugged as if to say *it wasn't relevant.*

"I didn't know," Brianna said. "But then, why would Chad share something so personal with me?"

Chad's hands twitched at his sides.

Brady got a speculative look in his eyes.

"I mean, we only just met," she said hastily.

"Takes about twenty years to get to know my son," Brady said cheerfully. "But it's worth it."

And Brianna had thought she knew him after three days!

"Thanks, Dad," Chad said, startled.

"Or you can choose to spend time with people who are uncomplicated and fun to be around," Trent said. He spread his hands. "Not naming any names."

Brianna grinned. "You mean, shallow people?"

Trent roared with laughter. "Remind me not to introduce you to Kelly—she'd like you way too much."

Brady chuckled. "So, you prefer the strong, silent type, do you, Brianna?" He darted a glance at Chad, obviously enjoying his discomfort.

Yikes, how had this got to be about her romantic preferences?

"I prefer *people*—" she stressed the word "—who love what they do and love to talk about it…rather than about themselves."

"Ouch!" Trent said to Chad. "I think she just nailed both of us."

"You, for sure," Chad said. Trent snorted.

Brady said, "Then I'm the man—the *person*—for you. It's nice to meet someone who speaks frankly, without tiptoeing around me in case I drop dead at their feet." He glared at his sons. "These boys spend more time worrying about me than doing their jobs."

"How girly," Brianna said.

A smothered sound came from Chad.

Brady looked alarmed at the thought of a threat to his sons' masculinity that didn't come from him. Then he chuckled again. "I like this girl," he announced. He took Brianna's arm. "Come with me. Look at this team through the eyes of someone who's lived on both sides of the steering wheel. When you decide to sponsor a Matheson car, you buy into something that's much bigger than that car, that driver. You're buying into a NASCAR tradition that started before you were born and I hope will go on long after I die."

He led her out of the office, talking nonstop.

"CAN YOU BELIEVE that?" Chad said, outraged, after his father had dragged Brianna off on his grand tour. "Dad jabbering away like he's known her forever?"

"What's going on between you and Brianna?" Trent asked.

"Nothing's going on." Chad focused on his computer screen, moved the mouse around meaninglessly.

"She's very pretty," Trent said.

Chad's head jerked up. "So is your *fiancée*."

"I'm not saying I'm attracted to her, you goofball." Trent clutched his hair. "Was I this bad when I thought you were flirting with Kelly last year?"

"Way worse." Chad leaned back in his chair, and the leather creaked. He grinned, remembering. "It was fun seeing you all bent out of shape over a woman."

"Yeah, well, much as I'd like to return the compliment, it's not fun thinking about you falling for Brianna," Trent said. "Your life is way too complicated to add that into the mix."

Chad clasped his hands behind his head. "Two things, little brother. One, you're the shallow guy in this family, remember— don't try and go deep. Two, I have no intention of falling for Brianna."

"Good," Trent said, more serious than Chad had seen him outside of a race car.

They spent the better part of the next hour talking about

Trent's planned sponsor appearances. Chad told himself to enjoy
the respite from Brianna's presence—it was exhausting the way
she set all his nerve endings on alert. Instead, he found himself
remembering the conversation they'd had before Dad arrived,
how she'd understood Chad's frustration with his father's attitude
toward his heart attack.

Then she'd got along so easily with Brady—and with Trent.
*Of course she did. I wouldn't have married a woman who
didn't like my family.*

Brianna's empathy with them was a good thing, he reminded
himself. She was big on making a personal connection—whether
Matheson Racing got the sponsorship or not might come down
to where she connected best. So Chad should be pleased, not re-
sentful…or worse, feeling left out.

When they came back, it appeared his wife and his father were
the best of friends. Even Trent, everybody's best buddy, looked
surprised at their rapid rapport—Brady could be charming in his
own rough way when he exerted himself, but he didn't usually
bother. Chad wondered how his father would have reacted if
he'd called home a couple of years ago and announced he was
getting married. Or that he'd just got married.

Brady shook Brianna's hand as he prepared to leave. "Great
to get to know you better, Brianna. I hope you'll come to our
practice in Kentucky."

Chad hadn't invited her. Or his father. "Dad, you're not
supposed to be traveling yet."

Brady's good humor fell away; his face darkened. "I feel as
fit as a driver—a *real* driver, from before they put power steering
in the cars."

"What does Julie-Anne say about you going to Kentucky?"
Chad asked.

His father scowled. "Just because I'm marrying the woman
doesn't mean I can't make my own decisions. If I say I'm coming
to the practice, then that's what'll happen."

Was something wrong between Brady and his fiancée? Chad

could only hope at least one of them was starting to see how foolish their hasty engagement was.

Julie-Anne was like Brianna. She'd concluded early on that Brady wasn't the sharing, loving kind of guy she wanted, so she'd ended their relationship. When Brady had his heart attack, he decided Julie-Anne meant more to him than his longtime independence, and, as Chad saw it, he'd been trying to be someone he wasn't ever since. With limited success.

Dad wasn't cut out to be married to a woman like Julie-Anne any more than Chad was cut out to be married to Brianna.

BRADY SLOWED his pace the moment he was out of sight of his interfering oldest son. He knew damned well he wasn't back to full strength yet. He didn't need Chad or anyone else making such a fuss.

As he traversed the few hundred yards between the team headquarters and the offices of Matheson Performance Industries, located in the same business park, Brady concentrated on getting some even breaths and ignored the fluttering in his chest. The fluttering had been happening on and off since the heart attack, but it didn't mean he was about to have another coronary. His doctor said it was due to panic.

Panic! Brady Matheson, former NASCAR Sprint Cup Series champion and stalwart of the sport, responsible for some of the fastest engines in history, was having panic attacks. It didn't bear thinking about.

Brady patted his jacket pocket, found the reassuring outline of a bottle of pills. Damned drugs. He'd been as strong as a horse all his life—he'd smoked cigarettes back when that was what everyone did, and he'd drunk his share of beer. Now he ate low-fat food and couldn't get through the day without swallowing half a pharmacy.

He told himself to be grateful he was still alive, not to complain because the team didn't need him in Kentucky.

The happiest moments of his life hadn't taken place on a race track or in the pits. His happiest moments had been the birth of each of his sons; quiet evenings with his adored second wife, Rosie; the day Julie-Anne had agreed to marry him, right after he'd acted like a jerk who didn't deserve her.

Grace moments, Julie-Anne called them, and she was right.

Brady gripped the iron railing as he walked up the steps into the MPI building. Since his heart attack, Julie-Anne had carried much of the burden at the company, with Brady providing input from the sidelines. An influx of capital from a new investor meant they had projects they needed to kick off. They couldn't wait for his health to return.

Julie-Anne came out the door just as he got there.

"Hello, sweetheart." Her warm, musical voice always gave Brady a lift. "I was on my way over to the team headquarters so you could take me to lunch."

Brady started to grumble about not being allowed into his own office, and she said, "I need your input on the engine contract with Cargill-Grosso Racing."

Unlike his sons, she wasn't trying to shut him out of his business. He smiled. "Okay, Gypsy, I guess I could do that." He'd given her the nickname soon after he met her, and it suited her. He kissed her mouth, and she responded with a mew of pleasure.

"Do you feel as good inside as you feel to me?" she asked when he lifted his head.

"I feel great." And he did. He had a wonderful woman who loved him, a business solid enough not to go broke when he couldn't make it into the office, and his youngest son about to marry a wonderful girl.

Julie-Anne said, "I bought a couple of T-bones yesterday." T-bone was his favorite steak; Brady tensed. She continued, "How about I come to your place tonight and cook us a cozy dinner for two?"

Cozy—or romantic? To Brady, they were quite different, but to Julie-Anne, they were one and the same.

"We could light the fire," she said, confirming his suspicions, "and snuggle up on that enormous sofa of yours."

They'd had a few evenings snuggled on that sofa right after he'd got out of hospital. He hadn't been up to anything more than watching TV. With Julie-Anne cuddled in his arms, TV-watching had become the most fun thing in the world.

"Brady?" Her voice was low, seductive. "What do you think?"

Brady pictured the scene: he and his beautiful, dark-haired Gypsy on the couch, her sexy curves, which he'd been dying to get his hands on since the moment he'd met her, tantalizing him.

The fluttering started in his chest again.

"Trent wants to stop by tonight and talk about the wedding," he lied.

"I can hold off on snuggling until after Trent leaves, if you think it'll embarrass him," she said humorously.

Brady sighed, thought about saying what he had to, then chickened out. Again. "Not tonight, Julie-Anne. Let's just stick with lunch."

The disappointment in her eyes was nothing compared to the disappointment she'd feel when she learned the truth.

CHAPTER SEVEN

THE NO. 548 CAR was booked in for wind-tunnel testing on Friday, Brianna's last day with the team.

At seven in the morning, Chad, Zack, Dave Harmon, the car chief and the engine specialist, along with one of the engineers and Brianna, met at the tunnel, a few miles from Matheson Racing's headquarters. They were allocated a private work bay that had its own bathroom and kitchenette, plus a workbench and power for the team's tools. They could spend the day here, making adjustments to the car in complete privacy between tests in the tunnel.

"Confidentiality is paramount," explained the wind-tunnel technician who met them on arrival. "Our other clients don't know you're here or what you're testing, and you don't know about them."

The No. 548 car was taken into the tunnel—more accurately a large, long room dominated by a huge conveyor belt—and the group filed into the control room that overlooked it.

Through the wide window, they watched as the car was secured. Then the conveyor, which the technician called a "rolling road," started up, accelerating from zero to 180 miles an hour in under a minute.

They made for quite a crowd in the control room. As a giant fan circulated air in the test area to simulate race-track conditions, Brianna hung back so the experts could watch the data appearing on the monitors.

Zack looked more relaxed than usual—maybe because the

pressure was on the car today and not on the driver. He laughed at something his car chief said. When he smiled or laughed, he was darned handsome, Brianna had to admit. Around the team offices, she'd noticed that several of the women couldn't take their eyes off him. Same with Chad, only more so. She stole a glance at Chad, who was talking to the wind-tunnel technician. To her mind, even taking into account Trent's undeniable charms, Chad was the best-looking guy at Matheson Racing.

They ate lunch, pizzas ordered in, back in the work bay. When the team had made some adjustments to the car, they sent it back out for testing. As the data started coming in, the mood in the control room was upbeat. They were getting what they wanted.

Zack moved back to stand with Brianna while the more technical team members hung over the computer screens.

"What's everyone so excited about?" she asked.

"When we drove at Halesboro, the car had more drag than expected," he said. "At least, it did until I crashed. After that, drag was the least of my worries." He spoke lightly, but she sensed the strain beneath the words. "We think we've found a fix."

Brianna wrinkled her nose. "It can't be easy, making a comeback."

He grimaced. "Not on this team, where Trent's the golden boy." He didn't speak with any resentment, more a pragmatic acceptance that he wasn't top dog around here. "I shouldn't have quit the first time around."

"Too bad we can't turn the clock back." Brianna's gaze drifted toward Chad.

Zack cleared his throat; she brought her attention back to him and found his sharp eyes on her.

"You're too young to have regrets," he said.

"No regrets," she replied, telling herself as much as him.

He looked skeptical.

"I guess this comeback is a way of dealing with your regrets," she said. "The next best thing to doing it over."

"Dad's illness was a wake-up call," he said. "He and I haven't gotten along in years—not in decades. But when I told him I wanted to rejoin the team, he didn't hesitate to say yes. I realized I shouldn't let resentment over the past get in the way of the future."

Whatever the past sins that had created the rift between them, Brady Matheson was a good father. His words about Chad flitted through Brianna's mind: *Takes about twenty years to get to know my son…but it's worth it.*

Brianna's father lost interest if he didn't get what she was saying in twenty seconds. When he'd called this morning, he'd questioned whether visiting a wind tunnel was good use of her time, then suggested she was taking too long on her evaluation.

At four o'clock, during the third round of testing, cheering broke out in the control room. The latest data were the best yet, better than they'd hoped for.

"This could be it," Zack said. "This could fix the problems I was having at Halesboro."

He gave that gorgeous smile, and spontaneously Brianna squeezed his arm. "I hope so," she said.

Chad said, "Fixing the aerodynamics doesn't let you off the hook, Zack. You've got a long way to go before you win a race."

Zack's jaw set tight; Brianna's blood boiled. Zack was at least trying to fix his past mistakes, which was more than Chad was.

"Don't be such a jerk, Chad," she said.

She'd thought the car guys were completely absorbed in their data, but every man in the room turned to stare at her. Dull color flooded Chad's face; Zack sucked in his cheeks and took a protective step closer to Brianna.

"Excuse me?" Chad said, menace in his quiet tone.

This was her chance to turn it into a joke. Or to apologize.

"You should just be…nicer to Zack," she muttered.

A ripple of interest ran around the small room.

"May I see you outside?" Chad said with jaw-breaking self-control.

"I'll come, too," Zack offered, worried.

"Stay," Chad ordered.

"He's not a dog," Brianna said crossly.

Zack groaned. "Brianna, honey, if I promise I won't let Chad push me around, will you please shut up and go with him?"

"Since you asked so nicely," she said pointedly to Zack, "and you said *please,* I'll go."

Zack looked as if he was muttering a prayer of thanks under his breath. Chad just looked mad.

Brianna followed him to the work bay. He closed the door behind them with an intimidatingly soft click.

No one will hear me scream.

"WHAT DO YOU THINK you're doing, telling me how to handle my brother?" Chad demanded the second the door closed. Okay, he'd pounced on Zack in a way he might not have if Brianna hadn't been hanging on to Zack's arm…but everything he'd said was true. She had no right to butt in.

Brianna stalked across the room—why was she wearing high-heeled boots to a wind tunnel, for Pete's sake? How was a guy supposed to concentrate with that *click-clack* distracting him every time she moved?

She perched her bottom on the workbench. "That wasn't handling him. That was insulting him."

"Someone has to tell it like it is," he snapped. "Zack has a long way to go before he's ready to race. He can't afford to lose focus."

"Sometimes people need encouragement. They need to know you see their good points, as well the bad." Her face was pale, her hands clenched at her sides.

The last time Chad had seen that mix of anger and vulnerability was the moment he'd met her—she'd just finished talking on the phone to her dad. He remembered her saying at dinner last week that she'd never lived up to her father's standards.

"Zack knows I see his good points," he said, less heat in his voice.

"How?" she asked.

"He…I…he just does." Chad paced toward the door. "You don't know Zack, Brianna. This isn't like you and your father—

he doesn't need my approval or some kind of connection." Though now that he thought about it, *disconnected* was a good word for his brother. "Zack needs to win races and I want to help him."

"He can't win if he doesn't feel part of the team."

"Of course he's part of the team," he said. "That doesn't mean we don't argue. You can't expect three brothers to always talk to each other like…like Barbie dolls." He raised his voice to a falsetto. "Omigosh, Zack, that race suit is the exact color of your eyes."

"You're being childish," she said. "You need to wake up and be thankful for your family."

"You need to remember that they're *my* family," he retorted. She recoiled as if he'd slapped her. Which was crazy, for there was no way she could think of his family as her concern, no matter how well she got on with them.

"I don't need your interference," he went on. Especially not the way she'd done it back there, so that everyone knew what she thought of him.

Her eyes flashed fury—he must have imagined that moment of hurt. "Pardon me for trying to keep the peace," she said.

"Keep the…? You just made things a hundred times worse," he snapped. "Every guy in that room is deciding whether he's on my side or Zack's, and the next time something goes wrong at a race track, one of us is going to cop the flak. Next time you want to keep the peace, go to the Middle East."

"Next time you want to insult your brother in front of the same people I apparently insulted you in front of, try shutting up," she said. "I take back every nice thing I ever thought about you."

He snorted. "What nice things?"

"None of your business. I meant what I said back there, Chad. You're a jerk." Brianna's eyes were suspiciously damp, her color high, as she stormed past him out the door. Which she did not close quietly.

What nice things had she thought, dammit? And when had she thought them? Two years ago…or more recently?

It didn't matter. What mattered was she was wrong about him

and Zack. He might have been a little tough on Zack…but Brianna didn't have the experience to see what Chad saw when he watched Zack out on the track.

A driver who'd lost his touch.

Chad wasn't sure his brother had it in him to make a comeback. Yet here he was asking Brianna's father to spend millions of dollars. There were no guarantees in NASCAR, of course, but Chad wasn't used to taking quite such a leap of faith. Small wonder he was on edge.

Still, he shouldn't have spoken so harshly to Brianna, either. It was just…he was starting to feel ganged-up on. As if Brianna liked everyone in his family except him.

I want her to like me.

As if she could like him after the way he'd spoken to her. Probably even made her cry.

"Damn." Chad grabbed his jacket from the workbench. He wasn't going to get a single thing done, let alone find another sponsor for Zack, when he knew Brianna was upset.

Outside, he scanned the parking lot. He saw her Mustang immediately, saw her chestnut hair above the back of the driver's seat. Relief flooded him.

As he neared the car, he realized her shoulders were shaking.

Brianna really was crying. And was apparently so distraught that she couldn't drive away. Chad didn't think he'd been that monstrous. Which just showed how little he understood women and why getting married had been such a stupid idea.

Guilt and annoyance rose as he pulled open the driver-side door.

"I'm sorry," he snarled. "All right?"

Her eyes widened with bewilderment, then she glared. "Are you telling me this is your fault?"

"Obviously it must be, or you wouldn't be flooding the parking lot."

A mystified silence, punctuated by a sniffle, greeted that. Chad whipped his handkerchief out of his pocket, handed it to her.

She blew her nose.

"I didn't mean to say that about you interfering in my family," he said belligerently. "You can't go getting upset every time I open my mouth."

"Can't I?" she said, annoyed. "Is that an order?"

She was back on her kick about him being bossy; his hackles rose. "Yes, it *is* an order. We're trying to work together here." Those tears were drying fast, he noticed, which made him feel a lot better—even if her eyes were sparking dangerously.

"I don't see how we can work together when you're so rude and obstinate," she said. "When I first met you I thought you were kind and...and soft."

Soft? Everything inside Chad revolted at the word.

She blinked rapidly, water welling up in her eyes again...and his heart twisted.

"I *am* kind," he said gruffly, then forced out, "and soft."

Which had the unexpected effect of turning her incipient sob into a hiccup, then a chortle.

"Okay, maybe I'm not soft, exactly..."

The chortle turned into a laugh.

"I'm trying to apologize here," he said, aggrieved.

"Chad, you're about as soft as...as a crash barrier."

He winced at the thought. The SAFER barriers they used in NASCAR these days were a hell of a lot softer than the old concrete, but they were still awfully hard. "How would *you* know how a barrier feels?"

She held up her hands, a peace offering. "I don't. But I do know you're not soft and—" she hesitated "—if you were, you probably couldn't run a NASCAR team."

He stared, surprised by her reversal. "You mean, I'm not the dictator you thought I was?"

"I mean," she said, "that team owners might have to be dictators some of the time."

He considered that a serious olive branch. "I'm sorry I made you cry," he said.

She smiled. "Actually, you didn't. You made me mad enough

to cry, but it was this thing that pushed me over the edge." She thumped the steering wheel. "My car won't start. It was the last straw in a day that started with my father hassling me and ended with you telling me to get lost." She turned the key in the ignition, and he heard only a click.

He decided not to reopen the discussion about his personality flaws. "You have gas, right?"

She gave him a look that said she would never run out of gas. Chad leaned in to look at the fuel gauge, anyway, and caught the scent of clean skin and her lily-and-lemon perfume. Got a close-up view of her lips, too—raspberry pink. It took him a good few seconds to focus his vision on the fuel gauge. Nearly full.

"Satisfied?" she asked coolly.

No, sweetheart, I'm not satisfied, not by a long shot.

The thought came out of nowhere and was reflected by a tightening in Chad's whole body. Hell, that crying jag had played havoc with his nerves.

"It might be your starter motor." He stepped away from the car before he did something stupid, like kiss her, and glanced at his watch. It was past four o'clock, and the guys would be wrapping up here soon. "I'll have someone tow this back to the workshop, while I drive you wherever you're going."

"You can't do that," she said.

"Brianna, you've just accused me of not being kind. I'm going to drive you whether you like it or not." He jerked his thumb in the direction of his Viper Coupe.

She glared. "Next you'll tell me this is your idea of soft."

"You got it." He turned and walked away, heading for his car, determined not to let her refuse. He could do with a chance to repair the damage he'd done that afternoon; he didn't want her last thought of him today to be that he'd never have made a good husband.

His dad and Rosie, Chad's stepmother, used to say it was best not to let the sun go down on an argument. Chad could take Brianna where she was going, grovel a little on the way, then be back at the office in time to review the budget estimates Tony Winters, the team accountant, had been working on today. The estimates were running a couple of weeks late, as were several other financial tasks. Tony had been apologetic, but the guy was on edge. Chad wanted to make sure everything was okay.

Brianna caught up with him before he reached his car—obviously she wasn't as averse to a little dictatorship as she thought. He helped her into the car and put her briefcase into the trunk.

"Where to?" he asked as he buckled himself in. He started the engine.

She stared straight ahead, her purse clasped demurely in her lap. "Atlanta."

Midway through reversing out of his parking space, Chad hit the brake. "What?"

"I'm going to see my father." That was definitely a smile tugging at the corners of her mouth. "I told him I'd be there by seven."

Chad pulled back into the space.

"Maybe next time," she said sweetly, "you should think twice before ordering me around."

He might have known she'd turn his helpful—make that *kind and soft*—offer into some sort of personality defect. Chad's hands tightened on the wheel. His plans for going over the finances this evening shuffled through his mind and he discarded them.

He reversed out of the space, executed a fast, squealy U-turn and headed out of the parking lot.

"What are you doing?" Brianna grabbed for her purse before it slid off her lap.

"Taking you to Atlanta." He flipped his turn signal, drove out onto the highway.

"Don't be ridiculous."

"You wanted to go there—" he consciously loosened his jaw so he didn't sound so uptight about it "—so that's where we're going. You're calling the shots, Brianna, not me." He managed to direct a carefree smile at her.

BRIANNA BIT DOWN on any further protest. She'd wanted to teach Chad a lesson about his domineering ways. She hadn't for one second imagined he'd take it into his head to drive to Atlanta.

"You are so stubborn," she contented herself with. "It's pathetic."

"Thanks," he said. "Where I come from, we call it kind and soft."

She clammed up.

When they hit the interstate, Chad said, "Since you're calling the shots, what do you want to talk about?"

She stayed silent.

"Come on, Brianna—" his knuckles dusted her upper arm, teasing her senses "—it's a three-hour drive."

She hadn't heard that coaxing tone in his voice since he'd asked her to marry him. She closed out the memory. But he was right, not talking for three hours would be childish.

"We'll talk about work." Which was the safest of the topics available to them. Not that talking business would stop her from noticing the timbre of his voice, or the thickness of his lashes in profile, or the molded fit of his jeans.

Darn it, Chad had been horrible today, and she still wanted him. She could only put it down to that vulnerability he'd shown when he'd come out to yell an apology at her and ended up trying to convince her he wasn't the super-tough, impervious guy he liked to pretend he was.

They conversed about the forthcoming NASCAR Sprint Cup Series season, about the other teams and their strengths and weaknesses. The conversation flowed surprisingly well, dissipating the tension, and the 250 miles flew by.

"So," Chad said as they reached the I-285 ring road around Atlanta, "who's the front-runner for the Getaway sponsorship?"

Brianna swallowed. If she wanted to be the consummate professional, she would tell him that her investigation was very much a work in progress, that both teams had considerable strengths.

She felt him glance at her. She couldn't keep their personal relationship out of this, couldn't treat him as just a business contact, much as she would like to.

"FastMax," she blurted, and when she heard his sharp intake of air, wished she hadn't. "Chad, I'm sorry to disappoint you, but their driver is more consistent, and their teamwork is impeccable. They're an excellent operation."

"And you're not divorcing Andrew Clark," he said sourly.

"That has nothing to do with it."

He shook his head. "Since the first minute you arrived at Matheson Racing you've been determined to see only the negatives."

The accusation stung. Her voice wobbled as she said, "That's not true."

He ignored her. "You accuse me of being a dictator whenever I apply a little team discipline, but if Zack does something out of line, you suggest he's undisciplined."

Okay, that might be true.

"You criticize me in front of the team, instead of trusting me to see the big picture."

"I made *one* comment." Admittedly a bad, very public comment. Plus a couple of other comments to Zack, she thought guiltily.

Chad stared at the road ahead. "You've made a big deal over the fact that back in Vegas I didn't want the kind of support you were offering as a wife," he said. "If what I've seen the past couple of weeks is a sample of that, then I think I'm vindicated."

The accusation shot through Brianna like a lightning bolt, jerking her back in her seat.

It was true! She'd been so determined to protect herself against her hyperawareness of Chad, against falling for him again, she'd emphasized every negative. And she'd let that spill over into her evaluation. Regardless of how much it might hurt him.

"Brianna?" He glanced at her sidelong.

She shook her head, wordless.

"Uh…did I upset you?"

The last thing she needed was him trying to make her feel better.

"I'm fine," she said shortly. After that, she didn't say another word, other than to direct him to her father's house. They pulled into the driveway right at seven.

"I'll be ready to leave by nine," she said, "if you don't mind driving me back." Right now, she wouldn't be surprised if he made her walk.

She opened her door.

Chad said, "I'm coming in."

CHAPTER EIGHT

BRIANNA STOPPED halfway out of the car. "Excuse me?"

Chad opened his door. "I'd like to meet your father, talk to him about the team."

"You can't." Her regret over her attitude toward him evaporated, leaving only alarm. "This isn't a business meeting." Unfortunately she couldn't sound convincing. With her father, everything was business. Quickly, she got out of the car, closed her door so that would be the last word on the subject.

Chad got out, too, and retrieved her briefcase from the trunk.

"Chad, I mean it. Go away."

"Hello, dear," a voice called. Once again, Margaret had seen Brianna coming.

Chad took the steps two at a time, leaving her scurrying to catch up. "Hi, I'm Chad Matheson." He shook Margaret's hand.

"Ooh, I'm a huge fan of your brother. Trent, I mean, though I'm sure Zack's very nice." The housekeeper laughed at her own rambling. "Tell me, is Trent as handsome in real life as he is on TV?"

"Handsomer," Chad said expansively. "He'd bowl you over in a heartbeat."

Margaret put a hand to her chest as if she could feel that heartbeat.

"Mr. Matheson isn't coming inside," Brianna said.

But Mr. Matheson was already over the threshold, chatting away to Margaret for all the world as if *he* was the charmer in the Matheson family.

Which he could be, she knew.

Margaret looked from one to the other, loyal to Brianna, but responding to Chad's natural authority. "Your father's upstairs, but he said he'll see you in his office," she said to the space between them. She led Brianna into the familiar, paneled room. Chad, naturally, followed.

After she left, Brianna turned on him. "I mean it, Chad, I don't want you talking to my father."

"And I meant it when I said I don't think you're giving Matheson Racing a fair shot."

Hot tears of anger pricked at her eyes. It was one thing to accuse her of bias—quite another to tell her father. As if her dad didn't doubt her enough, without Chad complaining she was mishandling the project. Good grief, he'd probably drop in a few choice words about what a terrible wife she was.

She was about ready to beg him to leave when her father walked into the room.

She almost didn't recognize him. Gone was the head of thick, silver hair, and in its place, sparse gray wisps. Thankfully, instinct had her stepping toward him without hesitation—she could only hope her shock didn't show on her face.

"Brianna." He sounded almost pleased to see her.

She hugged him, felt his reassuring bulk. Then she absorbed the grayness of his complexion, the faintest tremble in his fingers, the wince when a horn blared in the street outside. Her father looked past her, at Chad.

"Dad, this is Chad Matheson," she said reluctantly.

When her father frowned, she felt a twinge of relief. Dad didn't like things happening that weren't part of his plan, and he didn't like people seeing him at less than his strongest. Not that Chad knew how ill her father was—for all he knew, this was her dad's normal appearance.

Chad shook hands with Brian, explained how he came to be driving Brianna to Atlanta.

"I suppose your car was overdue for its annual service," her dad said. He waved them to sit on the leather couch that flanked the fireplace, and took a seat in the wing chair she'd used last time she was here. That he hadn't chosen to sit behind his desk told Brianna he wasn't himself. But she knew better than to ask how he was feeling in front of Chad.

Brian said, "How's the project going?" He glanced at Chad. "Perhaps I should have Margaret show our guest to the living room."

"Good idea," Brianna said.

Chad said, "Sir, before you do that, I want to comment on Getaway's NASCAR-sponsorship plans. From what Brianna's said, you intend to take a strategic, long-term approach to your sponsorship decision."

"Of course," Brian said.

"As the season gets closer and the drivers spend more time in their cars, the pressure increases to favor a driver with more recent NASCAR Sprint Cup Series experience than my brother Zack has. I'm here to advise you not to forget the bigger picture when you choose a good match for Getaway Resorts."

If there was anything her father liked less than unplanned interruptions, it was being *advised*. Brianna folded her arms and relaxed against a cowhide cushion.

She took the opportunity to examine her father. Was his face thinner? She couldn't be certain. His shoulders were a little hunched, though, where normally he sat tall and proud. He'd re-iterated on the phone just this morning that his doctors were wrong, that the chemo had a good chance of curing him. She hoped so.

She realized Chad's tone had changed, become confiding, and that her father was leaning toward him, listening. Uh-oh. She snapped her attention back.

"What I'm saying," Chad said, "is that you have a chance to create a legacy."

"I'm not going anywhere," Brian Hudson said. "Why do I want a legacy?" But to Brianna, his voice lacked its usual certainty.

"You might live for years or you might die tomorrow," Chad said with a candor she could see her father liked—though Chad could have no idea how likely the second part of his sentence was. "So might I. It's never too soon to start creating something that will last more lifetimes than your own."

Brianna's father grunted, and unconsciously ran a hand over his hair.

"Some people sponsor NASCAR because they want the glory this year," Chad said. "They want to be on TV when their driver wins. They want their name in the newspapers."

Her dad dismissed those attention-seekers with a sneer. He and Chad smiled at each other. How did Chad know which buttons to push talking to her father when she constantly got it wrong?

Because they're two of a kind. Two men whose businesses matter more to them than anything else.

Except…Chad did care about his family, she knew that. He just didn't have room for a wife.

Chad said, "A visionary knows things change from year to year—winners come, losers go. But there's one thing that lasts."

Going by the lift of his eyebrows, Brian was hanging on for the answer in his own restrained way.

"Sportsmanship," Chad said. He paused, let the word sink in. "The reason NASCAR is still one of America's favorite sports after sixty years is because it's about winning fair and square. It's about taking it to the track every weekend and battling your peers, no holds barred. It's about the best man winning."

Brian nodded.

"Sponsoring NASCAR—the *right* kind of sponsorship," Chad corrected himself, "is about investing in the values that have made the sport great. I urge you to choose a team that embodies those values. That's what you'll get with Matheson Racing."

Brianna felt as if she'd been manipulated into letting him say his piece, and now he was hijacking her job. "I should point out—" her voice was thin, and she swallowed before she continued "—that FastMax also embodies those values, as do many of the teams." She gave Chad a tense, *I'll kill you later smile.* "If Matheson Racing was the only one that did, those wouldn't be seen as the sport's values."

"Matheson's right," her father said. "It would be easy to give too much weighting to driver performance."

"That's why you and I agreed on the criteria before I started."

"How do I know you're sticking to those?" her father asked, turning toward her. "I'll get one of my marketing guys in there to take a look." He steepled his fingers. "Perhaps I should put someone else on the project with you."

Brianna's face flamed. From the corner of her eye she saw Chad shift on the couch—doubtless he planned to jump in and undermine her further. She swallowed over a lump in her throat. What was the point? She would never meet her father's expectations, never earn his respect and love. Why had she thought agreeing to do this job would open his heart?

Her father had shown more warmth, more *connection* to Chad tonight than he had to her.

"If you have someone else you think would do a better job," she said stiffly. "I'm willing to step aside."

Chad must be cheering inside—he wouldn't have to deal with her anymore. Dad would put one of his bright young men on the project, the kind of man Chad could relate to, someone who thought this was all about business and nothing more.

Her father folded his arms. "If you think that's best."

Then Chad said, "You don't want Brianna quitting this project, Mr. Hudson."

CHAD WISHED he could pick up those words and stuff them back down his throat…but no, he'd sent them rolling into the room at 180 miles an hour, and there was no getting them back. He believed every word he'd said to Brianna on the way here, about her prejudice against him and against the team. So why was he trying to help her keep her job?

Because he knew how important it was to her. No matter that she was steely-eyed as she threatened to quit, she had some crazy idea that completing this project for her father would earn his love.

Brian Hudson, who a minute ago had looked as if he would

lick Chad's hand if it got near enough, now appeared more likely to inflict a serious bite. "Don't tell me what I want."

Give it up, Chad told himself. *You don't get anywhere when you butt into a family argument.* He should know.

He heard himself say, "Brianna has been very thorough in her assessment so far."

She gave a hiss of annoyance, which he considered most ungrateful.

"I don't need you reporting on me to my father," she said.

Didn't she? It seemed to Chad that if he didn't stop her, she would throw away this big chance of hers.

"It's just, she's a tough sell—" her dad would like that "—so I wanted to make sure I got a hearing from you, too."

"I thought you were suggesting she wasn't looking at the big picture."

"All I want is a fair shot for Matheson Racing," Chad said.

"That's what you'll get," Brianna replied. There was a meaning in her voice Chad couldn't decipher. Had she accepted she was judging Matheson Racing by a different, more personal standard than she was applying to FastMax? Was she willing to change that?

Brian let out a beleaguered breath. "Is she doing a good job or isn't she?"

"Why don't you ask me?" Brianna demanded.

"She is," Chad said.

"You don't need to doubt you'll get a fair shot from me," Brian said. He glared at Brianna. "You'll stay on the project. Just don't lose focus—you know what you're like, flitting from one thing to the next. I want this job done properly."

Chad's hackles rose. He had a sudden glimpse of why Brianna objected to him ordering people around. Not that he was as unreasonable as her father, of course, but constant exposure to this could make anyone oversensitive.

"Sir, I'm sure you didn't intend to be rude to your daughter." Chad didn't normally have a problem with his mouth running away with him, but tonight it was as if a dozen green flags waved every time he opened it, and he had no choice but to put his foot to the floor. "But I'm sure she'd appreciate your apology."

Brianna's jaw dropped. Brian Hudson went so silent and his color rose so high, almost purple, that Chad wondered if the man had swallowed his tongue. Instinctively his mind raced ahead, working out what to do: get the guy on the floor, clear the airway, have Brianna call 9-1-1. And later, assure her he hadn't intentionally tried to kill her father.

He half stood, but it turned out Brian was just building a head of steam.

"Get out," he commanded, and once again, Chad found the bellowing of orders grew tired fast. "How dare you tell me how to talk to my daughter!"

Chad recalled saying something along the lines of *How dare you tell me how to talk to my brother!* to Brianna a few hours ago.

He might as well try her argument with her father. "Encouraging Brianna will do more for her than insulting her," he began.

Then Brianna wrapped her fingers around his wrist.

The contact was so unexpected, its effect—his blood pooling beneath her fingers—so startling, that he let her tug him to his feet.

"I need to get back to Charlotte, Dad, if I'm to deliver the results you want at the speed you want," she said. "Please look after yourself. I'll call you in a couple of days."

"If rudeness and arrogance are the values your team embodies…" Brian said ominously to Chad.

Brianna released Chad long enough to kiss her father's cheek, then towed him toward the door. Chad said a hasty goodbye over his shoulder.

Two minutes later they were on the road. Neither of them spoke until they were on the interstate. Chad was still kicking himself for having screwed up the chance to get Brianna's father on his side.

As they passed Atlanta's city limit, Brianna said, "I thought you'd be pleased to have me off the project."

"So did I."

She fidgeted, briefly drawing his attention to her slim fingers and his mind back to the feel of them against his bare skin. How could he remember that so clearly?

"So why did you convince him I should stay?" she asked.

He flicked his turn signal and passed a truck. "For someone so keen to tell me what I do wrong with my family, you're not smart when it comes to your own dad."

"My dad's difficult," she said.

"You told me this was a chance to connect with him, then you ran at the first sign of trouble. You can't make a connection if you quit."

"I've been trying for years," she protested.

Sudden rain pelted the windshield, and Chad concentrated on trying to see through it. If the rain didn't stop, the journey home would likely be longer than the trip down. He really didn't need to spend any more time cooped up with Brianna.

Neon lights drew his attention; he pulled in at a service area diner. "We never got to eat. Let's grab something here."

BRIANNA FOLLOWED Chad into the diner. Anyone would think today was the national Expose Brianna's Faults Day. First Chad's accusations of bias, and now this. *Did* she run the moment it looked as if things might not pan out with her dad?

Of course, she did. That was how their relationship worked.

Was there a better way?

They sat in a red vinyl booth by the fogged-up window. The previous occupant had drawn a heart with an arrow through it in the condensation.

Chad pulled the menus out of their holder, passed one to Brianna. "I don't know how ill your father is…" He paused, but she didn't fill in the gap. If she told him her dad might have only a couple of months to live, he'd feel awful about the argument he'd just had. "But I know that if you have things to tell him, you shouldn't wait. I learned that when Dad had his heart attack."

"Tell me what happened," Brianna said.

He pushed the salt and pepper aside, rested his forearms on the table, hands clasped. "When Julie-Anne called to say Dad was in surgery, I didn't think about what he was going through, the fear and pain he must have been suffering. All I could think was that I hadn't hugged him in months, that the last time we spoke I was mad about something Trent had said." He shook his head at his own selfishness.

She reached across, covered his hands with hers. "That doesn't mean you weren't worried about him. You were afraid of losing him."

He pressed his lips together, then said, "I was afraid of the guilty conscience, too. Not that I think you have anything to be guilty about where your father's concerned. But I figure, if you give up on this job, sooner or later you'll be kicking yourself."

Brianna swallowed. Chad was right. And it would be sooner, rather than later. In the pain of the moment, she hadn't seen beyond the fact that once again, she wasn't good enough for her father. But Chad, who barely knew her, had looked ahead—that big picture he was so fond of—and despite the hurt she'd doled out to him earlier today, had taken steps to protect her from future hurt. Hurt that would have been far worse than tonight's.

The waitress arrived to take their orders. Brianna chose a burger and fries; Chad had settled on the double bacon burger and double fries.

"I'll have a milk shake too, please," he said. "Chocolate."

Brianna stared at him.

"Want one?" he asked.

"Strawberry, thanks," she told the waitress. When the woman left, Brianna said, "As I recall from Las Vegas, you 'grew out' of milk shakes when you were twelve."

"Did I say that?" He shifted in his seat. "Turns out they're a great source of calcium."

"I know." She challenged him with her eyes.

"What?" After a second he let out a breath and leaned back

in the booth. "Okay, after you left, I ordered a milk shake once or twice. Must have been thinking about you, I guess. Decided I liked them."

Just when she thought she had him pegged, he surprised her again.

"You were right about what you said earlier," she said. "I haven't been as open to Matheson Racing as I should have been. I plan to fix that."

He nodded, watchful.

"And I wasn't very appreciative of your attempts to help me with Dad during that meeting," she said. "I'm sorry. What you did was really sweet."

He grimaced, looking almost as revolted by *sweet* as he'd been by *soft*. "Your dad was so spitting mad, he'll probably tell you not to bother with Matheson Racing. If you're lucky, you won't have to see me again."

Why did that make her feel bereft?

She forced a smile and said lightly, "I doubt it. Once Dad gets over the shock, he'll admire you all the more. I suspect you remind him of himself at a younger age."

Chad sat back to allow the waitress to set down their meals and milk shakes. "I get the feeling that's not a compliment."

"I love my father," she said defensively. And remembered she'd once told Chad she loved *him*. "He's strong," she said, "and so are you."

"Still waiting for the compliment."

She sipped her shake, eyed him over her straw. "I've accused you of changing for the worse since we broke up. But now I'm thinking maybe some things have changed for the better."

"If you're basing that on the fact that I ordered a milk shake, I have to question your logic." He popped a French fry into his mouth.

Brianna took the top off her burger and began to eat the filling with the bottom half of the bun. "There's never been much logic to you and me."

He chuckled.

"It's not like I'm saying you turned into a saint," she said. "You barged into Dad's house tonight and told him how I should do my job."

"That was a terrible thing to do," he agreed. "That would be like you telling me how to get the best out of my brothers."

She couldn't help her snort of laughter. He was entirely focused on his double bacon burger, but he was smiling, too. And suddenly this roadside diner felt like the toastiest, safest place in the world.

Chad was bossy and controlling, but he was also fiercely loyal and protective of those he loved. She'd seen that tonight. *He doesn't love me.* No, but he felt protective of her. Despite a couple of lapses, he'd arguably shown more loyalty to her than she had to him.

She was tempted to revel in that protection, to shelter her bruised heart in its warmth.

Brianna straightened in her seat, stabbed a French fry with her fork. What was she thinking? Chad hadn't budged on his view that he didn't want to work with her—he'd said it again just hours ago. It would be dangerous to fantasize about anything more.

She caught him watching her, speculation in his eyes. She wondered if he could read her mind—and cringed inwardly.

She grabbed her milk shake. "Race you to the bottom of the glass."

And although he rolled his eyes and muttered something about *childish,* he couldn't resist the challenge. They drained their glasses until their straws gurgled.

Brianna won…but only just.

THEY ATE FAST and were back on the road within half an hour. The rain stopped as they traveled north, but the night grew steadily colder. By the time they arrived back at Matheson Racing headquarters, a frost crisped the parking lot's grassed verges.

One of the mechanics had called Chad's cell phone to say he'd replaced the starter motor in Brianna's car. Chad drove right up to the Mustang.

"Wait here while I get it started," he said. He found the key inside the wheel rim and got into her car. The throaty roar of the engine confirmed all was well.

Brianna hunched her shoulders as she stepped out of Chad's warm Viper.

Chad turned on her heater and directed the blast at the fogged-up windshield before he got out. "Okay, you're good to go."

"Thanks." Brianna slung her briefcase into the back seat. Chad was so close to her she could feel the heat of his body in the cold night air. His breath was visible, mingling with hers.

She shivered. He chafed her arms through her jacket. "Get in the car or you'll freeze."

She nodded. But he didn't take his hands away, and she couldn't move—it was as if they were locked together.

Brianna tilted her head, parted her lips. Chad read it as an invitation—which she now realized it was—and lowered his mouth to hers.

Sweet. Tempting. Demanding. His kiss held a tenderness Brianna couldn't remember experiencing with him before, a newness, a sense of adventure. He coaxed her mouth open, entered. It was slow and languorous—crazy, given how cold it was out here.

She pulled away first, with difficulty. "Um…like you said, I'd better go."

He slid his hands down to cup her elbows and they stood, very close to each other, for several long seconds. She thought he might kiss her again.

Then someone called Chad's name, startling them both.

He cursed, stepped away from Brianna and lifted an arm in greeting to Zack, who was crossing the parking lot toward them. "Where did you come from?" Chad asked.

"I've been in the office going over the data from the wind tunnel."

The office Trent and Zack shared was at the end of the workshop, around the back of the building, which explained why they hadn't seen any lights.

Zack grew closer, and in the orange glow of the streetlamp, Brianna saw the gleam of curiosity in his eyes. Had he seen them kissing?

"Where have you been?" he asked. "I was afraid you might be burying Brianna in a shallow grave."

"Off-site meeting," Chad said. "Brianna's just leaving. I need to pick up a few things from inside." He held her door wide so she could get in the car.

Zack stood there, not going anywhere, so Chad said, "Good night, Brianna." Lightly, he thumped the roof of the car; then he walked toward the building.

Brianna clipped her seat belt. Zack closed her door, but just when she thought she was home free, he rapped on the window.

She opened it.

"You can tell me it's none of my business," he said, "but there was a vibe in the air between you and Chad just now."

"It's none of your business," she said.

"There was something going on earlier, too." Apparently she could tell him it was none of his business, but he didn't have to listen. "You seem like a nice lady, Brianna, so I want to warn you—Chad's not a good bet for a relationship."

"I'm not…" The protest began automatically, then her desire to know more won out. "Why not?"

Zack hesitated. "He's involved with someone."

CHAPTER NINE

"WHAT?" THE NIGHT chill seeped into Brianna's bones despite the heater blasting in the car. "He told me he's not." Great, she'd just let slip that she and Chad had got really personal.

Zack's eyebrows shot up. He scratched his head, grimaced. "I'm surprised he'd say that. Chad doesn't make a habit of lying. But…well, the guy's such a mess, maybe he doesn't see it the way I do."

"Chad's a mess?" Brianna asked. Not possible. If he was any more together, he'd be cement.

Zack's fingers wrapped over the window opening, as if he was bracing himself. "Brianna, Chad's married."

For one absurd moment, she thought he meant Chad was married to someone else, besides her. The confusion was a blessing, because her recoil and her stunned silence effectively stopped Zack guessing she knew anything at all about Chad's wedding.

"He got married in Vegas a couple of years ago," Zack explained. "We don't know who she was, but she hurt him pretty bad."

Brianna blurted, "*She* hurt *him?*"

Zack looked insulted on his brother's behalf. "Chad's a strong guy, but he cares deeply." He loosened his grip on the car. "All I'm saying is, I understand why he's attracted to you, but you need to know he would never cheat on a woman, not even one who left him." He looked troubled, as if he'd just realized that by kissing Brianna, Chad had indeed cheated on his mystery wife.

Brianna didn't want to lower Zack's opinion of his brother—

and she longed to know more about Chad's "hurt." But she couldn't say anything without clueing Zack in. Instead, she said, "I appreciate the warning. But there's no chance of anything happening between me and Chad." Now she just had to keep telling herself that.

He looked relieved, then skeptical. "What I just told you is confidential, okay? No one outside the family knows Chad is married."

His whole family knows?

"I'm only telling you because he's been acting…odd," Zack said.

"He's lucky to have you looking out for him," Brianna replied.

Zack shoved his hands in his pockets. His blue eyes turned cold. "Yeah, well, Chad's done a lot for me. If I ever meet the scheming piranha who ran out on him, she won't be so lucky. I don't know what she wanted, but she sure did a number on my brother."

CHAD HAD DRIFTED off to sleep around 4:00 a.m., after he'd finally realized what he had to do next. Difficult though the admission had been, he'd got out of bed to type the e-mail. Hitting the send button had brought him a measure of peace.

He awoke early on Saturday, despite the long drive to and from Atlanta and the late night. But not, it seemed, as early as Brianna, who thumped on his front door at 7:00 a.m.

How did she know where he lived? he wondered as he surveyed her from his bedroom window. Oh, yeah, he'd given her his address before they'd left Las Vegas, in case she needed him.

Obviously she'd held on to it.

The pounding on his door intensified. She was a bundle of outrage in jeans and boots, and a sweater the red-pink of glacé cherries. Chad wondered if she was ticked off because, like him, she hadn't been able to sleep, courtesy of the memory of that kiss. Crazy that one kiss could do that—it was a sign of what he'd acknowledged in the night, that he'd allowed Brianna too far into his heart again.

Thank goodness he'd recognized it in time.

He pulled on his navy, terry-cloth robe and headed downstairs barefoot.

She whirled into his house with an energy that reminded him of their time in Las Vegas—except this energy definitely radiated hostility.

"Uh, good morning?" he said.

She flapped the ends of her striped, multicolored woolen scarf at him. "How can it possibly be a good morning for you, given you're the innocent victim of a scheming piranha?"

Her chestnut hair bobbed with indignation.

Chad woke up his brain. He'd expected a difficult conversation with her today, but in his imagination it hadn't gone like this. Shouldn't *he* be doing the talking?

"The piranha," he guessed, "would be you?" In that figure-hugging sweater she looked about as predatory as a color-confused goldfish.

Her lips clamped together, but not for long. "Why didn't you tell me your family knows you're married?"

Chad's sense of humor went back to bed. Dammit, Zack must have said something.

"If we're going to fight, I need coffee." He headed for the kitchen, certain she was mad enough to follow without waiting for an invitation.

"Zack was talking as though I'm some kind of…of Jezebel." She set her purse down on the island.

Chad paused in the act of putting the kettle on the stove. "You didn't tell him you're my wife?"

Of course she hadn't. If she had, Zack would have been here by now, along with Brady and Trent.

"I couldn't," she said. "I was speechless."

"You seem to have got over that," he observed as he scooped coffee into the French press.

Her eyes flashed fire, and he wanted to take her into his arms. *No more of that. Not after that e-mail.*

"*Why* did you tell them?" she asked.

Chad leaned against the stove. "I blurted out that I was married right after Dad's heart attack. Trent was steamed because he thought I was making a play for Kelly—"

"Were you?"

"I'm *married*," he reminded her. "Trent and Kelly were falling apart, so I confessed to keep the peace."

Brianna grimaced. "Doesn't sound very peaceful to me."

Chad barked a laugh. "Damn right. I was lucky to get out of Dad's hospital room without being injected with truth serum."

"So…how much do they know?"

"Only that I married someone in Vegas, that we split up right away and that we're getting a divorce."

Pretty much all there was to know. Given he could never tell them how exquisite it felt to make love to Brianna, could never describe the lurch in his heart when she smiled…

The way she was doing now.

"You're not mad?" He squinted so he wouldn't get the full wattage of that smile, wouldn't be blinded to the fact that they were wrong for each other.

"I'm glad you didn't say anything bad about me," she admitted. "Though I'm not sure why your brother assumes I'm the villain."

"He's protective."

"Runs in the family," she said, resigned.

The water boiled, and Chad filled the press. He glanced at his watch to time the coffee brewing. "Could you grab a couple of mugs from that cupboard behind you?"

Brianna did as he asked. She turned back slowly, looking around as if she'd been so preoccupied with the reason for her visit she hadn't observed her surroundings. Chad tried to see the kitchen through her eyes. The old house had been a large farm-house when it was built, but it wasn't on the scale of Brian Hudson's mansion.

"This is lovely," Brianna said. Her gaze took in the rustic, oak-beamed ceiling, the flagstone floor. The kitchen counter was new granite, the appliances—including a state-of-the-art milk-shake maker—stainless steel. But the cabinetry was more wood. Elm, from trees felled in an era where timber was plentiful and houses were few.

Light from the low winter sun streamed through the French doors Chad had designed to match the old-fashioned, multi-paned windows.

"I imagined you living somewhere stark and functional," Brianna said.

"Is that a comment on my personality?"

She colored. "This is so cozy."

Cozy wasn't a word Chad applied much to his existence. He loved this house because it was so different from the atmosphere at work—it was a refuge from the rest of his life. He took the mugs from her, his fingers brushing hers, and poured the coffee.

He added cream and one sugar to hers. "Are we still fighting?"

"That depends." She took the mug, blew on the contents. "Did you tell your brother I screwed you over?"

"No," he said, shocked. "But I'll screw *him* over. If I can think of a way to do so without alerting him to the fact we're married…"

She touched his arm—dammit, how did her touch sear him every time?

BRIANNA WAS STANDING so close to Chad, she wondered if it occurred to him that if he put down his coffee, he could pull her into his arms. Her gaze dropped beneath the sudden intensity in his…then caught where his terry robe had parted. Dark hair curled over a chest that she knew felt hard and muscular…

Assailed with wanting, with longing, Brianna closed her eyes. Somehow, she managed to take a step backward.

"Brianna," he said, his tone intense.

She took a sip of her coffee, sheltering behind the mug. "I know," she said, trying to be sensible, "we shouldn't keep…but I find myself wanting to kiss you…again."

His eyes were dark with frustration, and good sense fled. She set her cup down on the island and reached out a hand to Chad.

"I e-mailed my lawyer last night—early this morning," he said. "I told him to file for a divorce."

The words thudded into her, each one a stone that bruised. Her hand fell away.

"We both know I should have done it a long time ago," he said. "We can't move on until we get the divorce."

"And…that's what you want to do? Move on?" Brianna had the crazy thought that if she'd known they were going to talk about this, she'd have worn makeup. She knuckled her cheeks, bare, exposed.

"We want different things," he said. "Yes, we both want to kiss each other, but nothing has changed since Vegas."

She tried not to look around at the house she now realized she'd wanted to picture herself living in. Caffeine burned in her throat, her stomach. She'd come here this morning angry that Chad's family blamed her for their split. Then she'd fallen into the usual trap of being seduced by her attraction to him, aided this time by his beautiful home…and it had ended with a slap in the face.

The slap stung all the more because last night was the closest they'd come to the tenderness they'd experienced in Las Vegas. That he would run from that, so hard, so drastically…

"Why apply for the divorce now?" she asked.

"Last night we were…close," he said. "But neither of us wants this marriage, not in the big picture. You want a guy who'll share everything with you."

"And you want companionship on those nights when you make it home early enough," she said stonily. "Conversation that doesn't demand your heart. Sex when you need it. Kids who won't disrupt your commitment to the team."

Chad stared out the French doors at a sparrow splashing in the birdbath on the lawn. "If you give me the name of your lawyer, mine will get in touch."

She swallowed. "It's not as if one of us is disputing the divorce or we're dividing up assets. I'm happy for your lawyer to represent both of us."

He nodded. The phone rang, but he ignored it.

"Why don't you get that?" she said, welcoming the distraction.

His eyes still on her, he picked up the phone. "Uh, hi, Dad." Then, "No, I didn't forget."

His eyes widened and he flicked a glance at Brianna. Obviously Brady had mentioned her.

"No," Chad said flatly.

No what? she mouthed.

"Absolutely not." Chad turned away from Brianna, made a few more comments, then ended the call.

"What was that about?" Brianna asked. Her cell phone buzzed, and Chad groaned.

"Don't answer that," he ordered.

She pressed the answer button.

"Brianna." Brady's voice boomed over the airwaves, sounding strong and healthy. "I want you to come to lunch today at my place."

"That's kind of you, Brady, but—"

"I'll have Chad pick you up," Brady interrupted.

"Do you think he'll want to do that?" Brianna asked. *What would his lawyer say?*

"Of course he will."

"Brady, if the invitation is because you want to talk about the sponsorship…"

"I expect that'll come up," he said easily. "When you're with the Mathesons, you talk NASCAR. It's one of those chicken-and-egg things. But mainly, I like you, and I'd like to spend more time with you."

A wave of nostalgia for something she'd never had washed over Brianna, taking her by surprise. She gasped for air.

"You still there?" Brady asked. "Damn cell phone," he muttered, "always cutting out on me."

"I'm still here," Brianna said, a wobble of amusement, and maybe something else, in her voice.

"So, you'll come for lunch?"

Chad was shaking his head at her and making throat-slicing motions.

"I'd love to come for lunch," she said.

"I TOLD CHAD to bring the sponsor girl with him," Brady said.

"Brianna Hudson?" Julie-Anne added chopped cilantro to the pan on the stove—a Thai chicken curry that Brady knew was delicious despite its newfangledness.

He stirred in the cilantro for her. Which was about the most useful thing he'd done in the past two months. It was nuts that a guy who, thanks to modern cardiac surgery, was perfectly healthy would be forbidden by his doctors to do anything more strenuous than *hover*.

Even more nuts that when he disobeyed, he was left short of breath.

"Anything else I can do for you?" he asked Julie-Anne.

What was the world coming to when a man needed someone's permission to be useful?

"You could set the table," she suggested as she ran the faucet over the chopping board.

"Carry all those knives and forks by myself?"

She laughed. "Don't be a grouch, dearest." Her smile was so sunny, so loving, that Brady couldn't hold on to his temper tantrum. Especially not when she turned off the faucet and walked across the kitchen, curvy in her T-shirt and ruffled skirt, hips swinging.

Brady managed to focus on the way watching her made him feel inside, in his heart, rather than on his physical reaction. Or his total, dispiriting, mortifying lack thereof.

Julie-Anne wrapped her arms around his neck; he tugged her closer. Their lips met in a tentative kiss that soon became urgent. Only Brady knew that his urgency was more desperation.

He cupped her face with his hands, explored her mouth thoroughly. She pressed herself harder against him and gave a little moan of longing.

When he broke away, he was breathing heavily.

"I love you, Brady," Julie-Anne said.

"I love you, too." It was easier to say than he'd ever thought it would be, after Rosie died. He never wanted to stop saying it to Julie-Anne. But would she feel the same when she realized...

Julie-Anne caught sight of the clock on the wall behind him and squawked. "They'll be here any second and this place is a mess!"

Her sense of organization was completely different from Brady's, so he knew better than to try to clean up with her. He was a tidy man himself, but the two of them never agreed on what went where. Even in his own kitchen.

He left her to it and went to set the table. Relieved to have once again escaped the inevitable conversation that loomed at the front of his thoughts.

All three of his sons would be here for lunch—it was great having Zack back in Charlotte, even if it was seldom easy. Nothing nicer than having the whole family around.

Not just family today. Brady was glad he'd circumvented Chad's objections and invited Brianna directly. For some reason, Chad was dragging the chain on the Getaway sponsorship. Which wasn't like his oldest son—Brady could only think Chad had too much on his plate. He'd been off the pace in his work, though not so as anyone other than Brady would notice, ever since he'd come back from Las Vegas two years ago.

What had possessed Chad to marry a woman he'd only just met?

Chad had insinuated that Brady was doing the same. But Brady knew Julie-Anne a heck of a lot better than Chad had known that little miss he'd married. He knew Julie-Anne would never walk out on him.

Which was the whole damn problem. She would stay with him out of loyalty, out of sympathy, but dammit, he didn't want that. He wanted a woman who saw him as the strong, take-charge man he was. *Used to be.*

This time last year, he'd have said he didn't want a woman at all. Which proved there was no certain way to happiness in this life. There was Chad, all upset because he'd rushed into a stupid marriage. Zack wasn't himself, either, but as far as Brady knew it wasn't anything to do with a woman; his middle son had some resentments to get over, but Brady didn't have a clue how to help him, wasn't even sure it was his job. Trent was as happy as a NASCAR Sprint Cup Series driver in Victory Lane, of course, but he'd always had a sunny nature. And Kelly was perfect for him. They were the exception to the rule.

Brady sighed. Family was too hard to think about. Better to focus on Zack's sponsorship—something tangible he could do for his son. Brady had hit it off pretty well with Brianna the other day, and he intended to build on that today.

He smirked at the way he'd outsmarted his son over getting Brianna here—proved he was still in charge of something. *Of lunch. I'm a legend in my own lunchtime.*

Chad and Brianna were, predictably, the first to arrive. Right behind him came Zack in his Ford F-150 truck. Trent, of course, would be late. He swore he never did it deliberately, but the simple truth was, the boy liked to make an entrance. Brady felt his face soften at the thought of his youngest son.

He went out onto the porch to greet the older boys and Brianna.

"Thank you for inviting me," she said.

He shook Brianna's hand, then kissed her cheek. Julie-Anne came outside, drawn by the noise, and Brady introduced the two women.

As always, he felt a glow of pride. Julie-Anne was so pretty, so youthful and energetic, she could easily pass for younger than her forty-nine years. She favored full skirts and figure-hugging tops that reminded Brady how desirable she was.

Brianna was a pretty girl, too, but she had none of the mature voluptuousness that made Julie-Anne so addictive. Still, Brady caught a spark of something in Chad's eye as he looked at Brianna that surprised him. Maybe his son was coming out of his self-imposed exile. Bad timing, though. He'd have to tell Chad to wait until after the sponsor deal was signed.

BRIANNA WAS INTRIGUED to meet Kelly Greenwood, the woman who'd tamed playboy Trent Matheson. She was prepared to be intimidated—none of the Matheson men were easy, not even Trent—but Kelly turned out to be low-key, even ordinary.

But when Trent looked at her, you realized she wasn't at all ordinary, not to put a light like that in a man's eyes.

Kelly was all smiles as she greeted Brianna on the porch where pre-lunch drinks were served. "Trent tells me you're quite something when it comes to keeping the Matheson men in line," she said.

"Now, sugar, that's not what I said at all." Trent's voice turned even more drawly than usual. "I said you'd like her."

"My point exactly." Kelly stumbled on a floorboard that stuck up a fraction from the porch.

Trent grabbed hold of her. "Dad, I offered to fix this board for you," he said, accusing.

Kelly swatted his arm. "Don't be silly. You can't expect people to Kelly-proof their homes." She said to Brianna, "I should warn you, some people run when they see me coming. I have two left feet."

"*Three* left feet, sugar," Trent corrected helpfully, which earned him another swat.

"I'm a klutz," Kelly said. "But I'm used to it, and if you stick around long enough, you will be, too."

I don't plan to be here that long, Brianna thought, wishing she could stay forever. Trent and Kelly had something between them—some kind of magic—that was irresistible. What would it be like to be so intimate with a man that it didn't matter if you and he were two entirely different kinds of people?

"Brianna's only here another two, three weeks, tops," Chad confirmed.

As if that was his decision. Brianna glared at him. His arms were folded, his shoulders rigid, his whole stance proclaiming *I asked my lawyer to get me a divorce.*

"Zack, tell me how the wind-tunnel testing went on your car," Brady said.

"We fixed some drag issues, and I think we really got a handle on the aerodynamics." Zack glanced at Chad. "Though if you believe some people, the driver's still a major problem."

"That's not true, Zack," Chad said, his voice a bit stiff. "You have the skill and determination to fix whatever's wrong. You just need more seat-time."

Everyone stared at him.

"Uh, thanks," Zack said cautiously. The shift in his brother's attitude didn't disconcert him for long—he seized the opportunity. "Do you mind if my team goes to Kentucky a day ahead? I know there's an extra cost in using the track, but I think it would help."

"Hey, not fair," Trent said immediately. "Ouch."

Brianna gathered that Kelly had nudged him hard. She knew money was tight at Matheson Racing right now—if they didn't sign a sponsor for Zack before Daytona, the team would have to fund him itself or pull him from the races. But Chad didn't dive in with the flat refusal to pay for another day's testing that she expected.

"I'll give that some thought," he said, still excessively polite. "Let's talk about it in the office on Tuesday."

Zack darted a glance at Brianna—she shrugged—then said, with equally exaggerated civility, "Thank you, Chad, I appreciate your willingness to consider the idea."

"My pleasure." The glint in Chad's eyes said the strain of speaking respectfully to his brother was starting to show.

"What's going on?" Brady demanded. "Why are you talking like constipated ballerinas?"

Chad gave Brianna a look that said *See? I can be encouraging.* As if he was doing this for her. Was he? Warmth spread through her…and came smack-bang up against her hurt that he'd filed for divorce.

CHAPTER TEN

THEY SAT DOWN to lunch late, almost two o'clock. The drinks had relaxed everyone—Brady managed not to groan out loud when the women moved to the subject of the forthcoming wedding, though he did exchange resigned glances with his sons. Kelly and her mom had everything planned, but apparently it was essential that everyone else hear all the details.

"I don't recommend it as a means of getting close to your mom, though," Kelly told Brianna. "Mom and I have almost come to blows a couple of times."

"My mom lives in Australia," Brianna said. "We don't keep in touch that regularly."

"That's too bad," Kelly said. "I mean, I know I complain about my mom, but I'm glad she's here."

Brianna gave her a reassuring smile. "I don't think my mother and I would have seen eye to eye about much to do with my wedding."

"Are you married?" Kelly's gaze traveled to Brianna's left hand.

Brianna blushed—Brady was interested to note that Chad immersed himself in the contents of his plate with an improbable degree of fascination for the Thai chicken curry. His son was definitely interested in Brianna. Goodness knows why that obliged him to stand ten feet away from the woman the whole time, rather than letting her see he was attracted. Brady shook his head at the ignorance of youth.

"I meant, if I ever get married," Brianna said. "I'd love to have a big wedding like yours. Even if I have to organize it myself."

Chad was chewing with a tension that suggested he might break a tooth. Well, well. Brady rubbed his chin. He knew his son wouldn't go after Brianna until he divorced the woman he'd married—as far as Brady knew, that hadn't happened. Still, it wouldn't hurt Chad to take things slowly next time around.

"How about you?" Brianna said to Julie-Anne, sounding slightly desperate. "Have you and Brady set a date?"

The light from the chandelier above the dining table caught the enormous diamond on Julie-Anne's finger. Brady was proud of that ring. But he wasn't so excited about Brianna's question.

"We want to wait until the doctors have cleared Brady to go back to work." Julie-Anne's musical voice was patient. "And until after Trent and Kelly's wedding. One set of imminent nuptials is enough." She smiled at Brady, a loving, knowing smile.

Except, she doesn't know.

"What do you think, dearest?" she asked. "Shall we pick a date and see if it works for the doctors?"

Chad looked about as sour at the prospect as Brady felt. Zack looked mildly interested; only Trent was enthusiastic. Along with the women, of course.

"Plenty of time for that," Brady said.

Julie-Anne's smile turned quizzical. "How about March? Or I guess the weather might be nicer in April."

"It rains in April," Brady said. "A lot."

The flatness in his tone communicated itself to her, and she sent him a worried look. Kelly did the same.

Brianna, thankfully, changed the subject, asking about the architect who'd designed Brady's house. From there, Kelly talked about the minor redecoration of Trent's place they planned.

Julie-Anne didn't join in quite as animatedly as before, Brady noticed. Damn, he was going to hurt her. If not now, then later. If he had any guts, if he wasn't a selfish jerk, he'd do it now.

Instead, he reached across the table and took her hand. And felt like a heel when she gave him a smile that radiated love, and faith in him.

It was five o'clock, almost sunset, by the time everyone left. Brady cleared the table while Julie-Anne worked in the kitchen. She hummed a Beatles song. He loved the way she sang or hummed all the time.

Drawn by the sound, he moved into the kitchen, where he stood, watching her.

She poured detergent into the dishwasher, turned it on. Then she straightened and looked at Brady. The gleam in her eye told him what she had in mind.

He said, "I'll make coffee."

She raised her eyebrows. "An energy boost. Great idea."

Unfortunately the coffee was done in five minutes, even though he went to the trouble of making it in a French press the way Julie-Anne liked. Brady would have been happy with instant.

They carried their mugs through to the living room. Julie-Anne sat on the enormous sectional leather couch and patted the cushion next to her.

Brady sat, and then found escape in the form of the TV remote control. "I want to catch the news, learn the latest about the Grosso baby." The kidnapping three decades ago of newborn Gina Grosso, Kent Grosso's twin sister, was recently in the news—rumors had surfaced that Gina was still alive and somehow involved in NASCAR. A mystery blogger kept adding fuel to the fire.

"Since when are you interested in the Grosso baby?"

He might have been fooled by Julie-Anne's casual tone if he hadn't happened to look at her and see her mouth set in a tense line, her eyes narrowed. He'd never been able to fob her off.

Still he tried to dig his way out. "I've known Dean Grosso twenty years. And Patsy."

"What's their other daughter's name? The youngest?"

What was this, NASCAR trivia? He tsked. "It's, uh, Susannah."

Julie-Anne folded her arms beneath her chest, pushing her curves up, and Brady willed himself to feel something. Anything.

"I'll be sure and tell *Sophia* your concern for her family next time I'm talking to her," Julie-Anne said.

"Just because I got the girl's name wrong—" there was probably a solid argument here, one he could drag on until Julie-Anne got so riled she'd forget all about cozying up together "—doesn't mean I don't care about her family."

"What's going on, Brady?"

It was a chance to tell her, but he couldn't do it.

"Have you heard from Amber lately?" he asked. A desperate attempt at diversion, and her indrawn breath told him it was a low blow. Amber was Julie-Anne's daughter, who was currently wandering the world somewhere. The two had been estranged since the death of Julie-Anne's unfaithful first husband, Billy Blake. Although she'd had an awful marriage, Julie-Anne had nursed Billy after an accident on the interstate paralyzed him. She'd sent Amber to stay with her sister to escape Billy's reckless behavior, and the girl had never gotten over the misguided belief that her mom didn't want her around.

When Julie-Anne had e-mailed Amber to say she and Brady were engaged, the girl had sent a furious reply about "not learning from her mistakes." Then nothing.

Julie-Anne found it painful to talk about Amber these days. Kids. You couldn't win.

"I'm sorry," Brady said. Because no matter how much he didn't want to discuss their relationship, there was no excuse for causing her pain.

"Is this prevaricating all because you don't want to set a date for our wedding?"

He gazed at the TV. "It's not that I don't want to."

She snatched the remote, turned off the set. "Have the decency to be honest," she snapped. "At least before your heart attack, you had the guts to say you didn't want me."

"That wasn't true. I said that when I was too stupid to know what was good for me." He would forever be grateful to his faulty heart for showing him how much she mattered to him.

"Do you love me?" she demanded.

"You know I do."

Her hands bunched into fists. "All I know is, every time I mention our wedding, which isn't a strange thing to do, given I'm your fiancée, you change the subject."

"I just don't see what the hurry is, when we're busy with Trent's wedding."

She gave him a searching look. "When you proposed, it was right after you almost died of a heart attack. Your proposal might have been a heat-of-the-moment thing, and now that the doctor says you'll be fine, you're regretting it."

"It wasn't the heat of the moment," he growled. He took her hand, squeezed it harder than he should, but she didn't seem to mind. "I love you, Julie-Anne. More than I knew I could."

Her smile was hesitant, watery, but still the smile that gave his heart a lift. "You don't have to sound so gloomy about it."

He kissed her hard, and she opened into his embrace with all the warmth and generosity he cherished.

Then she pulled away, buried her face in his neck. "I want you so much," she said, her voice muffled. "The sooner we get down the aisle and into bed the better."

The doctor hadn't cleared Brady for sex yet, but that should happen in the next month. Then he'd have no excuse.

"Maybe we shouldn't worry about the weather and get married early March," she said. "It doesn't have to be a big event if you think it'll strain your health. As long as you and I are there, that's all that matters."

Dammit, he had to tell her.

"Julie-Anne," he said, "there's a reason I can't set a date."

She paled, then visibly braced herself. "Tell me."

Brady squirmed. How could a guy say this and keep any kind of dignity? "The medication they put me on after the heart attack, the beta blockers…it turns out they have a few side effects."

Her eyes widened. "The doctor mentioned dizziness," she said, "and fatigue."

"Yeah, well, there are some others he didn't mention. I guess at the time there were more important things to worry about."

She swallowed, but her gaze held steady.

"It seems that on these pills, I can't get, uh…" Brady sought refuge in jargon and said, "Beta blockers can cause a reduction in libido."

His face burned hot as a T-bone on a grill.

"You're worried about our *sex* life?"

He couldn't tell if she was horrified or just plain surprised. He nodded.

Julie-Anne laughed and flung her arms around his neck, knocking the wind out of him. "Brady, my dearest idiot, if that's all it is, we can get married tomorrow."

"Do you understand what I'm saying?" He disentangled himself. "As things are now, there's no way I can, uh, satisfy you."

It was humiliating to even talk about something he'd always taken for granted, about his basic ability to be a man.

Brady ran a hand over his face. "Gypsy, what if the effect of these pills is permanent?"

"Is it?"

"I don't know," he said, frustrated. "I only found out they were to blame for this libido thing by searching on the Internet. I don't know how long I'll have to keep taking them, or if I'll recover to the extent that I can…or if that particular side effect will clear up."

"Why don't you ask your doctor?"

"I'm not going to talk to him about—"

"He's your *doctor*," she said. "You're supposed to tell him that kind of thing. For all you know, there might be a simple fix."

She was right, of course. Brady felt better already. He drew a breath. "Okay, I'll tell him."

"Regardless of what he says," she continued, "we can set a date."

"I want to wait until I've seen him," Brady said.

Julie-Anne turned away, dashed a hand over her eyes.

"I'm sorry," he said miserably. "I know this is disappointing."

"I don't give a damn about whether you can make love to me or not," she said fiercely. "What upsets me is that you think it would make a difference to how I feel."

What could he say? She might not think it made a difference now, but who knew what the future held?

CHAD WAS THANKFUL for the breathing space afforded by the team's practice at Kentucky—even though they had to share the track with two other teams, and even though his dumb-ass brothers were responding to the tension of testing by acting as if they were about to launch preemptive nuclear strikes on each other.

He drew in a breath of the Kentucky air, redolent of gasoline, as he walked toward the garage. And felt happier. This was what racing was about—the rubber meeting the pavement. If he could just keep things this simple...

It was so much easier than being at Matheson Racing, wondering when Brianna might call or turn up, his dad prowling around like a suspended driver. Brady was a walking advertisement for why a guy shouldn't jump into marriage with a woman he didn't know very well, and why he shouldn't marry someone who was integral to his work.

This season was falling apart before it started, but Chad couldn't get his brain into gear to put his focus where it should be. He'd be crunching the numbers with Tony Winters, and instead of searching for ways through their sponsor difficulties, he found his mind wandering to Brianna and the way she'd fitted right in with his family on Saturday. To the way neither of them was good at handling their own kin, but it seemed they could give each other a few pointers.

Chad's cell phone rang; a glance showed it was his lawyer. He shut off the call. It was about the divorce, no doubt, and he couldn't think of a damned thing he wanted to say on that particular subject.

"Chad, wait up," Kelly called from behind him.

He stopped. She walked briskly toward him, her clumsiness not allowing her to risk anything faster, like jogging.

"Hey, Kel." He grinned at her. One thing about Kelly, she could cheer him up. She was so levelheaded, and she had Trent's number so completely, it was a relief to have her around.

"I enjoyed meeting Brianna at Brady's place," Kelly said.

Uh-oh. Kelly was a sports psychologist, so you had to watch yourself or you'd find your thoughts pegged open for inspection.

"Good," he said cautiously.

"I talked to her some more after lunch, but she was a little guarded."

Go, Brianna. "You can be scary when you're doing your lie-down-on-my-couch thing."

Kelly chuckled. "She seems to like you."

Chad stopped. "How do you figure that?"

"I have my ways." She tapped her nose. "Thing is, if you're interested in her—"

"I'm not," Chad said.

"—then you need to know she's not the independent type, like you."

"You think?" he said.

"I'm not saying she's not strong—I think she's very strong. But when it comes to a relationship she's going to be looking for a guy who'll give a lot."

"Did she tell you that?" he demanded.

"Are you kidding? She doesn't know me from a hole in the ground." Kelly put a hand on Chad's arm to slow him down—unconsciously, he'd sped up. "I gathered both her parents are emotionally distant. She's craving an antidote to that."

Chad had never been the antidote for anyone's emotional problems. "Thanks for the heads-up. I'll make sure I don't give her the wrong impression."

"That's not what I meant," Kelly scolded, "and you know it."

"I'd be more interested," Chad said deliberately, "to hear your views on Zack."

She sighed and went with the change of subject. "That guy is a closed book with a padlock on it. And I thought it was hard getting Trent to open up when I first met him."

"Do you think Zack can race well this season?" Chad asked. He knew from Trent's losing stretch before Kelly came along that a driver whose head was in the wrong space was going to struggle on the pavement.

She considered the question. "I'm trusting your and Trent's opinions that Zack is a great driver, at least sometimes."

He nodded.

"Anything's possible," she said, "but my impression is Zack has a lot happening beneath the surface. There's a danger it'll boil over at the wrong times."

That meant bad decision-making. Lack of focus in crucial moments. Wrecks. Damn.

They stepped into the garage area.

"Thanks for your thoughts," he told Kelly. "If you could keep trying to get Zack to talk to you on an informal basis…"

"I'll try. But Zack doesn't trust his family," Kelly said. "Right now, I'm not quite family, so he's said a couple of things. But I guarantee you that'll change after the wedding."

Great, another problem—an even more reticent Zack—on the horizon.

FULCRUM RACING and FastMax were also testing at Kentucky on Friday. FastMax had brought Brianna with them.

At the sight of her in the FastMax garage, bands tightened around Chad's chest. Was this how his dad had felt before that heart attack?

This wasn't about his physical health, Chad knew. This was about the fact that he was divorcing a woman he'd once been crazy about, a woman who was everywhere he looked, strolling around in tight jeans and a casual fur-lined jacket, her chestnut hair swinging. She was in his face. She was in his thoughts. She was in his soul.

Chad didn't need this. Not with Trent seething about Zack squeezing in an extra day's testing yesterday and Zack acting all smug about how well his car was running. Not with Brady here against doctor's orders, and the strain between him and Julie-Anne painfully obvious.

As Chad watched Brianna, Garrett Clark broke away from the TV-news crew he was chatting to and made a comment to her. She laughed and Chad's stomach knotted. No way was he going to let Clark charm her out of that sponsorship money. He strode down the garage.

Maybe she sensed his intention to forcibly drag Clark away from her, because when she saw him, her chin shot up in the air, defiant.

"I didn't expect you here today." Even Chad heard the accusing note in his voice, and the TV cameraman was giving him an odd look. He dialed it back and said, "Welcome to Kentucky."

"As you can see, FastMax invited me."

He should have done the same, of course. Chad cleared his throat. "I hope you'll have time to come by Matheson Racing. Maybe you could join us for lunch. Zack can tell you how things are going with the car." Since his brother got on so well with Chad's wife.

"I'm busy at lunchtime." The way she kept her eyes fixed firmly on Chad, not letting them stray to Garrett, told Chad who she was lunching with.

Testosterone surged. "Dinner, then. Are you staying over?" It was a two-day session.

He'd been trying to keep his distance from her since he'd spoken to his lawyer. But what was he supposed to do? Stand aside while his wife ate lunch and did goodness knows what else with Garrett Clark?

"Dinner with Zack?" she asked.

"With me."

"Thanks, but I thought I might go into Cincinnati for a look around."

She hadn't hesitated to turn up for lunch with his family when he didn't want her to, but now that he asked her to a meal, she refused.

Still, he wasn't going to argue in front of Clark. "Then I'll see you in our pits later."

BRIANNA DIDN'T REACH the Matheson Racing pits until after her lunch with Garrett, having spent an enjoyable morning with Andrew Clark and his team.

Trent was done for the day—his team had a list a mile long of things to fix—but Zack was still out on the oval, and his crew chief, Dave, was hunched over a screen on the war wagon. Chad and Trent watched the lap-time monitor down below.

"How's Zack doing?" she asked Chad.

He smiled, which was an improvement on his surliness earlier. "His last two laps have been faster than Trent's best."

Trent muttered, "There's a first time for everything."

Even Brianna could see Zack was driving better than he had at Halesboro, holding his line into the turns, then out again.

The dour Dave Harmon whooped as Zack posted an even faster lap. Chad spoke into his headset. "Great job, Zack." He grinned at something his brother said in reply.

Zack kept up his sterling performance, and when he pulled into the pits, he wore a grin a mile wide. Trent's trademark charming smile was markedly absent.

Zack got out of his car, pulled off his helmet, then vaulted the pit wall. He sauntered up to Trent. "I tell you, little brother, I'm going to whip your—" Zack glanced at Brianna "—behind at Daytona."

"In your dreams," Trent said. "Any fool can drive a fast lap when he's the only guy on the track."

"Any fool except you, it seems," Zack said.

Trent snorted. "When you're out there with forty-two other cars, you'll be buried so far back in the pack you won't have a chance to clock up anything other than a mediocre time."

"I plan to start up at the front," Zack said. "Ahead of you."

"Not a chance," Trent scoffed.

"Guys…" Chad issued a warning, but his brothers ignored him. Chad's momentary relaxation was gone, replaced with the assertive style that so often drove Brianna crazy.

This time, she saw the infinitesimal sag of his shoulders before he squared them again, the bleakness in his eyes as he realized a couple of the myriad balls he was juggling were about to come tumbling down. The poor guy. If only he didn't feel he had to carry the load by himself. A lesser man would have buckled by now. Brianna's heart went out to him. He was stubborn and bossy, but he would do his darnedest for his family, even if the effort tore him apart.

"If by some miracle you do make it to the front—" Trent heaped coals on the fire "—you'll never stay there."

Zack folded his arms. "Because you'll smash into me and make sure I don't?"

Any hint of bantering was gone—this was stark accusation. Zack had to be referring to the crash that had put him out of contention for the Chase for the NASCAR Sprint Cup four years ago. He'd walked away from his wrecked car, but he'd lost his chance to make the Chase. He'd quit Matheson Racing, joined another team. After the next season, he'd stopped racing altogether.

"Can it, you guys," Chad snapped. Which, Brianna thought, was like telling two snarling tigers to play nice.

Going by the jut of his chin, Zack wasn't about to back down, and Trent looked ready to inflict some serious damage on his brother's handsome features. One of the TV crew members who'd been hanging around in the garage picked up on the tension from fifty feet away and said something to his colleague. Both men watched the Matheson brothers.

In about two seconds, this squabble would turn into the kind of fracas that would hit the headlines and would have any sponsor with a scrap of sense washing its hands of Zack Matheson.

Someone needs to do something.

Zack shoved his brother. Trent drew back his fist.

Now.

CHAPTER ELEVEN

BRIANNA WASN'T DUMB enough to insert herself between two super-strong NASCAR drivers with throwing punches on their mind. Instead, she let out a loud moan and swayed dramatically on her feet, her knees crumpling.

She was counting on lightning-fast NASCAR-driver reflexes to save her before she had to fall to the ground. She hadn't counted on *three* Matheson men rushing to grab her. Trent and Zack each grabbed an elbow, while Chad wrapped his arm around her middle. "Brianna? What's wrong?" he demanded.

She blinked woozily. "I feel faint…"

Chad cursed. "Trent, go find one of the track doctors. Zack, let's get her to the hauler." He scooped her up into his arms, she clutched at his shoulders. Then she heard a cry of excitement from the TV crew and realized she was likely to end up on the evening news: *Deranged Sponsor Collapses in Kentucky.*

"I'm fine now," Brianna said in her normal voice. "You can put me down."

"You're not fine," Chad said. "You fainted." He was pale beneath his year-round tan—he really was worried.

"It's just a thing I get," she said, "at the sight of violence."

He stopped walking, stared down at her, brows drawn together.

"And that sight has gone now, so I'm fine," she said.

"A thing you get." Chad enunciated clearly—he looked as if he was ready to write the *Deranged Sponsor* story himself. "So, you faint at the sight of violence?" He said the words with relish.

She kept her eyes innocent. "Uh-huh."

Chad called, "Hey, guys, guess what? Brianna faints at the sight of violence."

Trent pulled up short from the sprint he'd just begun and walked slowly back.

"Or sometimes at the thought of it," Brianna inserted.

Zack rolled his eyes. "Aw, man, we've been had."

"Suckered," Trent agreed, disgusted.

"Outmaneuvered," Chad said with what sounded like pride. He lowered Brianna so her feet hit the ground, but kept an arm around her waist. "Now, if you kids have finished scrapping in the playground, how about you go and see Dad. He went back to the hotel for a rest, but he'll want to know how practice went."

"I want to look over my stats from this afternoon," Zack said.

"I'll bring them to the hotel," Chad said. "You can pick them up from my room later."

Brianna wondered if she should move out of Chad's embrace. Reluctantly she wriggled a little; Chad tightened his grip. That answered that question. She avoided his brothers' eyes as they discussed tomorrow's test schedule.

At last they left her alone with Chad—as alone as they could be, with the crew chief up on the war wagon, and the pit crew pushing the car back to the garage.

She felt the brush of something against her hair—Chad's lips?—then he released her. "I must be the only guy in NASCAR whose wife faints at the sight of violence," he mused. "I'm trying to figure if that's an asset or a liability."

"It was the only way to stop them killing each other and getting themselves plastered all over the TV news."

"I never would have thought of it…but it worked." He touched her cheek. "Great work, Brianna. That could have turned nasty." His voice softened. "Thank you."

"Hey," she said, suddenly awkward, "what are wives for?"

His blue eyes darkened. "Have dinner with me tonight," he said. "I'll take you into Cincinnati, if that's where you want to go."

She was torn. Dinner with him would be wonderful—if they could get through it without arguing.

"You asked what wives are for," he said. "I hear one thing they're excellent for is sharing an evening with their husbands."

How could she refuse?

CHAD TOOK BRIANNA to Chez Marc, a fine restaurant in downtown Cincinnati. It was exactly the kind of classy venue she deserved, he thought as he surveyed the candlelit tables laid with fine crystal and silverware, the patrons talking quietly amid the discreet strains of classical music.

The maître d' helped her out of her coat, and Chad wished it was his hands on her shoulders, on the straps of her midnight-blue dress, silky, with a deep V neckline that showed her curves. Too tempting.

They followed the maître d' to their table. Chad couldn't take his eyes off Brianna as she tucked her purse at her feet, then shook out her napkin and slid it onto her lap.

He shouldn't have insisted on dinner, but with the memory of the delicious weight of her in his arms this afternoon, with the warmth that had filled him after her crazy scheme to stop his brothers from killing each other, he hadn't been able to resist.

She caught him looking. "Is something wrong?"

"You look amazing," he said. "Perfect."

She grimaced.

What had he done wrong now? Chad accepted a leather-bound menu from the waiter. "That was a compliment, by the way."

"I have a thing about the word *perfect*," she said.

"Another *thing?*" he asked. "I had no idea you have so many things. How does this one fit with your fainting-at-the-thought-of-violence thing?"

"This one's for real."

"Perfect." He tried the word out. "It seems…perfectly harmless."

She smiled at his word play, but she looked tense. "My dad's motto—literally, it's on his office wall—is Make It Perfect."

Chad couldn't see a thing wrong with that. In fact, he was tempted to borrow Brian Hudson's motto—you didn't win NASCAR races unless you were as near to perfect as possible on race day. But from the tension in Brianna's voice, he gathered he'd miscalled that. He made a sympathetic noise.

Her eyes narrowed. "You have no idea what I'm talking about."

"It's, uh, frustrating? Having to be perfect?"

She sighed. "Not so much frustrating as too much pressure. I can't live up to Dad's standards."

"That sign on his wall doesn't mean *you* need to be perfect," Chad said.

She rested her chin on her hand. "All I know is, sometimes Dad acts as if he'd like us to be closer, but something holds him back."

"You think that something is that you're not good enough?"

She shrugged.

Chad couldn't scarcely imagine feeling like that. He and Brady had their fights and didn't hesitate to point out each other's flaws, but there was a deep bond between them that allowed them to weather those storms. If they let a lack of perfection interfere in their relationship, they wouldn't *have* a relationship.

"Maybe your dad's just not good at showing his feelings," he suggested. "Maybe he feels he'd lose control, be too vulnerable, if he opened up."

But that was no reason not to show your kid you loved them, Chad thought. *Or your wife,* a voice inside said. He shook his head. This wasn't about him.

"Maybe," she admitted. "Or maybe he just doesn't have those feelings for me. The only time I remember Dad saying something kind to me was when I brought home straight-A report cards."

Chad eyed the woman he knew to be smart, caring, fun, beautiful. What more could anyone want? Anger against Brian kindled inside him.

The waiter arrived to take their orders. Brianna chose the swordfish steak, Chad the rack of lamb, along with a pinot noir to complement both their meals.

"There's no way any father could be disappointed in you as a daughter," he said as soon as the waiter left.

She darted him a quick glance. "Thanks."

"Is that why you haven't worked for him before now?" Chad asked. "Because you can't be perfect?"

She sipped her water. "I don't want to lose what little I have of his love by falling short on the job."

"So what changed that made you agree to do this project?"

"It's my last chance to get it right," she said. "And Dad's last chance to figure out he loves me and tell me so."

"What do you mean?" He paused while the waiter poured the wine. Realization hit; his jaw firmed. "Just how sick is your father?" he demanded.

BRIANNA PICKED UP her wineglass, took a fortifying swallow. "Dad has cancer. The doctors don't think he'll recover. He has maybe three months."

"What?" Chad exploded, drawing glances from the neighboring tables. "Your dad is dying and you let me pick a fight with him?"

"You were defending me," she said. "Do you regret that?"

"Of course not, but I might have said it more gently."

"Dad doesn't do gentle, and neither do you." Though that wasn't strictly true. Chad had been gentle, tender, the night they'd married. "Dad wouldn't appreciate you going easy on him because he's sick. He's convinced this won't kill him."

He puffed out a breath. "And what do you think?"

"When Dad says it, I believe him. But logically…"

"It doesn't stack up," he completed. "Your dad and mine sound a lot alike. My father refused to accept he was having a heart attack. If Julie-Anne hadn't dragged him to the hospital, he would have died." He reached across the table for her hand. "Stubborn old men, huh?"

"Can't live with them, can't live without them." She meant it as a quip, but her voice broke.

Chad lifted her fingers to his lips, kissed the tips. "I might have gone easier on you, too, if I'd known about your dad's cancer," he said ruefully. "You have enough to deal with, without my bad temper making things worse."

"Dad won't let me sit at his bedside," she said. "I might as well be here fighting with you."

They broke apart while the waiter delivered their meals. When he was gone Chad said, "Brianna, your problems with your dad are about his inability to connect, not about you not being good enough."

The thought had occurred to her before, but she'd never given herself permission to examine it. She turned it over in her mind. If Chad was right, the rift between her and her dad wasn't her fault. But that meant…

"Which means," Chad said apologetically, "trying to win his approval with this sponsorship project is trying to do the impossible."

Bingo. She blew out a frustrated breath. "I seem to make a habit of that. Like—" she focused on cutting a spear of her asparagus served with hollandaise sauce "—marrying someone I've known three days and hoping to live happily ever after."

Chad said, "In that instance, you weren't the only one who tried the impossible."

His eyes held hers, the deep blue she'd fallen in love with, along with every other thing about this man. Brianna swallowed. That was then.

She read regret in his face, a reflection of hers. Over the past two years, she'd never thought he might be sharing some of her pain.

"I assumed you thought of our marriage as just a glitch in your perfectly run life."

"That would be the life in which I'm struggling to find a sponsor for Zack, worrying about my dad, panicking about my brothers on their way to becoming sworn enemies…" He paused, looked horrified at his own indiscretion. "I didn't just admit to a potential sponsor that my brothers hate each other's guts."

"Your potential sponsor didn't hear a thing." She hesitated.

"Your wife heard it, though, and appreciated the confidence." She laughed lightly, feeling more carefree than she had in months, even though she was in the middle of a divorce and she'd just figured out she couldn't do a darned thing to make her father love her. "If you need any more help keeping your brothers in line…"

"Let's not talk about them," Chad said. "I'd rather talk about you. About how I love your laugh."

"You do?"

"It makes me smile inside." He wasn't smiling on the outside. Instead, he was frowning at his own admission.

This kind of talk didn't come easily to him. Brianna had to offer him something, some reward for that openness, before he turned distant again. "When I'm with you," she said, "you make me feel like I matter."

"Really?" He sounded surprised, pleased. "Even though you think I'm bossy?" His voice deepened, and the words brushed over her, making her shiver.

"You know you're bossy."

He took her hand; his thumb swept her knuckles. "Guess that puts me out of the running with you, huh?"

She gulped. "Bossy isn't the worst thing in the world." *Not when you took charge of our lovemaking.*

His eyes darkened. "If I was bossy, I'd drag you out of here right now, drive you back to the hotel and make love to you."

She saw the desire in his eyes, the tightly reined passion in the tense muscle of his jaw. "Chad—"

"Maybe we rushed into marriage," he said, "and maybe we were too different to make a go of it, but I've never had a night like that one." He kissed her knuckles, and she shivered. "Neither have you."

Helpless with longing, she said, "I don't have anything to compare with. For all I know, any night could be that good…with any man."

Not that she believed it. No other man had turned her to mush just with his touch, with the melting heat of his eyes.

"I still want you, Brianna," he said. "I never stopped. I don't think I can survive another day without making love to you."

She laughed shakily. "Of course you can." But as seduction lines went, it was right up there.

"Come back to my room," he said.

She licked her lips, saw him fight a groan. "Is that an order?"

"Hell, no," he said. "I'm begging." He tightened his grip on her fingers. "Please, Brianna, stay with me tonight."

She saw the hunger, near desperation, that told her he really was begging. For the briefest second, she wished he'd stopped after *me. Please, Brianna, stay with me.*

But they both knew better than that. One night, she thought. She could do one night. She *wanted* one night, more than she'd ever wanted anything. Except to marry Chad in the first place.

"Yes," she almost whispered.

CHAD COULDN'T BELIEVE Brianna had said yes. They attempted to eat more of their meals, but gave up after a few minutes—the atmosphere was too thick, too heavy to allow anything as mundane as eating. He drove like a madman back to the hotel, not saying a word in case he said something that made her change her mind.

Silence was definitely the best policy. The plan was still intact as they hurried through the lobby, as the elevator rose sixteen ex-cruciatingly slow floors, as they half ran along the corridor to his room, as he fumbled the card key so badly he couldn't get the damned door open.

He cursed; Brianna laughed softly, and somehow that did the trick. The green light flashed, and he opened the door.

He ushered her in, then closed the door behind them, leaning on it for good measure.

She was here. She was with him. They would make love.

She dropped her gaze, and her sudden shyness was reminiscent of their wedding night. If he remembered rightly—and he hadn't forgotten one moment of that night—the shyness hadn't lasted long. Chad shrugged out of his jacket, hung it on the hook on the back of the door and moved toward his wife.

He wished they were at his home, with the antique four-poster bed, with the beamed ceilings and shutters over the windows.

"Next time we do this," he said, "it won't be in a hotel room."

"One night," she reminded him. "Just one night."

They'd argue that point later. Chad took her in his arms, and after a still moment she let out a soft breath and leaned into him.

"Brianna." He murmured her name against her temple, inhaled the lemon scent of her hair. Her arms came around his neck and she pressed closer, setting off a reaction primeval in its fierceness.

He claimed her mouth, hard and hungrily, and instantly she met his fire with her own. She tasted of honey and spice and lingering wine. Chad wove one hand through her hair, let the other go exploring. Mmm, the curve of her back…

She made a little sound of need, and he walked her toward the bed.

BRIANNA LAY in the haven of Chad's arms, feeling the rise and fall of his chest against her back. Their lovemaking had been incredible. She'd have said it was impossible to improve on their wedding night, but she'd have been wrong.

His tenderness, his passion, had robbed her of all inhibition. She knew he'd found it just as sublime.

In the darkness of the room she heard a click—familiar, but she couldn't quite place it. She had no trouble placing the next sound— the swish of the door opening and the flick of a light switch.

An intruder!

She shrieked and Chad jerked instantly awake…just as the room flooded with light.

Zack, Trent and Brady Matheson stood just inside the door, all three of them gaping like tourists at the Taj Mahal.

CHAPTER TWELVE

BRIANNA DIVED beneath the covers—they might not have noticed her, or at least not have recognized her.

Chad cursed. "What the hell are you guys doing here?"

"What the hell are *you* doing?" Brady growled. Then, "Don't answer that. I have eyes in my head."

"You're sleeping with my sponsor?" Zack demanded, incredulous.

In her hiding place Brianna groaned. So much for the hope they hadn't recognized her.

"How did you get in?" Chad demanded.

"You gave me your spare key," Zack said. "You told me to come by and pick up the track stats to discuss with Dad."

"I meant earlier," Chad snapped.

"Excuse me for not knowing you were entertaining," Zack snapped back. His voice sounded closer—shouldn't they be leaving, rather than advancing?

"I suppose I should be grateful you didn't bring Kelly and Julie-Anne with you," Chad muttered.

"They went to the mall to eat," Trent said. His voice turned accusing. "They were looking for Brianna to invite her along."

Brianna ran out of air beneath the duvet. Reluctantly she stuck her head out. Zack's ironic expression reminded her of the night when she'd told him nothing would happen between her and Chad.

Trent ran a hand through his hair. "I can't believe you'd…" He stopped, fixed his brother with a harder look than Brianna had seen on his usually carefree face. "You *wouldn't.*"

Beside her, Chad tensed—even more than he had already. "Can you guys give us some privacy?" he asked.

But Trent wasn't a quitter, on the track or in life. "You wouldn't cheat on your wife, even if you haven't seen her for a couple of years." He turned to the others. "You know what this means?"

Going by their blank expressions, neither Brady nor Zack shared Trent's insight.

"I can't believe it, but I know I'm right." Trent grinned, smugly certain of his instincts. "Brianna is Chad's wife."

OH, HELL.

Chad sent Trent a look that should have shriveled his pain-in-the-butt youngest brother on the spot. Not only did Trent remain unshriveled, but his shrug of apology was far from sincere.

"Is that true?" Brady demanded.

Chad had never realized how much dignity clothes and a desk lent a guy. Talking to his family while he was naked in bed with a mortified, equally naked Brianna, was about the most lowering thing he'd ever experienced.

He mustered what shreds of his authority remained. "Out," he said, "all of you. We'll get dressed, then we'll let you back in. Whether we talk to you about this or not is our decision, so don't hold your breath."

It felt weird using words like *we* and *our* about him and Brianna.

Trent at last showed he was good for something, as he took charge of shepherding his shell-shocked brother and father out the door.

Brianna threw herself down into the pillows, the sheet pulled up to her chin. She moaned.

"I'm sorry," Chad said. "It never occurred to me Zack would turn up."

"If it had been just Zack…" She trailed off as if she'd realized that would have been no better.

She was pale, and her lips trembled in a way that made him

want to kiss them again, for reassurance, for comfort. Although doubtless that would soon turn to something hotter…

Chad red-flagged that line of thought. "We'll have to tell them," he said.

To his relief, she nodded. "Trent was so certain you'd never cheat on your wife, we have no choice."

"We don't want any confusion over where this is going," Chad said. "We'll tell them we're getting a divorce."

She nodded. He began searching for his clothes—how had his pants ended up on the TV set? Oh, yeah—he smiled at the memory. Brianna had been excitingly assertive about getting him naked—he'd had no chance to fold his clothes the way he'd done on their wedding night.

"You think this is funny?" Brianna stepped into her dress. "Because it's the worst moment of my life."

What happened before his family arrived had been the *best* moment of his life, Chad realized with a shock.

"If my father hears that I…slept with the owner of one of the teams I'm evaluating…" She hiccuped.

"You slept with your husband," Chad said. He moved behind her to help her with her zipper.

Her hands froze, then made way for him. "And if he hears that I got married without telling him…"

"What? He won't love you anymore?" Chad kicked himself for his lack of tact. "Sorry. I know things are tough with your dad." The zipper slid into place; he had no more reason to keep his hands on her. "He won't hear anything. My family might be nosy and interfering, but they're loyal."

She turned to face him, all anxiety, no trace of the uninhibited lover with whom he'd shared incredible intimacy tonight. He had a feeling he wouldn't see her naked again for a very long time. If ever. His throat constricted.

"Ready?" he managed.

"Nearly." She pulled a comb from her purse and tugged it through the hair he'd mussed. "Okay, I guess so."

Chad looked down at her, at her cheeks flushed with embarrassment, at the pink curve of her mouth. He dropped a kiss on her lips. "We can do this," he said. "Together."

He opened the door.

Any hope that his family might have grown tired of waiting was quickly dispelled. His brothers and his dad practically fell into the room.

"Is it true?" Brady demanded. "Are you two married?"

"Have a seat, guys." Chad didn't want this to turn into a stand-up argument. He indicated the small meeting table and chairs. Brianna perched on the end of the bed—she shot Chad a grateful look, which he guessed was because he'd pulled up the covers. After a second's hesitation, he sat next to her.

His father was about to bust a gut, so Chad said, "Trent's right. We're married."

Three voices fired questions. Chad held up his hand.

"We got married in Vegas after Trent won there in April two years ago." They knew that; he'd told them last year. "We both realized right away—" *but not before it was too late* "—we'd made a mistake."

Beside him, Brianna's head twitched, as if he'd surprised her. What was that about? She'd been as adamant as Chad that they'd made a mistake. Hadn't she? A cold wind of doubt whistled through him. She'd said it first, he was certain.

Or had she only agreed with him?

Or simply not argued with him?

Which of them had *thought* it first?

Chad's eyeballs suddenly felt too big for their sockets; his throat dried up and his hands felt clammy. "We—" the word was a croak, and he felt Brianna's gaze on him "—we decided to split up."

It had been a joint decision, he was certain. He cleared his throat. "We didn't see each other again until Brianna arrived at Halesboro. She didn't even know for sure we were still married. I'd told her I'd organize a divorce, but, uh, I've been busy."

Lame. That was how it sounded. His father's snort confirmed it.

"If you want a divorce, you get a divorce," Brady said. "You don't shack up in the nearest hotel room."

Brianna flinched and Chad said, "Dad," with a level of threat he didn't know he could employ with his father.

Brady reddened. "Sorry," he muttered to Brianna.

"We filed for divorce last week," Chad said. When both his brothers, usually so quick to take opposing views, sniggered, he realized he'd made a mistake.

"You filed for divorce even though you're sleeping together?" Brady demanded.

"Once." Brianna found her voice. "It was once, that's all."

Chad felt bad that she had to explain anything at all. "Dad, we're adults, we're married, and if we want to sleep together once, twice or a thousand times, it's our business."

"It's *family* business," Brady said. "Brianna is my daughter-in-law."

"And our sister-in-law," Trent said helpfully. Never one to let well enough alone, he added, "Welcome to the family, sis."

Chad shot his brother a glare that promised he'd be washing race cars for a month if he didn't shut up.

"Why did you decide it wouldn't work?" Zack sounded curious, rather than condemning, but Brady jumped in with an emphatic, "Yeah, why?"

"That's not your business," Chad said firmly.

"Was it your idea to break up?" Brady asked Brianna. "Did someone talk you out of staying married to Chad?"

His belligerent tone had Brianna stiffening. "No one talked me out of it."

"Because Chad's been moping around ever since," Brady said.

"Dad…" Chad began.

Brady ignored him, of course. "Took me a while to notice it, but he definitely went off the boil after that Vegas race."

"If you have any problems with my work…" Chad said tightly.

"I'm not talking about your work, and you know it," Brady fired back. "I'm talking about the way you quit smiling, the way you took Trent's shenanigans too seriously, the short fuse you've been on. You clammed up and wouldn't tell us what was wrong."

Hell, Brianna must think he was a total wimp. Nothing, Chad told himself, could be further from the truth. Sure, he'd been disappointed—in himself—but to suggest he'd spent two years moping...

"Dad, I'm not sure we made much effort to find out what was wrong," Trent said.

Brady brushed him off. "We may be kin now," he said to Brianna, "but that doesn't mean I won't get mad at you when you hurt my son."

Chad was taken aback by the ferocity of his father's expression and the matching scowls on his brothers' faces. Dad was wrong to suggest he was an emotional wreck, but still, his family's concern was touching. Even if it was hard to get used to, given he was usually the one doing the worrying.

But he couldn't let his dad get away with talking to Brianna like that.

"None of this was Brianna's fault," Chad said. "I'll thank you to speak to her with respect."

Zack gave him a thumbs-up; Brady was unchastened. "Then if it wasn't her fault—" Chad's heart sank "—it must be yours."

More sniggering from his brothers. This felt like the time Chad had been caught taking Trent and Zack for a ride in Dad's car when he was fifteen. They'd begged and pleaded so much, he'd given in. Then when Dad caught them up in his truck and pulled them over, his little brothers had donned angelic expressions and let Chad take the rap.

"I like this girl." Brady nodded at Brianna.

"I like her a lot," Trent chipped in. Chad ignored that—Trent was trying to get back at him for giving him a few anxious moments last year over Chad's friendship with Kelly.

Brady ignored his youngest son, too. "Given she's exactly the kind of girl a guy with an ounce of sense might be expected to marry and be crazy about, how the hell did you screw up so fast?"

This was why he hadn't admitted he was married until he'd blurted it out back in November in an attempt to calm Trent down.

"Look at her—she's pretty, she's smart, she loves NASCAR…" Brady began to list Brianna's attributes, with Trent and Zack nodding agreement to each.

Go ahead, Chad thought, *agree with each other. Any other time, you'd be throwing punches by now.*

"What I said to her about hurting you goes the other way, too," Brady said. "You must have done something pretty bad to scare her off."

"He didn't do a thing," Brianna said, her voice clear and calm in the seething atmosphere. "Chad was a total gentleman from the moment I met him until the moment we parted."

Zack muttered something that might have been, "Sounds boring."

Brady quelled him with a look. But Chad couldn't help agreeing with his brother—there'd been nothing gentlemanly about the way he'd made love to her….

Tentatively Brianna took Chad's hand. She squeezed it, offering reassurance he hadn't realized he badly needed. He laced his fingers through hers.

"We got married, we realized we made a mistake, so we separated," she said calmly. "Soon, we'll be divorced."

Yeah, that was it exactly. They were both on the same page about this. Except…her fingers against his sent threads of longing through Chad, tying him to her.

"But why do you have to get divorced?" Brady asked, bewildered. "You like each other well enough to go to bed together."

"That comes under 'none of your business,'" Chad said.

"You don't throw away any marriage without working hard to save it," Brady said.

"Like you did with my mom?" Chad regretted the words the instant they left his mouth. He hadn't even realized until now that the resentment still lurked in him.

Brady's jaw set. "Your mother and I *did* try."

Chad wasn't about to point out that once Brady met Rosie, the woman who became his second wife, he'd made no further effort to repair his separation from Chad's mom. He said, "I know, Dad." So what if it didn't sound a hundred percent convincing.

"You two are young, healthy," Brady said. "Whatever problems you have, time is on your side." He steepled his fingers. "I want both of you to make me a promise."

Chad grunted. No way was he committing to what he suspected his father was about to say.

"Marriage isn't something you jump in and out of like a swimming pool. I want you to think hard about whether you can stay married," Brady said. "Reconsider your decision, or at least give it more consideration than the five minutes you appear to have put into it so far."

About to tell his father a flat no, Chad noticed a faint tremor in Brady's fingers. Now that he thought about it, Dad looked tired, his eyes a little sunken. Hell, sometimes Brady's assertiveness made Chad forget he wasn't operating at a hundred percent.

"I'll consider it," Brianna said.

THE WORDS TUMBLED out of Brianna's mouth. Brady looked terrible; her instinct was to reassure him. "I…I mean, I'm willing to think about it—" she was aware of Chad's shocked gaze "—but I can't promise anything beyond that."

"That'll do for now." Some of the color seeped back into Brady's face. "What about you, Chad?"

Brianna winced. She'd pushed him into a corner, left him with no place to go.

Tight-lipped, Chad said, "I'll think about it, too."

Brady relaxed visibly, and he no longer looked as if he was about to slump onto the table. "That's a good start."

"Now you all can do something for us," Chad said. "You can leave."

Brady stood; Trent and Zack did the same.

"Brianna's father doesn't know anything about our being

married," Chad said. "Nor does anyone else. I don't want it to go beyond this room."

Brady frowned. "I have to tell Julie-Anne."

"I have to tell Kelly," Trent said.

Everyone looked at Zack.

He shrugged. "Heck, even if I had a girlfriend, they always complain I never talk about anyone except myself."

Chad smiled reluctantly and some of the tension seeped away. "Fine, tell Julie-Anne and Kelly."

"Brianna needs to come to the wedding next weekend," Brady said.

Trent nodded. "Kelly will want you there, and so do I."

Brianna gave Chad half a second to agree with them. When he didn't, she said, "I don't think that's a good idea."

"You're family," Brady said, and the rough declaration blossomed in a place in her heart. "You're coming."

What could she do but nod meekly—and avoid Chad's eyes.

Finally the three men left. Brianna sagged back on the bed. "That was awful."

Chad stood, stuffed his hands in his pockets. "Why did you say you'll think about staying married?"

He sounded irritated. Did he think she was going to hinder his precious divorce?

"Your father looked as if he was about to have another heart attack. I didn't want him stressing about us."

"So you don't plan to think about it?"

"I told your father I will, so I will. But right now, it's a no-brainer," she said snarkily.

His eyes narrowed. "You seemed to enjoy yourself tonight."

She attempted the uncaring shrug that Zack did so well. "I don't have much basis for comparison."

"You don't need comparison." His finger jabbed the air in front of her. "I'm telling you, it doesn't get better than that."

"I don't know why we're having this conversation. You made

it clear you don't want to stay married to me. You couldn't even say you wanted me at your brother's wedding."

He blinked. "I never said I didn't want you there."

"You didn't say you did."

He raked a hand through his hair. "Brianna, we're getting a divorce. Telling my father you'll think about staying married, coming to Trent's wedding—that's not going to convince anyone our marriage is over. It's not logical."

"So making love was just about the sex?" she said. "Nothing more?"

"Of course it was more," he said. "You and I connected tonight. We talked over dinner, remember? We talked about deep-down personal stuff."

"We talked about *my* deep-down personal stuff," she said on a note of revelation. "You were great, Chad, talking to me about my dad. You were kind…but we didn't talk about you."

"We discussed the team…"

"One comment," she said, "then you said you didn't want to talk about it anymore. Whichever way we turn, it's always me being willing to bare my soul, and you…not."

"We talked, dammit," he said. "It might not have been good enough for you, but it was as good as I get."

They stared at each other, neither backing down. Chad let out a breath. "Guess that thinking we promised Dad won't take too long."

BRIANNA HAD DISCOVERED there was no going against Brady Matheson once he made his mind up about something like her attendance at Trent and Kelly's wedding. She called him from her hotel room on Monday to suggest maybe it wasn't a great idea for her to go, but he refused every argument. "I want you there," he said.

Chad had said that since the heart attack his dad was operating at about sixty percent of his usual assertiveness—she couldn't imagine dealing with Brady in full flow. No wonder Chad was so controlling. He'd inherited the full whack of his dad's genes and must have had to hone them further so he could stand up to his dad.

An entirely different tactic from Brianna, who, rather than force her way into her dad's affections, had retreated.

Did that make Chad braver than she was or just more stubborn?

Her cell phone rang five minutes after she hung up from Brady. It was Zack.

"Calling to offer my services as wedding escort on Saturday," he said.

"Uh…" Brianna said intelligently.

"Your husband didn't look that excited about the prospect of you attending."

See? She wasn't the only one who'd noticed Chad's reticence.

Zack said, "I'd be delighted to accompany you—as your brother-in-law, of course."

"Thanks," she said. "I'd like that." She knew she was getting to like the Matheson family too much, but she couldn't bring herself to break the tie before she had to.

She'd just plugged in the hair dryer to blow-dry her hair when Chad called.

"Why the hell does my brother think he's taking you to Trent's wedding?" he demanded.

Brianna set the hair dryer down and perched on the edge of the bathtub, knees weakening in that telltale way. "Because he invited me and I accepted."

"You can't want to go with him," Chad said, outraged. "He's even less open than I am. He'll be terrible company."

"I like Zack. And unlike you, he does want me there on Saturday."

"I want you there," he sputtered.

"No, you don't."

"I do, dammit. I just didn't want to send mixed messages to my family. And they'll be a lot more mixed if you show up with my brother."

"Then I'll go solo," she said.

"You won't want to go solo," he said with his usual I-know-everything authority. After a moment he added, "Neither do I."

"Your whole life is a commitment to going solo."

The noise coming down the phone might have been his teeth grinding. "I am *trying* to do the sharing, caring thing. Like I was trying to at dinner the other night, though that apparently fell on deaf ears."

"Why bother?" she said. "We're getting divorced, remember?"

"I don't know why," he said flatly. "But I do know you're going to the wedding with me."

"Because you don't want your brother showing you up?" she suggested.

"Because you're *my* wife."

"You won't be able to use that excuse for your dictatorial behavior much longer," she said primly. She knew he hated the word *dictatorial*.

When he ended the call, Brianna stayed perched on the edge of the tub. She didn't want to think about Chad *trying* to be caring and sharing. Because when it came down to it, he couldn't do it—and she didn't want to get her hopes up. Because if she started to hope, she might fall in love with him again.

"Not going to happen," she warned her reflection in the mirror. She yanked the comb through her hair.

She wouldn't let herself fall in love with Chad again, because even if he cared for her in his own Chad-like way, it was a dead-end street.

"I need to finish this assessment, impress the heck out of Dad, see if he's ready to admit he loves me," she said aloud. "Then leave Charlotte and never look back."

But first, she had to get through Trent's wedding.

CHAPTER THIRTEEN

THE WEDDING was held at a historic church in Concord, with the reception planned at the race track afterward.

The church was packed to the rafters with NASCAR folk, family and friends of the happy couple. Brianna sat up front with Brady and Julie-Anne. Chad and Zack were both in the wedding party, along with Kelly's younger brother and a good friend of Trent's. Which, Brianna assumed, meant there would be four bridesmaids.

The scale couldn't have been more different from her and Chad's wedding in Las Vegas, witnessed only by the receptionist at the Two Hearts Chapel. Brianna glanced down at her tea-colored silk dress. It draped softly over her curves, then flared out to end above her knees. She was far better dressed for Trent's wedding than she'd been for her own. So was Chad—he looked incredible in his tuxedo. Brianna had noticed several women craning their necks to get a better view. *He's mine. Hands off.*

The organ struck up "Here Comes the Bride." In Las Vegas, Brianna had marched the dozen steps down the wedding-chapel aisle to a CD of "I Will Always Love You"—with no understanding of how ironic the song choice would turn out to be.

At the minister's request, the congregation stood to welcome the bride.

It took a while for the procession to reach the front, with Kelly walking very slowly so she wouldn't trip over her feet—but it was worth the wait. Kelly looked gorgeous, her cream silk dress fairy-tale romantic. The bridesmaids, dressed in lilac silk, were equally stunning.

As Brianna watched them line up at the altar, she caught Chad's eye. She couldn't read his expression—rueful, maybe?

The minister began the service, and she was caught up in the timeless romance of those powerful words of love, of promise, of commitment.

Trent, even more gorgeous than usual, wore a huge grin on his face. Kelly's smile was loving and pinch-me excited.

The minister asked the couple to say their vows, which they'd written themselves and been brave enough to memorize.

"Sugar…" Trent began. Laughter rippled through the congregation at his use of the pet name that had bugged Kelly like heck when they first met. "I love you so much and I always will. I promise that when you need me, I'll be there. You'll be number one in my life, ahead of any race, any championship. The race that matters most to me is our marriage."

Brianna's eyes misted, but she delayed blowing her nose so she wouldn't miss any of Kelly's words.

"Trent, I love you and I always will. I promise that wherever you go, I'll go, too. I will always support you and honor you. We're a family and we're a team—nothing will break us apart."

CHAD COULDN'T BELIEVE he felt a pricking behind his eyes as Kelly finished her vows. They were corny, for Pete's sake! But something about the couple's joy, their obvious love, had plenty of people in the church sniffling.

He chanced another glance at Brianna. She was wiping her eyes, like most of the other women. She blew her nose into a tissue.

Would they still be married if their wedding had been like this? No one would have wiped their eyes at their ceremony in Las Vegas.

He shook off the heavy mantle of regret that threatened to settle. He and Brianna would never have got as far as this kind of wedding, he told himself. Because people didn't put this much effort into it without being absolutely certain they were doing the right thing.

And that took time. With a little more time, he and Brianna would have seen what had been so obvious after the wedding.

He'd thought he was sure, that day in Las Vegas. But not so sure that he'd called his family to tell them the good news. Not so sure that he'd told Brianna the truth about the family business before the wedding. And not so sure that he'd made the slightest effort to convince her to stay.

JULIE-ANNE BLINKED away tears as Trent and Kelly spoke their vows. The young couple were besotted with each other, and even though they'd had some major obstacles to overcome to get here today, they hadn't let those things stop them.

Unlike Brady who, despite being an unstoppable force at Matheson Performance Industries or on the race team, had allowed a temporary problem with his libido to derail his and Julie-Anne's future.

She cast a sidelong glance at him, at his stern profile. As always, her stomach tightened like a schoolgirl's. He sensed her observation and looked back at her. Unsmiling.

He'd been worse, rather than better, since he'd done as she suggested and consulted his doctor. Brady had told her the visit had gone "fine." Julie-Anne had seen that as clearance to go ahead and set a wedding date.

He'd refused. "When I'm better, that's when we'll get married."

The stubborn man wouldn't be shifted. It had finally dawned on Julie-Anne that her insistence that it didn't matter if they couldn't make love in the conventional way was hurting rather than helping. So she'd clammed up. Which meant neither of them was saying much.

Up at the altar, Trent murmured something to Kelly that made her giggle and had the pastor's lips twitching. Kelly leaned in to Trent, and Julie-Anne fancied she could feel from here the heat of the love blazing in his eyes.

It used to be that the most important thing in Trent's life was winning the NASCAR Sprint Cup championship. But after he fell in love with Kelly, he'd been willing to sacrifice that to save her, interrupting his buildup to the final race to defend her in the media. He'd figured out what was truly important.

Love.

Not sex.

Too bad Trent's father still had his priorities skewed.

Or maybe it was something else, something more sinister. Because if Brady really wanted to be with Julie-Anne, if he really loved her, wouldn't he agree that they should get married and work everything else out later?

EVERYONE WAS READY to celebrate when they arrived at the enormous tent set up at the race track for the reception. Once again, Brianna sat with Brady and Julie-Anne, along with some of Kelly's family, at a table next to the bridal party. The older couple seemed to be in a quiet mood—maybe the festivities had tired Brady.

When it came time for speeches, the bride's father paid tribute to his daughter in terms so glowing they put Kelly's mascara to the test.

Then it was Chad's turn. He made a great speech, witty and warm about both his brother and Kelly. He wound up by saying, "There were times when I thought, no matter how right for each other Trent and Kelly were, there was no way they could get together. Kelly was too smart, Trent too dumb—" that got a big laugh, because the couple had met after Kelly called Trent an airhead on national TV "—and whenever they got close, something happened to tear them apart. But each time, they got back on track. Their love is much, much bigger than anything life can throw at them." He turned to the couple and raised his glass. "Trent, Kelly, your race is going to run and run."

Applause broke out, with some whistling and hollering from the back of the room. Brianna was certain Trent's eyes glistened as he lifted his glass in thanks to his brother.

The band struck up the first dance, and Trent led Kelly onto the floor. They looked made for each other, Brianna thought. Then, as tradition dictated, Chad escorted the maid of honor, Kelly's sister, for a dance.

As the last words of the song faded, Chad appeared at Brianna's side.

"Dance with me?" he said, and it came out half command, half question, as if he was trying to be less determined to have things his way, but wasn't sure his life would still work.

Brady beamed at the suggestion, looking happier than he had so far tonight, so Brianna got to her feet. As they stepped onto the dance floor, the next song started. "I Will Always Love You." Brianna froze.

Chad swore. "This must be a common song at weddings."

She was surprised he'd remembered. "Uh-huh." She bit her lip.

"You're upset." He took a step toward the stage. "I'll ask them to play something else."

"No!" Brianna grabbed his arm. "Chad, that'll be way too obvious."

"Can you dance to this?" he asked.

In response, she held out her arms. He tugged her close to his lean length and they began to dance. The haunting song filled Brianna's senses, obliterating everything else. She closed her eyes, swayed against Chad.

With no visual distractions, she saw the truth in crystal clarity.

The problem with this song was not that she was dancing to it under false pretenses.

The problem was she was afraid it might be true.

BRADY TOOK Julie-Anne's hand and led her to the dance floor.

A few feet away, Trent and Kelly swayed, locked in a tight embrace that, as the minister had said, no man would put asunder.

I want that. The thought sprang into Brady's mind. Dammit, he didn't need to take love lessons from his son. He'd proposed to Julie-Anne before Trent had even thought of marrying Kelly.

"They look so happy," Julie-Anne said wistfully.

Brady grunted. "Our turn will come."

Silence as she moved to the music. Then, "When?"

Brady let out a frustrated breath. "When I'm…better." When he could give her the wedding night she deserved.

"What if you don't get better?" Her question slammed Brady in the gut, all the harder because it was the same question he'd been holding off for weeks. It had all the pent-up force of a race car heading out of pit road.

His palms turned sweaty, his heart thumped with the irregular *whump-whump* of a loose tire. Another panic attack. Brady tried to even his breathing.

"The doctor said…" Dammit, he was talking too loudly, almost croaking. He cleared his throat, lowered his voice. "The doctor said I'll almost certainly be fine."

She didn't look particularly happy. "But if you're not fine, will you still marry me?"

"Of course I will." But he'd hesitated long enough to betray his uncertainty.

"Then there's no reason not to marry me now."

Brady pretended an interest in the tune the band was playing, hummed a few bars.

Julie-Anne pulled out of his arms. "You say this is all about wanting to please me in bed—" Dean and Patsy Grosso, dancing past, stumbled when they overheard "—but that's not true."

Brady glanced around. "It is," he hissed.

"You don't believe we can survive this problem if the doctor's wrong."

He couldn't say a word to that.

"My love for you is strong enough to survive anything," she said, quiet now. "So the problem is your love for me."

"It has nothing to do with how much I love you," he blustered.

"Before we got engaged, you always said you didn't want the kind of emotional commitment that I did," she said. "I thought we'd moved past that."

"We did." The words didn't ring true.

"Then commit to sharing your life with me now. The good and the bad and the truly, unmentionably awful."

He stared at her, frozen, as the song ended. The band switched into a swing segment and started to play "Ain't Nobody Here But Us Chickens."

Brady began to move again, woodenly.

"Tell me we can get through anything," Julie-Anne persisted, automatically adjusting her steps to the new song.

His legs trembled like jelly; he held her tighter.

He felt the rise and fall of her bosom in the new red dress that made her look young, vibrant, full of energy. He kissed her hair. Had she noticed that he hadn't said those words?

"Brady," she said, "I can't marry you."

She'd noticed.

Brady's stomach dropped; panic clawed through him, taking him over body and soul. "You don't mean that." *Too rough.*

Her voice filled with tears. "I love you so much, but I can't marry a man who'll shut me out when the going gets tough. Who's afraid to trust me."

"Gypsy—" words came back, only platitudes, but he clutched at them "—this is a temporary—"

"I can't trust your love," she said. "Brady, we're finished."

Every word cut Brady like a knife, left him bleeding a little more. She stood still, waiting, as if giving him the opportunity to put everything right.

He couldn't. He couldn't do a damn thing.

She turned on her heel, left the dance floor. He saw her pick up her red silk purse from her chair and walk slowly, with dignity, out of the tent.

Leaving Brady, the biggest chicken of them all, alone.

Anguish almost doubled him over, hollowed him out with pain. He clutched his middle, fighting to breathe, ignoring the anxious glances of people nearby. He concentrated on putting one foot in front of the other, heading out of the tent, the opposite direction from Julie-Anne.

As he neared the exit, his pace picked up. Because stronger than the anguish was the relief that he would never have to be less than a man to her.

CHAD AND BRIANNA saw Brady leave. They found him outside, breathing so hard Brianna wondered if they should call 9-1-1. But when Chad offered to drive his dad home, Brady bit his head off with enough energy to suggest he wasn't ill. He did at least let Chad call him a taxi. While they waited for the cab, Brady told them he and Julie-Anne had argued and their wedding was off.

The taxi arrived before they could get more details.

Brianna let out a slow breath as the cab pulled away. She ached for the older man. "He's hurting so badly."

"I hate seeing him like this," Chad admitted. He draped his jacket over her shoulders.

She pulled it close around her. "Haven't you been hinting heavily to your dad that he shouldn't marry Julie-Anne?"

"If they're going to break up," he said defensively, "it's less painful now than later."

She blinked. "What about those things you said about Trent and Kelly, the obstacles they overcame? Why can't your father and Julie-Anne do the same?"

He ran a finger around the stiff collar of his tuxedo. "They don't really know each other," he said. "Maybe they only just got around to talking about the things people should discuss before they tie the knot. About what they want out of life, how their relationship will work."

"You mean, the things we didn't talk about?"

He lifted his face to the night sky as if the secret of a happy marriage was written in the stars. "Hard to believe, isn't it, that we missed something so fundamental."

His implication—that he'd never have married her if they had—hurt.

"At least the way we did it, you had the perfect excuse to get out of the marriage," she said, her tempter flaring.

Chad's gaze jerked to her. "What does that mean?"

"You said I give up on my father too easily, that I'll quit the relationship rather than risk more hurt," she said. "You were right. I'm starting to realize I gave up on us too easily, too, for the same reasons."

"We knew each other three days," he said. "Getting married was a stupid thing to do. In our case, quitting was the sensible option."

"People do stupid things all the time," she said. "Sometimes they put it right, make it work. Like Zack's trying to with his racing career."

"What are you saying?" he demanded. "You think we should have stayed married?"

She caught a breath, half sob, in her throat. "I don't know." Because if she did, the terrible mistake hadn't been getting married, it had been giving up.

"How could it have worked?" He ran both hands through his hair. "We had completely different ideas about marriage."

"You never wanted to make it work," she said quietly. "Did you?"

He drew back. "The divorce was your idea."

"I mentioned breaking up first," she admitted. She pushed her hands into the pockets of his jacket. "But, Chad, I didn't wake up that morning—I didn't go into that conversation—wanting our marriage to end or in any way regretting what we'd done." She paused. "Did you?"

Silence. Heavy, pulsating with memory and regret. Chad spun away from her, took three paces. Then turned back and stared her down like an old-time outlaw.

"I did," he said at last. "Before I said one word, before you did, maybe even before I opened my eyes that morning, I was wondering if our marriage was all wrong."

Brianna hadn't expected him to admit it. Now his confession weighed on her like a stone. He had known from the start he didn't want to make it work.

"I'm sorry." He sounded dazed, as if he could hardly believe what he'd said. He took a halting step toward her. "Brianna, I'm sorry. We made vows and I discarded them because I was… scared. I was a jerk."

"You were a jerk, but you were also right," she said dully. "You weren't ready for marriage. Neither was I." Her teeth chattered uncontrollably, though wearing his jacket, she had to be warmer than he was.

"Sweetheart, let's get you inside."

She didn't need him being *kind and soft,* darn it!

"I j-just realized," she said. "I thought I knew it was too late, but it's only just hit me." Her breath came in short, shivery puffs, visible in the night air.

"What has?" He grasped her shoulders, gave her a tiny shake. "Tell me."

"All this t-time, a p-part of me has hoped we might be able to fix our marriage." With a huge effort of will, she stilled her shivers, her chattering teeth. "But we can't. Chad, it really is over."

IRONICALLY, NOW THAT Chad had admitted he'd never been husband material, by Tuesday morning, rumors had started flying about his relationship with Brianna. The gossip was contained within Matheson Racing at this stage, but he knew the rumors could go further. Given human nature, they definitely *would* go further—it was just a matter of time.

Chad thought about the problem, found a solution, implemented it.

Like everything else so far this year, it didn't go as planned. Which meant he had another confession to make to Brianna.

He knew she was meeting with FastMax Racing's accountants. Reluctantly he called her. She recognized his number, because her voice when she answered was guarded in the extreme. Which was less intimidating than that shivering she'd done the other night.

"Our receptionist overheard Julie-Anne on the phone to Dad this morning," he said.

"Those two are talking again?" Her wariness dropped away.

"Uh, I don't think so. It was about work." Julie-Anne was still in her job; Brady was still at home recuperating. Chad continued, "Julie-Anne said something about you and me. Not specifically that we're married, but the receptionist interpreted her words that way."

Brianna's defeated sigh suggested she couldn't take much more bad news about their marriage.

"Zack told me the story was going around the cafeteria," Chad said. "I went down there and made enough of a joke that I don't think anyone's taking it seriously."

"That's not so bad, then," she said.

Hold that thought, Chad pleaded silently. He gripped the phone tighter. "I, uh—" a sweat broke out on his forehead "—I did something else that I thought would kill the story stone dead."

"Great," she said. "What was it?"

Chad swallowed and wished he could turn back the clock. "I, uh, asked the human-resources manager for a date."

Deathly silence.

He waited.

More deathly silence.

"Brianna? It was the only thing I could think of."

"Very clever." She spoke so quietly he could hardly hear.

He closed his eyes. He'd known the second he asked Liz out for dinner it was stupid. He'd asked via e-mail, to make it easier for her to spread the details of the invitation around her friends in the office. That had already happened. Which was useful for the rumor of his marriage. Not so useful for the marriage itself.

We won't have a marriage much longer.

"But people are still talking about you and me," he said. "I think—" he hated doing this to her "—we need to tell your father."

She hissed. "Tell him that you're dating the HR manager?"

He didn't imagine the acid in her words. Angry was better than defeated, he told himself. "You know what I mean. And I'm not dating Liz." He would call her as soon as he got off the phone, cancel dinner and apologize.

When Brianna spoke, her voice was shaky, and Chad longed to take her in his arms. "I guess you're right. I should tell Dad."

"We'll go together."

The phone clattered as if she'd dropped it. "There's no need."

"I know how much you care about your dad," Chad said. "And how easily he can hurt you. I won't let that happen."

"How thoughtful of you," she said politely. Then, "When shall we go?"

He hadn't expected such easy acquiescence. He began typing an e-mail to his secretary, telling her to cancel his appointments. "This afternoon. We'll get away right after lunch."

She agreed without enthusiasm. He knew she wasn't looking forward to telling her father the truth. He wanted to tell her he would protect her.

But she had zero reason to trust him.

CHAPTER FOURTEEN

BRIANNA'S FATHER had not a hair left on his head, not even eyebrows. The chemotherapy had taken it all. His face had thinned, too, emphasizing the lines running from his nose to his mouth.

Brianna kissed him and tried to hide her dismay. What effect did sudden bad news have on cancer patients? If she could be certain her father would never hear she was married, she wouldn't tell him now.

She sat down on the couch; Chad joined her. "Dad, I need— *we* need to talk to you."

"You're going with Zack Matheson for the sponsorship?" Brian's mouth tightened. "I have to admit it's not what I expected." Brianna's reports to him so far all pointed in the direction of FastMax.

"This isn't about the sponsorship. It's personal." Brianna leaned forward, hands clasped on her knees. Something in her tone silenced her father.

"I first met Chad nearly two years ago in Las Vegas," she said. "And we, uh, the fact is, Dad, we…" The words stuck in her throat.

"We got married," Chad said. The admission hung in the air.

Brian's mouth worked. "You *what?*"

"We got married," Brianna confirmed. "We separated right away, and we didn't see each other again until a couple of weeks ago, but we're still married."

"We're divorcing," Chad clarified.

Brianna nodded.

Her father rubbed his temples. "Why did you do a crazy thing like that?"

"We were in…we thought we loved each other," she said.

Her father looked incredulous, as if that was the stupidest reason for getting married he'd ever heard.

"Why didn't you tell me?" he demanded.

"I'm telling you now."

"I suppose I should be grateful," he said. "Who's your lawyer?"

"We're both using Chad's lawyer," Brianna said. Chad gave him the name.

That got her father going again. "Don't be such a fool. I'm one of the wealthiest men in the country."

"I didn't marry *you,*" Chad said sharply.

"I'll bet you didn't make him sign a prenup," Brian accused Brianna.

"Of course I didn't. And I never will, no matter who I marry," Brianna said. "Chad's not making any financial claim on me, and I'm not going after his fortune, either, which right now is considerably larger than mine."

"This is the stupidest thing you've ever done," he said.

"Don't speak to your daughter like that," Chad said. "I'm sorry to hear how ill you are, but I've told you once before, Brianna deserves your respect. That hasn't changed."

"You don't get to—" Brian began.

"As long as she's my wife I decide how you get to talk to her," Chad said.

"No, *I* decide," Brianna said. "Dad, he's right. That was deliberately hurtful, and you should know better."

For a long moment her father stared at her, his chest rising and falling.

Then he said, "Don't blame me if he takes you to the cleaners."

"I won't. Dad, if you want me to continue with the NASCAR project, I want to assure you there's no way my personal situation will affect my judgment about the sponsorship."

"I wouldn't expect it to," he said. Of course not—he never

pulled his punches with family; he wouldn't expect her to show her husband's team any favoritism.

"But what I'd rather do is hand the project over to someone else and be with you," she said.

"I don't need—"

"Dad, you're sick."

"I'm having chemotherapy," he said. "Of course I'm sick. The whole idea is that it almost kills you while it cures you. I don't want you here."

"Because I'm not good enough," she blurted.

He tsked. "Don't be silly."

"Have I ever been good enough to be your daughter?" she asked, holding his gaze.

There was a long, charged silence. Chad squeezed Brianna's hand.

"I had to be firm with you." Brian sagged into his chair. "You've seen how some of my peers' daughters have ended up— driving drunk, posting their sexual exploits on the Internet for the world to see."

"I wouldn't have let you down like that," Brianna said.

Her father nodded. "You've been good, a good girl."

It was more praise than he'd given Brianna her whole life.

"Then trust Brianna to be the daughter you need while you're ill," Chad said.

It meant a lot to her that he said that.

Brian addressed his words to her. "I do, but you need to trust me to know my own health. I'll be around to see this NASCAR season, and I want to be sure I'm backing the right driver. I want you back in Charlotte, doing your job." He paused. "So far, I've been quite impressed with the reports you've sent through."

For her father, this was gushing. She couldn't help beaming.

"If I go," she said, "I need your word that you'll let me know if your medical condition changes."

"I told you, I'm not going to die."

She eyeballed him, and at last he said, "Very well."

"Thanks, Dad." Brianna rose and hugged her father, who patted her shoulder. As she leaned into him, tears rose. She blinked them away before she straightened. "I'll be back to see you next week."

CHAD WAS COUNTING the days until Brianna would walk out of his life. No more of this unsettling feeling that he should be someone he wasn't. That he might have thrown away his best chance at happiness. Life could go back to blessed normality.

Only, right now, normality didn't feel that blessed. It felt... empty.

"Cut it out, you guys," Chad called across the Daytona garage to his brothers, who were engaged in an increasingly heated argument about who would do best in today's exhibition race. Entry was restricted to the top six cars for each manufacturer, ranked on team owner points from the previous season. Zack had been invited to drive the No. 597 car of Klein Racing. Jerry Klein, the team's owner, was an old friend of Brady's, and when his driver had broken his leg on a skiing vacation, he'd done Matheson Racing the favor of offering Zack some race time.

Today's race wasn't a points race, but everyone took it seriously as a gauge of the season to come...and of the big race here next weekend.

Trent and Zack had calmed down, but now the ferocious one-upmanship between their teams was getting too vocal. When his brothers had drawn adjacent pit positions, Chad's first thought had been of the convenience. As he watched one of Trent's tire guys cuff one of Zack's, he wasn't so sure.

"Stop that!" Chad roared. They did, but not without some shoving and cursing. Chad scowled. Used to be that when he said jump, guys jumped without hesitation. Used to be that his brothers could be called into line when necessary and his father would listen to his opinions.

When exactly had he lost control of the team? Of his life?

At around the moment that he'd lost control of his feelings for Brianna, he realized.

Stunned, Chad strode away from the pits, headed back toward the hauler, his mind buzzing. Lost control of his feelings for Brianna? What else could he call it when he thought about her all the time, when his frustrations paled against the pleasure of remembering the sight, the smell, the taste of her? When making love with her seemed more essential than breathing? Yet somehow, he'd screwed things up so much that was no longer a possibility.

Chad knuckled his temples. What was wrong with him?

One answer sprang to mind, but he dismissed it. He wasn't about to admit he was in love—he'd said that two years ago, and look where that had got them—but he could admit one thing for sure.

I can't let her go.

BRIANNA MADE the short walk from Garrett Clark's pit area to Zack Matheson's, fingering the hot pass she'd been issued for the event. Unlike the cold passes given to most people lucky enough to visit the garage and the pits, her hot pass allowed her to stay in the pits during the race.

Although it was exciting to be here for the exhibition race, it was also a sign she hadn't completed her task within her original deadline. Her father had thrown a bunch of scenarios at her that he wanted her to consider, including whether the return per dollar spent would be greater if Getaway sponsored a NASCAR Nationwide Series car…or even two. Should they spread the investment, and the resulting profile, across two less costly cars, or go all-out for the glory of a NASCAR Sprint Cup Series sponsorship? Interesting question, not quickly answered.

Her dad had waved away Brianna's objection that Getaway would miss out on sponsoring the exhibition race and maybe even next week's big race. "From what you've told me so far," he said, "FastMax is the stronger team. Their car's not available until after Daytona, anyway."

It gave her another week or so with Chad. After that, she wouldn't see him again. The thought sucked her energy, left her listless.

"Brianna."

She looked up to find Chad descending the war wagon. He jumped the last few steps to the ground, landing lightly for such a big man. It was both pleasure and pain to look at him, gorgeous in the team shirt that made other men look the same as everyone else. Chad would always stand out.

"Are the guys ready?" she asked.

He shrugged—a strangely casual gesture for Chad, who took everything about racing seriously.

"Chad, is everything okay? Your dad?" She reached out, touched his arm. Because she could, and very soon she wouldn't be able to.

He looked down at her hand, didn't answer the question. When he returned his gaze to hers, his eyes were very blue. "Watch the race with me."

The words were a command, yet the tone was almost a plea.

Was he trying to torture her with his proximity? "You think your commentary will sway the sponsorship?" He had to have heard what her father had said the other day about expecting to hear a recommendation for Matheson Racing. She wondered how he felt, if she'd only added to the pressure on him this week.

"I want to watch the race with you." No inflection, no clue as to why.

She wanted it, too.

After the prayer and the national anthem, after the drivers had climbed into their cars and obeyed the time-honored command to start their engines, Brianna sat atop the pit box with Chad and Zack's crew chief.

The drivers started to circle the track. The race was broken into two segments, the first just twenty-five laps. The ten-minute intermission at the end of the first segment was a bonus for the teams, who could find a hundred changes to make to the car setup in that time. The second segment ran fifty laps, and drivers inevitably had to make a fuel stop.

Although the exhibition race didn't count toward the NASCAR

Sprint Cup Series points, the fans were just as excited, and the roar that went up from the crowd when the green flag dropped was deafening, even from here.

Trent and Zack started seventh and eighth. Trent passed the car in front of him, Kent Grosso's blue-and-white No. 414, almost immediately, which had Chad beaming. He made a comment into his headset, then switched to monitor Zack's communications with his crew chief.

Zack took a little longer, but he passed Grosso, as well, by which time Trent was running fourth. Brianna willed Zack to find the passing opportunities he needed. Garrett Clark had qualified for the pole in this race and was still out in front.

Every meeting she'd had this week, every encounter with Garrett Clark, had suggested FastMax was the team to sponsor. She almost wished he'd crash, put a dent in his perfection.

At the end of the first segment, Garrett was running second, having fallen behind Trey Sanford. Trent was running third…and Zack had slid back to fifteenth.

"It's his first race in four years," Chad reminded Brianna as they watched the over-the-wall guys make adjustments to the car.

"I know."

He looked closely at her. "Is his result today going to make or break it for you?"

She shook her head. "No, but a good result would be a big help," she said honestly.

She hated the hurt look that came into his eyes, as if he expected some kind of loyalty from her. "Chad, I just…"

"You just want to get this right for your father," he said.

She nodded. "I have to." To her surprise, he took her hand, threaded his fingers through hers. He didn't say anything else, but returned his attention to the race.

In the second segment Zack slid farther down, to twenty-second place. Which wasn't great, considering there were fewer cars here than in a NASCAR Sprint Cup Series race. Brianna found herself praying for him; she suspected Chad was doing the same. Brady, over on Trent's pit box, didn't look as happy as he should, given Trent was alternating between second and third.

On lap thirty of the second segment, it happened. Justin Murphy, driving the No. 448 car in the semireckless style everyone thought he'd grown out of, attempted a slingshot maneuver. He misjudged and clipped the rear of Zack's car. Zack spun across the track, taking Justin with him. The two cars crashed, parted, then crashed again, this time with a crunch. Locked together, they slid onto the infield.

Both drivers immediately lowered their window nets and raised a hand to show they were okay. But it was clear both cars were out of the race.

Chad cursed, probably thinking of his dad's money as much as his brother's career prospects.

"Could Zack have avoided that?" Brianna asked, fairly certain of the answer.

Tight-lipped, Chad said, "He could have and he *should* have."

She'd thought as much. Justin Murphy might have started it by attempting a pass he had little hope of pulling off, but Zack's lack of skill or judgment had put himself and Justin out of the race.

Trent finished third, which had the team elated, but that wasn't relevant to Brianna's task. By then, Zack's team had already packed up and left the track. Because of Daytona's Speedweeks, most of them would remain between this race and the big race next Sunday.

The longer race would cost Brady considerably more to run. Brianna put that out of her mind.

As they watched Trent giving media interviews with his usual aplomb, Chad's cell phone rang. He stepped away from the throng to take the call. Brianna saw his brow furrow. He walked a few steps farther, talking vehemently.

The call lasted maybe three minutes. After it ended, Chad looked at his phone in disgust, then stuck it in his pocket.

Brianna joined him. "Something wrong?"

"No, I…" He stopped, closed his eyes. When he opened them

again, there was something in his face Brianna hadn't seen before. A new kind of determination, one he seemed uncomfortable with. "Country Bread just called. They're eliminating Zack from their list of potential drivers."

She winced. "Because he crashed today?"

He nodded. "Right now, I don't blame them. But—" he seemed to be forcing the words out "—I admit, I'm upset."

Chad was telling her how he felt? Without being asked? Brianna glanced at the sky, wondering if she might see pigs flying overhead.

BRIANNA HAD TRAVELED between the hotel and the race track that morning with Brady, who'd invited her to fly down on the team plane with him. But Chad insisted on taking her back.

He said little as he drove, but when they reached town, instead of continuing along South Atlantic toward their hotel, he took a left down a small street toward a tiny parking lot above the sands of the famous Daytona Beach.

"What's going on?" Brianna asked.

"Let's walk," he said.

He must still be down about Zack's result today and about Country Bread pulling out. As far as she knew, that made Getaway Resorts the team's only hope for a primary sponsor. Her stomach sank as she got out of the car, and her mood turned as dark as the sky above.

She could commiserate with Chad if he needed sympathy. But if he was looking for any kind of encouragement about the sponsorship...

He held her hand as they headed down the steps to the sand. Brianna rolled up her pant legs, and Chad did the same. She caught him looking at her ankles, and then his gaze traveled slowly up. He swallowed.

They walked toward the low tide. As they hit the line between dry sand and wet, Chad stopped, took her hands in his.

"There's no easy way to say this," he said, "so I guess I might as well just spit it out." He squeezed her fingers. "I feel as nervous as a rookie in his first race."

"What's this about?" The wind blew her hair across her face; she pushed it aside.

"Brianna—" his voice dropped, serious "—I'd like us to stay together. To stay married."

What? Warmth flooded Brianna, protecting her from the wind. Chad had asked the question she most wanted to hear. The one she'd given up on.

And yet…he didn't look warm. His jaw was tense—*he's nervous, that's understandable*—and his face held none of the joy she might have expected. None of the urgent excitement that had accompanied his first marriage proposal.

"Why?" she asked.

His foot scuffed the damp sand. "We've tried ignoring our marriage, we've tried working around it, but nothing can get you out of my head. I figure maybe it's time to accept it. I…care about you."

As a declaration of his feelings, his words fell far short of what she wanted to hear.

"I care about your brothers, but that doesn't mean I want to marry them." Hurt leached into the words, though she tried to contain it.

"This isn't the same, and you know it." He let go of her hands, at the very moment she wanted him to hold more tightly. "We're already married, it's on record that we cared enough about each other, in the right way, to commit to each other."

"Cared, past tense."

"Care, present tense," he said firmly.

"Do you love me?" She held her breath.

Chad rammed his hands in his pockets. "Yes," he said, "I do."

She'd asked the question, but she hadn't expected a direct answer. Brianna dug her toes into the sand, trying to find a solid place she could trust. "You sound very sure of that. Which you weren't, say, a week ago."

"So I only just realized it," he said. "But what other explanation is there for the way I think about you, the way I want you?"

"Lust could be an explanation." Her jacket flapped in the stiffening breeze, and she zipped it up.

"I've felt lust before. This is all that and more."

His words were heading in the right direction—but there was something missing.

"You said you loved me back in Vegas," she said. "Why would our marriage be any different this time around?"

"Because this time," he said, "I'm willing to do it your way. The whole sharing, talking, emoting thing."

He looked her in the eye, and she could see he meant it. It was like a dream, hearing him say those words—and like many dreams, it didn't feel real.

"Well?" he said. Then, obviously realizing how sharp he sounded, "What do you say, Brianna? Are we together forever?"

Unfair! was her first thought. How was she supposed to think clearly in the face of that lure?

"So you're telling me—" she felt her way, wanting to believe, but looking for the catch "—you'll share with me. All your hopes and fears and problems and dreams."

"Whatever you want," he promised.

"Share one with me now."

"Huh?"

"Give me an example of one of your fears."

He squinted into the distance. "I can't think of one off the top of my head."

"Really? Because I could tell you one of mine."

"I'm new to this," he said. "Give me time."

She nodded. It wasn't an unreasonable request. "Chad, last time around, you refused to consider the idea of us working together. Now that I understand how much NASCAR demands of you, I think it's even more important for me to be involved in the team."

"We've survived the past few weeks," he said. "I'm negotiable on that if it's what you want."

Suddenly Brianna realized what was wrong. "Do you need me, Chad?"

He reared back. "What kind of question is that?"

"A simple one." *All you have to do is give the right answer.*

He folded his arms. "I'm not generally a needy guy," he said. "In NASCAR, *needy* doesn't get you far." Consciously he unfolded his arms, shook them loose. "Surely what's important here is that I love you. I hope we'd both be more mature, more realistic, this time about making our marriage work."

"Needing someone isn't about being clingy or insecure or incapable," she said. "When you love someone, being with them, even when times are tough, makes your life better in every way. Who doesn't need that?"

A flash in his eyes told her he didn't.

In that moment of his denial, the truth hit Brianna.

She'd fallen in love with him all over again.

CHAPTER FIFTEEN

I LOVE HIM.

A gust of wind whipped spray off the ocean; the salt stung Brianna's face. She closed her eyes against the elements and against the knowledge of the pain of separation that she was about to experience.

Only this time, it would be worse.

This time, she'd fallen in love with the real Chad, a man she knew like her own heart.

She knew he didn't want to share the most meaningful parts of his life with her. She knew he could be insensitive and bossy and domineering.

She knew he cared about his family—he'd probably be horrified to realize how much. His attitude toward Brady was all about protecting his father from hurt. His love for his brothers kept him trying to unite them and make the team work when anyone else would have given up.

She also knew Chad was loyal and protective, that he understood what hurt her and would do his utmost to keep her safe. She knew he was a wonderful lover, both gentle and demanding.

She knew he wasn't about to become the man she needed. But she had to try.

"I don't want you opening up as some kind of favor to me or as a bargaining chip," she said. "I want you doing it because your life is better when you do." Her voice rose in frustration. They were so close....

"Those're just words," he flung at her. "I could promise you

I'm doing it for the right reasons, but it's how we make it work every day that counts." He hunched his shoulders as he faced into the wind. "I just…love you," he said tightly. "Accept it, dammit."

She gazed out to sea, where a boat, a tiny blaze of light, headed for the dark ocean. "I see what this is about now."

"Great," he said sarcastically. "For a minute there I thought I simply meant what I was saying."

"You do care for me. But you care more about protecting your world."

He snorted.

"The team," she said. "If you and I stay married, you'll get the sponsorship."

Chad's face darkened and he said very quietly, "If you think for one minute I want us to stay together because of the money…"

She quailed before his anger, but she said, "Your timing suggests it does."

"This has nothing to do with Getaway's money."

She took a step backward. "I'm not accusing you of deliberately asking me to remain your wife for that reason. But if we do stay married, all your problems are solved."

"I DIDN'T HAVE any problems until I met you!" Chad said, hurt and furious.

She flinched. To his horror, tears sprang to her eyes, but she brushed them away.

"I want the kind of love Trent and Kelly have," she said. "I want us to need each other above all else."

"They're not like most people," Chad said, frustrated.

"You believe we can never have that?"

"I don't want us to be Trent and Kelly," he said. "I want us to make our own way." Damn. It felt as if he was offering her the runner-up prize. "Will you stay with me or not?" He sounded like his father in one of Brady's worst moments.

"No." She spoke before he could find a way to rephrase the question, and that one word hit him so hard it winded him.

He opened his mouth a couple of times, but no sound came out.

"We're done, Chad." No shivering this time, no tears.

Chad called on every reserve of strength, of stoicism, in the effort to stay still, to stay on his feet, to keep his face from contorting with despair. "Then I have to respect your decision."

It sounded wooden, but that was a whole lot better than letting her see how her refusal had devastated him. Shocked him, he amended. That was all it was, a shock. And if this was how it felt to end things with a woman he didn't *need,* then there was no way he was ever going to be dumb enough to actually need her.

"WHERE'S JULIE-ANNE?" Brady asked his new secretary, the woman Julie-Anne had hired for him.

"She had a meeting with the piston supplier."

"I'll wait," he said, and headed into his office. Even the thrill of Speedweeks hadn't been enough to keep Julie-Anne off his mind. He'd commandeered the team plane first thing this morning and flown home.

"Mr. Matheson, Julie-Anne said you're not allowed back at the office yet."

"My doctor said I could come in for a couple of hours," he lied. He should be annoyed that Julie-Anne was keeping him away from his work, but it was a relief to know she still cared enough to lay down the rules.

More likely, she doesn't want another heart attack on her conscience.

If she'd stopped caring, that was his fault. But he was here to fix that.

His office shrieked her presence. Brady breathed in her spicy floral scent, fingered the scarf slung over the back of her chair. *His* chair. The desk was a mess, but he knew it was an ordered mess, and that Julie-Anne would know exactly where everything was. Thank goodness she'd agreed to stay on at the office, despite their break-up, until he was fit for work again.

He sat in the chair and picked up a folder marked "NASCAR Nationwide Series" and began flicking through it. It was a relief to fill his mind with engine-dyno statistics and forward orders. He'd had far too much time to think *relationship* thoughts.

He'd been there maybe half an hour when he heard Julie-Anne's voice in the outer office. Brady's fingers trembled on the page he was reading.

She'd been alerted to his presence, going by the frown on her face as she entered the office. "Brady, what are you doing? I don't believe for one minute your doctor said you could come in here."

Her voice washed over him, the sight of her—hands on hips, indignation in her eyes—filled his senses, poured into a cavernous hunger he hadn't even realized was inside him. A glorious, welcome warmth filtered through him. This was what it must have been like when the sun came out after the Ice Age.

"I wanted to be here," he said, aware that *here* meant wherever she was, rather than this specific building. His face was one big goofy grin. Anyone would think he was a high-school senior, not a middle-aged man with a rickety heart.

She glared a moment longer, then, reluctantly, her mouth curved. Just that hint of a smile set Brady's heart thudding better than any defibrillator. Why had he thought he could have any kind of life worth living without Julie-Anne?

She dropped her gaze, reminding him she didn't yet know the decision he'd made, and stacked the folders she was carrying on a shelf where they weren't supposed to go. No doubt in some kind of random order that made sense to her but would drive Brady nuts when he got back to work.

He let out a satisfied sigh.

"How long do you intend to stay?" she asked.

"Forever."

She blinked. "Excuse me?"

He grabbed her hands, tugged her away from the shelf. "Julie-Anne, I'm a fool."

She stared.

"Don't argue with me." He grinned, because plainly she had no intention of disagreeing. "I love you so much my life doesn't make a scrap of sense when you're not around."

"Brady, we've been here before." She sounded impatient, resigned, but he didn't miss the thread of hope in her voice.

"You're right," he said. "Once before, I had the good sense to propose to you, then I let my stupid pride get in the way of making you mine. I told myself I was doing it for your sake."

"Idiot," she said lovingly.

He pulled her into his arms. "But from now on I'm going to be totally selfish. You were dumb enough to say you want me for better or for worse, and I'm going to hold you to it."

"I want that in writing."

"You'll get it," he promised. "I'm going to sign a marriage-license application and then I'll sign the register as your husband—call it a contract for life."

He saw in her eyes how he'd hurt her with his intransigence. Saw, too, the forgiveness she offered so readily. His heart swelled. "I don't deserve you," he said roughly.

"No, you don't." But she didn't make any move out of his arms. Instead, she burrowed into his shoulder.

"Is there any chance I haven't killed your love for me?" he asked.

"You gave it your best shot," she said, "but it seems my love for you is a survivor. Just like you."

"Just like us," he said, and lowered his mouth to hers.

She tasted like nectar and honey and tomorrow. Brady reveled in her unshakable love for him, gave her all of himself in his kiss, promised his love always. Gave her his patched-up, second-rate heart and knew she treasured it like solid gold.

When they pulled apart, he felt healed.

"I want to set a date for our wedding," he said. "How about a month from today?"

"That sounds wonderful." She kissed him again. Then her

eyes narrowed. "Wait a minute. When do you come off those beta blockers?"

"Uh…three more days."

"You're doing it again," she accused. "You're thinking soon you'll know whether or not you'll be able to make love, and if you can't, you'll try to talk me out of marrying you."

"I'm not," he said. "I won't." Not very convincingly.

She shook her head, half laughing, half exasperated.

"Brady Matheson, do you still like kissing me?" she asked. "Holding me, touching me?"

"Of course I like it—I love it." He caressed her. "But, sweetheart, right now the part of me that matters doesn't give a damn."

"The part that matters is here." She thumped his chest.

Half laughing, half complaining, he said, "Hey, I just had a heart attack."

"And here." She tapped his head.

He kissed her deeply, because those parts were in full working order. When the kiss ended, Brady said, serious now, "You can't tell me being able to make love—to make love *fully*—doesn't matter."

"It matters," she agreed. "But it doesn't matter more than my love for you. Brady, I plan to marry you for better or for worse, whether you like it or not. You need to accept that right now, and as far as I can see, there's only one way to make sure that happens."

He knew what that was. He'd been expecting it. He'd planned to argue, to put his foot down, but suddenly, he didn't want to. His heart kicked like a mule, and he found himself smiling like a loon.

"Okay, Gypsy," he said. "You win."

A STIFF-NECKED PRIDE that Brianna could only assume came from her father's genes had her dressing up the next night for Dean and Patsy Grosso's thirty-first wedding anniversary party.

The party promised to be an extravaganza—the Grossos had reunited a couple of months ago after a separation, and they wanted to share their rediscovered happiness with the world.

Chad had asked Brianna to accompany him back when they'd been on kissing terms. He hadn't called to pull out of the date, so she assumed he still planned to pick her up at seven.

She could only hope that stiff-necked pride would hang in there long enough to keep her from betraying the realization that had struck her yesterday, that had forced her off the beach, unable to spend one more second hearing Chad explain why the kind of love he was offering should be enough.

Brianna put on her diamond-drop earrings, followed by their matching pendant, and surveyed the glittering effect in the mirror. The jewels were impressive enough that they might distract people from seeing how little party spirit she'd been able to muster.

She wanted to flee back to Atlanta…but Chad had called her on her habit of running away from people who didn't love her the way she wanted them to.

She would stick this out until it reached its natural end, so she would know she'd given it her best shot. Even if right now there seemed little point.

Because the love he'd offered her would never be enough. He might have let her through the front door of his heart, but he had no intention of inviting her in further. Tonight's party wouldn't change that.

Chad showed up on time, his face blank, his greeting as neutral as Switzerland. He didn't look like a man who'd had his heart broken by her refusal of his proposal.

Because he wasn't, she reminded herself. To have a broken heart, he'd have to have risked it in the first place.

CHAD WAS RELIEVED to find that the anniversary party, held at one of Daytona's top hotels, was the huge affair he'd expected.

Because although he'd stuck with the plan of escorting Brianna to the party—if he hadn't, Zack would probably have jumped in—tonight had to be the first step in getting his old life back.

He'd offered Brianna all he had to give and she'd turned it down. How many more clues did he need that their marriage was never going to work?

In a way, accepting that was a positive step. Brianna had been right about closure all along: he was relieved not to be hiding anything from his family anymore, that the divorce was in progress. He could see light at the end of the tunnel that led back to his old self. Soon he would be able to put all his focus on this year's NASCAR season. Where it should be.

Brianna left his side almost immediately and went to talk to Hugo Murphy and Patsy Grosso. Judging from their animated discussion, they were speculating about who had the wherewithal to win this season's NASCAR Sprint Cup Series championship.

Chad spied Zack across the room, but didn't see his dad anywhere. Brady had said he'd attend, but he'd been grumpily antisocial since the breakup with Julie-Anne, so maybe he hadn't bothered. Giving up on his dad, Chad went to congratulate Adam Sanford, owner of Sanford Racing, on his brother Trey's win in the exhibition race.

Adam's new fiancée, Tara Dalton, was with him—they stood so close together, it made people smile. Even Patsy Grosso's cynical cousin, Jake McMasters, on the periphery of the conversation, caught Chad's eye and grinned.

Chad had thought all he wanted was to talk NASCAR—simple racing talk, minus any by personal complications. But after they covered the race, he found himself asking Adam and Tara about their wedding plans…and listening to their replies.

Maybe he'd evolved into a *softer, kinder* version of his old self.

BRIANNA TRIED not to watch Chad out of the corner of her eye all evening, but it was difficult. As she mingled with people she'd got to know the past few weeks, then later as she ate dinner and listened to the speeches—laughing and almost crying along with everyone as Dean paid tribute to the wife he adored—she was always aware of Chad's whereabouts.

Toward midnight, as the crowd began to thin, she found herself just a few feet away from him. The circles in which they were talking swelled and merged, until they were loosely in the same group of partygoers. She turned away so she couldn't see him. Which put her in the middle of a conversation between Andrew Clark and Patsy Grosso.

Brianna had heard the two weren't close, but right now, Patsy was talking intently to her brother. Brianna murmured an apology for the intrusion, but before she could retreat, Patsy said, "If my own brother won't be honest with me, perhaps you can cast some light on this, Brianna."

Yikes. Brianna had an awful feeling she knew what this was about—she'd overheard some gossip earlier in the evening and dismissed it.

"In the past half hour at least a dozen people have, I don't know, shied away when I came near," Patsy said. "What's going on?"

"I told you, you're imagining it," Andrew said hastily. He shot Brianna a beseeching look.

She imagined he was trying to spare Patsy some pain on the night of her big party, but Brianna guessed the other woman would hate to discover tomorrow that she'd unknowingly been the butt of gossip.

"I think," Brianna said apologetically, "a few people are talking about the latest blog post. Apparently there was one early this evening." A mystery blogger was continuing to perpetuate the rumor that Patsy and Dean's stolen daughter, Gina, was still alive. "I can't imagine how difficult these rumors are for you and Dean." Brianna squeezed Patsy's arm.

Patsy blew out a frustrated breath. "Dean's certain the blog is all lies and we should ignore it. What's that jerk saying now?"

"I didn't see it myself, but I gather it's something about Gina's blood type being B positive."

Patsy's fingers closed around Brianna's wrist like talons.

"What did you say?" Her face had gone white and she spoke loudly enough that several people broke off their conversations to stare at her.

"I, uh, assumed the blogger looked up Kent's blood type," Brianna said, "and made something up based on that."

"Kent's not B positive." Patsy swayed on her feet. "But Gina was. *Is.* That information has never been in the public domain."

Tara Dalton spoke up hesitantly. "A lot of people are B positive… my sister Mallory, for one."

"Not…not that many." Tears welled in Patsy's eyes, and she squeezed them closed as she pressed her knuckles to her lips. Feeling her pain almost like a physical wave, Brianna stepped backward, horrified that she'd sprung such momentous news on the poor woman so publicly, so precipitously. She should have followed Andrew Clark's lead.

Chad appeared between them. He slid an arm around Patsy's shoulders. "Let's go find Dean," he said. He caught Brianna's hand. "Come on, sweetheart."

She wasn't his sweetheart, but his words felt sweet right now.

They delivered Patsy to her husband. Jake McMasters went with them—Dean and Patsy had hired him in his capacity as a private investigator to check out the rumors about Gina.

Chad gave Dean a quick rundown on what had happened, and at Dean's insistence, Brianna contributed what she'd heard of the latest blog post.

There was a silence while Dean assimilated the information.

"Nine percent of the American population is B positive," he said. "If the blogger was guessing, it's not an obvious choice."

He dropped a kiss on his wife's hair, and she leaned against him. "Patsy and I need to leave," he said. "We'll check out the blog for ourselves, get in touch with the FBI. They told us that if something truly new came out, they'd get serious about investigating."

The couple left, but Jake McMasters stayed, lost in thought.

"Any more information we can help you with?" Chad asked.

It took Jake a second to reply. He shook his head. "Tara Dalton said her sister Mallory is B positive. Mallory's the same age as Gina would be."

Chad stared. "There's no reason to think her parents were involved in Gina's disappearance, is there?"

Jake shook his head, but he looked thoughtful. "I checked out the family when Tara brought up the rumors with Dean and Patsy. My first thought was that she was behind them. She wasn't," he said hastily. "But I did learn that Mallory Dalton looks nothing like the rest of her family. I can't say she looks like Dean or Patsy, either," he said fairly. "But her parents are obsessive NASCAR fans. I bet they haven't missed a race weekend in years. Maybe even thirty years."

"You mean, they were in Nashville when Gina was stolen?" Brianna asked.

Jake shrugged. "Seems likely. And guess who the Daltons' favorite driver is?"

"Dean Grosso," Chad said.

Jake didn't answer, but he made a "gotcha" pistol gesture. He walked away, heading for Tara and Adam.

Brianna's shoulders sagged. "What a night. Poor Patsy and Dean. I ruined their anniversary party."

Chad lifted her chin with his finger. "I think you made Patsy's night. To learn that the blogger does actually know something is a big deal."

"Still, it wasn't the way to find out."

"It was a shock," he agreed. "But Dean and Patsy will know you don't have a malicious bone in your body—and if they don't, I'll tell them."

Darn it, Brianna thought, did he have to act so…*married?* She'd messed up, and Chad had been there. Reassuring, helping, defending her. It was one-half of what she'd always wanted. If only he would welcome her doing the same for him.

"I think I'll call it a night," she said. "I'm driving down to see Dad tomorrow, which means an early start."

She'd finished her report, all bar the conclusion, which

shouldn't take long. In the weeks she'd spent in Charlotte, it had become obvious that FastMax's driver was more reliable, more charming, more media-worthy than Matheson Racing's. Andrew Clark was a pleasure to do business with, and he ran a harmonious, efficient team.

There was only one recommendation Brianna could make.

Chad reached into his jacket pocket for his keys. "I'll drive you home."

"I'll take a cab," she said. "I still feel bad about the Grossos. I don't feel like chatting."

"I won't talk," he said. "You know I'm good at that." He gave her a crooked smile. "I'm worried about you."

She pressed her hands to her cheeks. "Chad, please don't."

"Don't what?"

"When you're kind, like you've been tonight…it makes it too hard for me to leave you."

Triumph flared in his eyes. "Then don't leave."

CHAD WATCHED Brianna go and realized the worst moments of his thirty-six years had been exactly this: watching Brianna walk away.

Because her leaving meant that from now on, even his best days wouldn't be as real, as meaningful as a bad day with her. That no matter how many people surrounded him, he would be alone inside.

He cursed as the truth hammered him.

Whose pigheaded, mush-for-brains idea had it been that he didn't need her?

He needed her, now and always. In his bed, in his life. On his team.

This wasn't about the pasty, plug-in version of love he'd offered her on the beach. How could he have been so stupid? His love for her was everything to him. He wanted it to be everything to her.

Chad buried his face in his hands and cursed again. He'd made a terrible mistake—two terrible mistakes. Letting Brianna go the first time and letting her go tonight.

He had to get her back right now.

Reason intervened, staying him.

Brianna had some crazy idea that he wanted her for the sponsorship. Telling her he'd discovered his *need* for her right before she reported to her father wasn't the way.

Though it killed him, he would have to wait. Let her make her decision about the sponsorship first. Then show her he was for real.

It wouldn't be easy, not when he thought about all the stupid things he'd said and done the past few weeks.

But there was one thing he could fix—*must* fix—right away.

CHAPTER SIXTEEN

"DAD, I CAN'T BELIEVE it." Brianna rubbed her eyes to make sure she wasn't hallucinating. "You look…"

"Better," her father said triumphantly. He kicked back in his seat. "I'm feeling good, too. The chemo's working."

His face looked fuller, more relaxed. He radiated vigor almost the way he used to.

"You're amazing." To think she'd doubted he could beat the cancer. "What did the doctor say?"

"He was surprised to hear me sounding so well," Brian said smugly. "I'm going in tomorrow for some tests so we can see if the numbers bear out the way I feel."

"Do you want me to…" She stopped. "No, of course you don't want me to come with you."

"I'll be fine." Was there a hint of apology in her father's tone? "Now," he said, "what have you got to say about my NASCAR sponsorship?"

Brianna pulled a bound copy of her final report from her briefcase. In a sudden attack of nerves, she fumbled the document, dropped it on the floor.

"Sorry." She bent down to retrieve it and used the moment to take a steadying breath. Then she handed over the document she'd worked late into the night to prepare after she'd returned from the Grossos' disastrous party.

After she'd left Chad, his concern for her wrapped around her like a shield during the taxi ride back to the hotel, she'd done a lot of thinking.

"You can read the report later. I'll tell you what it says." She squared her shoulders, lifted her chin. "I'm recommending Zack Matheson for Getaway's sponsorship."

"What?" Her father flicked through the document, read the conclusion, then tossed the report onto his desk as if its next destination was the trash. "Whenever we've talked about this, you've said Garrett Clark is the most exciting driver around, and that the only reason he doesn't have a sponsor yet is because his stepfather is hanging out for the highest bidder. Which I can afford to be."

"That's right."

He looked taken aback, but he carried on. "While Zack Matheson is a moody, crash-prone son of a gun, about as safe a bet as me walking on Mars next year."

"If you tell me you're going to walk on Mars, I believe you."

Brian almost smiled. "Talk me through your thinking here, Brianna," he ordered. "Because from where I'm sitting, it looks faulty."

"I'm thinking," she said, "with my heart." Unconsciously, she put a hand to her chest. "I love Chad, and I want to do this for him."

"You're getting a divorce," her father said, incredulous. "And no matter what you *want* to do, this isn't your money to use as some kind of alimony. This is Getaway's investment in NASCAR."

"Of course," Brianna agreed. "But more than anything, NASCAR is about passion, about people doing what they love, supporting what they love. And who they love." She laughed, amazed it had taken her so long to reach this decision. "Dad, I love Chad, so I'm giving him my full support and I want you to do the same."

Her father snorted. "You might love him, but I sure as hell don't."

Brianna took a deep breath. "No, but you love me." Silence. "At least, that's what I choose to think. And I say that if you love me, you'll sponsor Zack Matheson."

"That's preposterous," he sputtered. "Not to mention blackmail."

She reminded him with her silence how he'd blackmailed her into taking on this project in the first place. His gaze slid away.

"If it'll make it easier," she said, "let me remind you that drivers come and go, but Chad Matheson is the best team owner in the business—and you don't have to be in love with him to see that."

Acknowledgment flashed in her father's eyes.

"Dad, for the sake of our relationship—yours and mine—you need to accept my recommendation."

"You're saying it's him or me?" he said ominously.

"I've told you how I feel. That's not going to change." Never had she spoken so directly to her father. If she hoped to see a dawning respect in his eyes, the kind he'd given Chad, there was none. Just irritation and outrage...and disbelief.

"I need your answer now." She pushed through her fear that his displeasure would turn to loathing, trusting Chad's call on this. "You've thought about this sponsorship a lot, so don't tell me you need more time."

She stopped there. She folded her hands in her lap and waited. The carriage clock on the mantelpiece ticked, measuring her father's regard by how long it would take him to back her or turn her down.

After what felt like minutes, he said, "Matheson is a good team owner."

Brianna caught her breath. She hadn't actually believed he would give in.

"I accept your recommendation," he said formally. "Getaway Resorts will sponsor Zack Matheson."

"Dad, that's fantastic!" She couldn't restrain herself; she rushed forward and hugged him, kissed him.

He kissed her cheek, his lips dry, and patted her back.

"I can't wait to tell Chad. I'll stay here tonight and fly back to Daytona tomorrow."

CHAD KNOCKED on his father's front door. A turn of the handle revealed it was unlocked, so he went on in.

Something about the silence unnerved him.

"Dad?" Chad picked up the pace, raced into the den, half expecting to find Brady laid out by another heart attack. The room was empty.

Fear sucked logic out of him. "Dad!" he shouted, and headed for the kitchen—*empty*—then the garage. His father's classic Mustang was there, but no sign of Brady. He strode back into the kitchen all set to dial 9-1-1—only to find his father sitting on a stool at the island.

Chad jumped a mile high. He cursed.

"Thought you were still in Daytona," Brady said.

"I thought *you* were. Until our pilot told me you flew out on the team plane on Tuesday. He wouldn't say where to."

"Ah." Brady walked across the kitchen to the sink. Chad noticed his feet were bare. "You look like hell," Brady observed conversationally as he poured a glass of water.

"So do you." Chad's reply came automatically, because Brady had looked like hell ever since he'd broken up with Julie-Anne. Then he realized Brady actually looked okay—tired, but more relaxed than he'd been since the heart attack.

Maybe, Chad thought, a guy could get over the pain of breaking up with the woman he loved. Or maybe it was just too early in the morning for Brady to have recalled his sorrows.

"Care to talk?" Brady asked. Which was a strange thing for his father to say, but Chad was too relieved to question it. He needed to repair the damage he'd done. If that meant getting up close and personal, well, he could do it.

"When you broke up with Julie-Anne," he said, "how did you feel?"

Brady made a sound of disgust.

"*Physically,*" Chad added. "Did your chest ache—I mean differently from your heart attack?"

Brady rubbed his chin. "Maybe."

"Did you have this kind of hollow feeling in your gut, and your legs were all heavy and leaden?" Chad's legs felt heavy enough to drag him under.

Brady was looking at him as if he were crazy. "The gut thing, yeah. Nothing wrong with my legs. But, son—"

"I can't believe you let yourself feel like this—like *that*." Chad didn't want his father knowing he was in the same pathetic state. He paced across the room and didn't stop until he reached the picture window that looked out over rolling green pasture. "How could you be so dumb as to let me or anyone else tell you Julie-Anne isn't right for you? Look how I messed up my marriage, for Pete's sake."

"I didn't exactly let—"

"Hell, Dad, you're old enough to know better." Chad hooked his thumbs over his belt. "You need to call Julie-Anne right now and apologize for being such a jerk."

His father gaped, and all the steam hissed out of Chad. "Please, Dad," he said. "You love that woman, she loves you. I'll never forgive myself if you let me break you two up."

Brady threw back his head and laughed. And laughed. The delighted roar brought a smile to Chad's face.

"Okay, maybe I sound a little crazy myself," he said sheepishly. "But when you meet a woman who turns you inside out, you need to hang on to her and not let go, even if it means you're in for the most uncomfortable ride of your life."

Brady wiped his eyes. "What's really crazy is that you think I'd let you decide who I should or shouldn't marry."

"But…I thought me going on about how you didn't know Julie-Anne well enough had finally gotten through."

"You're a great team boss, son, but you're the last guy I'd take advice about my love life from," Brady said. "I've got a few years on you and I already figured out for myself that I couldn't live without Julie-Anne."

"So you've spoken to her?" Chad asked hopefully.

"I've done better than that." Brady paused for effect, then said with a grin, "I've married her."

"You're kidding, right?" Chad started to laugh.

"We took a leaf out of your book—we flew to Vegas." Enjoying his son's stunned expression, he called, "Sweetheart, guess who's come to congratulate us."

Half a minute later, Julie-Anne entered the room. She was dressed, but the way her thick hair was tousled, Chad guessed she'd just got out of bed.

She walked into the shelter of Brady's arms as if this was the place in the world she most wanted to be.

"Brady's told you our news," she guessed. Her voice quivered with happiness, but also, Chad sensed, apprehension.

"I couldn't be more delighted," Chad told her. "You two are great together. I'm only sorry I was too much of an ass to see it earlier."

"I blame it on your Matheson genes." Julie-Anne blew a kiss to Brady, who patted his new wife lovingly on the bottom. "It's not your fault."

"You're too kind," Chad said, and meant it.

Brady tugged Julie-Anne closer as if he literally didn't want to let her go ever again. "Chad, going by the lecture you just gave me, you should be somewhere else right now."

Chad's problems returned in a rush. It was all very well telling his father how to fix his love life, but things weren't that simple between him and Brianna.

"I'm already fond of that wife of yours," Brady said. "So don't you let her slip away."

"I always told her I didn't want to mix work and marriage," Chad said. "But with Brianna it's all-in or all-out. Which means it's all-in. It's what I want. I just have to figure out how to make it work."

"The problem between your mom and me wasn't that we worked together," Brady said abruptly. "If that's what you're thinking."

He seldom talked about the breakup with his first wife, Chad's and Zack's mom.

"I don't remember much, except you guys fighting," Chad said. "Mostly about work."

"It might have seemed like that." Brady grimaced. "Truth is, we fought about everything. You know your mom and I had to get married, with you on the way—we were never love's young dream."

"That can't have helped," Chad agreed.

"Thing is, we never would have got married otherwise. When I think how I felt about Rosie and now about Julie-Anne—" the smile he directed at his new wife was so full of love Chad got a lump in his throat "—your mom and I never had those feelings for each other. If we had, they would have given us something to hold on to when things turned bad. The way you look at Brianna, I think you two have those feelings." Brady reddened, embarrassed by his own soppiness. "Not that I know anything about it," he muttered.

Chad looked out the window. "She wants…more than I thought about giving."

"Take it from me." Brady joined him at the window, and they both took a great interest in the neighbor's goat, grazing a hundred yards or so from the house. "Give her what she wants and you'll be the happiest guy alive. Next to me."

Chad was sure no man could be happier than he was when he had Brianna in his arms, but who was he to argue with a newlywed?

As he left, he shook his father's hand, kissed Julie-Anne. This was one Las Vegas wedding that would last.

BRIANNA FLEW into Daytona from Atlanta at lunchtime on Saturday.

The balmy Florida weather meant she could roll up the sleeves of her light wool jacket and let the sun warm her wrists. Weak though the rays were, they promised springtime, and to Brianna it felt like hope.

Which was crazy, because she and Chad were finished. She loved him, knew in her heart she always would, but she couldn't live with his idea of a marriage.

That didn't stop the anticipation fizzing in her stomach at the prospect of seeing him again.

A mechanic grilling burgers outside Zack's hauler greeted her with a wave. "Chad's inside."

"Thanks." Brianna grinned, hardly able to contain the good news that would have the entire team celebrating tonight.

As she stepped into the hauler, her cell phone chirped. The display showed an Atlanta number. Her dad had said he'd have someone from Getaway's in-house PR team call her about announcing the sponsorship. She pressed to answer.

"Miss Hudson? This is Dr. Martin Greer from Emory University Hospital, calling about your father."

"How did his tests go this morning?"

"We didn't need to run the tests," the doctor said quietly.

"What's happened?" Brianna clutched the counter that ran down the right-hand side of the hauler, her legs shaking.

"Brianna, is that you?" Chad came out of the office. One look at her face and he raced to her. He grasped her shoulders, sustaining her.

"Your father collapsed at home and was admitted to the hospital," the doctor said.

"But…I was with him just a few hours ago. He was a thousand percent better."

"It's quite common for terminal patients to rally briefly to what seems like full health," Dr. Greer said. "When that happens, it's followed by a total relapse…and death."

CHAPTER SEVENTEEN

WHEN SHE ENDED the call, Brianna slumped against Chad's chest.

He stroked her hair, his big hand soothing. "Your dad?"

"I have to go. He's in the hospital. He's not going to make it." Her vision hazed and she stepped blindly forward. Chad steered her toward the door. "I don't know if there's a flight from Daytona now, and I might need to go to Orlando. Will you drive me?"

Asking Chad for help came as naturally as breathing. However Chad *didn't* feel about her, he would protect her with his last breath, she knew.

"We'll take the team plane." He pulled out his cell and made a call, only to discover the team plane was right now bringing emergency engine parts from Charlotte.

"I'll try Brent Sanford, see if his plane's free." Chad scrolled through the numbers on his phone. He talked fast to Brent, whom Brianna assumed must be associated with Sanford Racing, and soon had the flight arranged. "Two passengers," he said.

"You're coming with me?" she asked, after he ended the call.

"No arguments," he ordered.

She was more likely to kiss him than argue with him, but there was no time for either. Chad summoned a helicopter to take them to the airport. Brianna was thankful for the noise of the chopper, which meant she didn't have to make conversation when her mind was consumed with worry about her father.

They took off in Brent's plane less than an hour after the doctor phoned. Brianna prayed they would get to Atlanta in time. Prayed it would turn out to be a false alarm, and her father would snap at her for believing he was frail enough to die like other people.

They flew over the speedway, the crowded infield. "You can be back here in time for the race," she said to Chad. "Even if you have to stay overnight in Atlanta."

"I'm not leaving you."

She swallowed. "Thank you." Her fingers tightened around her purse at the thought of her father.

Chad's hand closed around hers. He pried her fingers loose. "Let me tell you some good news. Dad and Julie-Anne got married in Vegas on Wednesday."

That did jerk her mind away from her troubles. "That's wonderful."

He grinned, and suddenly he looked younger. "Dad woke up to what he was throwing away just in time. He groveled enough that Julie-Anne agreed to marry him."

"How do you feel about it?"

"Relieved," he said. "Those two are crazy about each other. I can't live with Dad making everyone miserable when they're apart."

Despite the flippancy of that last remark, Brianna could see he was genuinely happy for his father. She wondered what had changed his attitude, but her mind soon strayed back to thoughts of her father. She blinked rapidly.

Chad ran a knuckle down her cheek. "Sweetheart, you should try to sleep. You might have a long night ahead of you."

About to protest that there was no way she could sleep right now, Brianna's eyelids suddenly turned heavy. So heavy, she couldn't keep her eyes open. Obediently, she leaned back into her seat.

She felt something soft descend on her and realized Chad had put a blanket over her. He raised the armrest between her seat and his and took her hand.

"You're being so sweet," she murmured.

"You're being so compliant." She heard the rumble of laughter beneath his words, and despite her worry, she smiled.

CHAD TRIED TO SETTLE in to sleep himself—this week had been short on shut-eye. But he was worried about Brianna. If her dad died now, she would feel as if she hadn't got that assurance of his feelings that she wanted.

He watched her as she slept. She was so beautiful he longed to hold her in his arms forever. Could he convince her of that somehow?

One thing was for sure, he was going to have to get mighty comfortable with talking about his feelings. What was it she'd asked him down on the beach when he'd botched that proposal? Oh, yeah. To name one of his fears.

His brain and mouth had dried up. Pathetic! How big a deal could it be to name something he was afraid of?

"Letting my family down." He spoke the words aloud.

He glanced at Brianna—still asleep.

Chad cleared his throat and continued quietly, "I'm afraid of letting my family down, and when things fall apart it'll be my fault. I know Zack and Trent are old enough to look after themselves, but I feel responsible. I always have, from when we were kids.

"I'm worried about Zack's comeback into racing," he said. "I lie awake at nights wondering if he's good enough behind the wheel, or mentally strong enough, to make it at the top level. Sometimes I think letting him back in was a huge mistake, but I couldn't turn him down. Not after the bad feeling of the past couple of years…and not after seeing how happy Dad was to have him return."

He tilted his head back, closed his eyes. "I just know there'll be animosity between Zack and Trent on the track, and that's going to be a strain on everyone. Including Dad, who doesn't need it right now. Dad'll be happy with Julie-Anne, but that doesn't mean he might not have another heart attack. And if he does, how will we run MPI and the team? Something's got to give."

Chad lifted his lids just enough to see Brianna was still asleep, then closed his eyes again. "When we get a sponsor for Zack— if we ever do—he's going to have to make nice to a lot of people, and that's never been his strong suit. I mean, sure, he likes you, but that's probably just to annoy me. No, everyone likes you," he corrected himself. "But Zack's concerned about you, too. He's too self-absorbed to be doing it for any reason other than to bug me. That makes me sound like a jerk, I know, but I also know Zack."

The words poured out of him. "Speaking of me being a jerk, most of all I'm afraid I'm going to lose you through my own stupidity. All my big ideas about us not working together—did you ever hear such garbage? I know we'll argue and there'll be pressures, but I'm starting to figure out that doing this all on my own is no life at all.

"When you came to Charlotte," he said, "you asked me if I'm happy. I lied. Sure, I have a kind of happiness, but it's not what it could be."

He peeked at Brianna again. Her eyes were still closed—but her mouth was curved in a wide smile.

Chad jerked upright. "Dammit, Brianna, are you awake?"

"No," she said, still grinning, eyes stubbornly closed. "I'm sound asleep, not listening to a word you say."

"Brat," he said, amused but embarrassed as hell. He leaned over and kissed her.

Still, she didn't open her eyes. "Maybe one day you'll be able to say this stuff to me when I'm awake, but until then, I'll just keep on sleeping."

Chad loved the sound of *one day*—it sounded like a future. He leaned over again.

Turned out Brianna kissed pretty well in her sleep.

THEY TOOK A TAXI directly to the hospital from Atlanta's airport.

"Brian Hudson," Chad told the nurse at the desk in the cancer ward. "My wife's father."

It took Brianna a second to process that he was calling her his wife, but the nurse caught on immediately. "Room 205," she said. "I'll see if I can get the doctor to come and talk to you."

Brianna half expected to find her father sitting up in bed,

railing against the incompetence of medical staff who didn't know a healthy man when they saw one.

Instead, she found a sunken-faced man, lying so still that if it hadn't been for his labored breathing, she'd have thought he was dead.

"Dad." She dashed forward, slowing as she reached the bed. His eyes opened, and after a moment they focused on her.

"Bri…anna." Sighed, more than spoken.

She took his hand, was shocked to find his fingers almost fleshless.

"Dad, you promised me you'd pull through," she said fiercely. "I'm holding you to that."

He nodded, and she thought his mouth moved in a smile.

"I'm going to sit with you," she said. "Don't tell me I can't, because I'm not going anywhere." At a movement behind her, she remembered. "Chad's here, too."

Her father's gaze moved to Chad.

"Sir," Chad said. "I'm sorry to see you so unwell."

Brian's mouth quirked with what might have been skepticism.

The doctor arrived and requested a private word with Brianna.

"Your father's organs are beginning to fail," he said. "I don't expect him to last the night."

Thousands of words—the myriad things she'd never said to her dad, never confided in him for fear of his condemnation or rejection—rushed over her. "Can I stay with him…until he goes?"

"Of course. Though he's on some heavy pain meds, so he won't have much to say."

"But I do," Brianna said.

HER FATHER, naturally, defied the doctor's prognosis and was still alive the next morning. He'd had a peaceful night, with the exception of one fretful stage where a nurse had administered more morphine and he'd slid back into unconsciousness. Brianna had stayed at his bedside, holding his hand, talking about NASCAR, about the hotel business—the kind of easy conversation they'd seldom had. The doctor had said her dad would have periods of lucidity; she wanted to wait for one of those to say the things in her heart.

Chad stayed, too. Twice, he'd told Brianna to get an hour's sleep, promising to wake her if her dad's condition changed. She didn't think Chad had slept at all, apart from a couple of ten-minute power naps.

Around lunchtime he brought her a milk shake from the hospital cafeteria. She flashed him a smile of gratitude. Together they observed her father in the bright afternoon sunshine.

He seemed smaller than he had last night, and Brianna guessed he was near the end.

She couldn't put off what she had to say any longer. She set her shake on the nightstand.

"Dad," she said, and perhaps the urgency in her tone communicated itself to him. Her father's eyes fluttered open, then closed, then open again.

She leaned forward, clasped his bony hand. "I love you, Dad," she said. "I haven't said it, I guess I haven't shown it much, and I'm sorry." She drew a deep breath. "Dad, I've always been scared of showing my love, in case I get hurt…but I learned recently that if I back down from something so important, I'll never get to give and receive the love we both deserve."

Chad squeezed her shoulder.

"It takes courage to love the way I want to," she said. "I'm sorry I didn't find that courage earlier. But please—" her voice cracked "—know now that I love you."

Her father's eyes met hers. She looked intently, trying to see his love, desperately willing him to find the strength to speak. His throat worked, then his mouth, as if he was forcing words to the surface.

Then her father's gaze flickered to Chad. "Look," he muttered.

Chad bent down.

"After…her." A tiny but emphatic nod of the head accompanied the words.

"I will, sir." Chad took Brianna's free hand, and the three of them were joined in an unlikely partnership.

"Dad…" *Say you love me.*

Her father's eyes closed.

A couple of hours later he stopped breathing. Chad called the medical staff, but Brianna knew it was over. Her father had slipped out of the world with an uncharacteristic lack of bombast.

Her eyes dry and burning, she kissed him goodbye.

Chad led her from the room, took a briefing from the nurse about paperwork and administration. He called her father's lawyer, and they learned Brian had left detailed instructions about his funeral and burial. His belief in his survival hadn't been as unwavering as it had seemed.

When there was no more they could do, Chad threaded his fingers through Brianna's. "Do you want to go back to your father's house?"

She shook her head. "That's not home."

"Let's go somewhere that *is* home," he said. "Or at least, closer to it."

She had no idea what he was talking about, but she let him find a taxi and negotiate a fare up front for what sounded like a long journey. She fell asleep almost as soon as they pulled away from the hospital. If Chad confessed any more fears or worries during the trip, she was oblivious.

When he gently shook her awake, they were at…

"A race track?" she asked. Not one she'd seen before.

"Yup. The one in Atlanta," he said.

He must have used the journey to make some arrangements, because they were allowed straight through to the empty stands. Chad led her up the first flight of stairs, and they gazed out at the enormous, slightly misshaped oval.

"One and a half miles," Chad said. "Trent and Zack both love this track. Dad does, too—several of his engines have won races here."

"What about you?" she asked.

"I crashed my truck here once. Looked spectacular, but I walked away."

"You said we were going somewhere closer to home," Brianna said.

He put an arm around her shoulders. "It's not Charlotte, but it is NASCAR."

She looked up at him, surprised.

"I'm sorry," he said, "about your dad."

"I wish…I wish he could have said what I needed to hear."

"Your father wasn't the kind of guy to wear his heart on his sleeve." Chad turned her to face him. "He asked me to look after you. I think protecting you, making sure I'll be around to protect you, was his way of showing his love."

"It doesn't seem—"

"Brianna," he said, "I know something about protecting the people I love. And maybe letting them see the protection, but not the love."

Recognition seeped into her. She wasn't quite able to trust it.

"I won't hold you to that promise to my dad," she said.

He chuckled. "No, but I'll hold you to it."

"Really?" she said hopefully.

"I'm holding you to a couple of other things, too." He took her hands. "Brianna, sweetheart, two years ago you promised to be with me for better or for worse, until death do us part. I'm holding you to those promises. And if you won't hold me to mine, well, I'll hold myself to them."

She bit down on a smile that would have turned into a joyous laugh. "What about our divorce?"

He groaned. "Didn't you listen to a word I said when you were pretending to sleep on the plane? There's not going to be a divorce. If you haven't figured out by now that I love you so much I don't have a life without you, that you *are* my life…"

Now she couldn't help grinning, because that was exactly what she'd figured out. "Okay, so I'm your life," she said. She went up on tiptoe and kissed him. "But am I on your team?"

"There's no team without you," he said. "Not for me. I wish that wasn't true. Life was a hell of a lot easier when I called all the shots and if anyone didn't agree with me I could steamroller over them."

She laughed at the image, at its painful honesty.

"But it seems—" a gusty sigh "—I no longer know everything. I need someone to talk to, to share my problems with, to tell me when I'm getting out of line with Dad, to pull my bratty brothers apart…" His eyes brimmed with tenderness. The tenderness Brianna thought she'd seen in Las Vegas, but this was deeper, truer, forever. "I need a teammate," he said. "A wife."

"And a sponsor." She was teasing, but his face darkened.

"Hang the sponsorship," he said roughly. "Dammit, Brianna, if that's going to come between us, I don't want it. I don't know who you've chosen, but if it's Matheson, I want you to un-choose us. Who knows, with your father gone, the whole thing may not happen anyway."

"But if Getaway doesn't sponsor Zack…"

"Then we'll make it happen some other way," Chad said impatiently. "We'll fund him out of MPI's pockets for a couple of months, and if he's not showing good-enough results to sign a sponsor by then, he can pull out. He won't like it, and Dad certainly won't like putting his own money in, but they'll have to live with it. I'm not going to risk our marriage."

She was laughing now in sheer delight.

"Hey," he protested. "This *thing* you have of laughing whenever I bare my heart is a little disconcerting."

"I never said baring your heart had to be painful," she said. "We do get to have fun on our team."

Suddenly he didn't look so certain. "What I'm not sure of is how you feel," he said. "I know I don't deserve to have you love me back after I've been such a jerk."

"You have been a jerk," she said severely.

But not severely enough. His lips twitched. "Brianna, darling, do you think you might find it in you to love me back?"

"I don't think I ever stopped." She didn't get to say more, for Chad caught her in a kiss that robbed her of speech, of air, of pain. And filled her with hope.

"Tell me," he demanded, when they surfaced. "Tell me you love me."

Her voice wobbled. "Chad Matheson, I love you. I love you more than I did the day I married you, which wasn't nearly enough. Now, I love you enough to work through every problem we have. Your dad says it takes twenty years to know you, but I'm giving it the rest of my life. I'm never going to quit."

She was laughing and crying and she'd have sworn he was doing the same. Their lips melded.

Chad's cell phone rang. He ignored it in favor of discovering the tender region behind her ear. It rang again, but the ridge of her collarbone proved far more interesting.

Just as they sank down onto the hard plastic seating, his phone beeped to say a text message had arrived.

Chad hauled the phone from his pocket, clearly intending to hurl it onto the race track.

Then his gaze was arrested by the message. His jaw dropped.

"What is it?" Brianna demanded. Knowing that even if it was bad news, he would share it with her.

His mouth worked. "It's Zack."

"Is he hurt?" She tightened her hold on him, her heart plummeting.

Chad's face broke into a grin. "He won Daytona!"

Brianna whooped along with him, gave him a smacking kiss for good measure.

"You realize there's no way Getaway will let you turn down the sponsorship now," she teased. "They'll throw millions of dollars at you whether you want them or not."

He kissed the tip of her nose. "Ah, well, if that's the way it is…"

"I love you," she said, and kissed him again.

Chad said, "Remember how I told you there's a moment in a race that your gut tells you is the moment where you'll win or lose?"

"Uh-huh. You said great race car drivers throw everything into that moment, no hesitation, no matter how crazy it seems." Zack must have done that today.

"That's where you and I are now," Chad said. "At that moment where we decide to win or to lose in this marriage. Brianna, sweetheart, we knew each other three days before our wedding, then we split up for two years—that's about as crazy as a marriage gets. I promise, from this moment, no hesitation, I'm all-in, for always."

She lay back on the plastic seats, tugged him down to her. "For always," she said. "Winner takes all."

* * * * *

*For more thrill-a-minute romances set against
the exciting backdrop of the NASCAR world, don't miss*

FROM THE OUTSIDE *by Helen Brenna
Available now!*

For a sneak peek, just turn the page!

OH. MY. GOD.

Mallory Dalton concentrated on making herself breathe. *In. Out. In. Out.* Roberto Castillo, *the* Roberto Castillo, was standing right in front of her. Her parents, die-hard NASCAR fans, weren't going to believe this.

And his agent was saying something, to her.

"We have a proposition we think you'll be interested in." The older woman, Patricia, went on to describe what sounded like no more than a publicity stunt, flawed in its fundamental premise that Roberto, a man considered one of the most eligible bachelors in the world, might possibly be interested in *her*.

"You're suggesting that *Roberto* wants to be seen dating *me*?" In truth, he wasn't her type any more than she presumed she was his. But there was another problem with their plan. "Why should anyone give a hoot what I do?"

"Are you kidding?" Patricia put out her hands and the large bangles at her wrist clattered. "You're America's Sweetheart."

Sweetheart. Right. Mallory barely kept herself from snorting out loud. But if she wasn't an amalgamation of all the virtuous characters she'd played through the years, then who was she, exactly?

That was the question she'd been burning to answer most of her life, and that's what had drawn her to acting. It should have given her the opportunity to try on different hats and faces, be different people. Someday, maybe, she'd get back to the business of finally figuring out who she was.

"Maybe we should let you two talk." Patricia dragged Mallory's agent several feet away.

Suddenly Mallory found herself alone with a man who'd been consistently voted within the top ten of the sexiest men alive.

The seconds ticked by without either of them saying anything. Finally Mallory gathered her nerve. "I'm not interested." She couldn't believe it, but she actually turned her back on him. *The* Roberto Castillo.

What had gotten into her?

"Hey, wait a minute," Roberto whispered close behind her. "Mallory."

Oh...my...God. His accent, his breathy *h*'s, the way his words flowed into one another like silk against suede, the way he said her name, softly rolling the *r,* had her almost pooling onto the floor in what would no doubt be a mound of loose joints.

"Forget our agents. You and I...should talk."

She turned back around. "I'm listening."

"I have been in the public eye a very long while." His smile was a little lopsided. "There is nothing the press likes better than a good girl putting a bad boy on the straight and narrow. That story is as old as time."

Her thoughts bounced back and forth, weighing the pros and cons. "I'm sorry, but you and I... I...don't do bad boys."

"Are you sure?" He grinned his trademark smile, complete with a dimple on his left cheek.

She swallowed.

Mentally stepping back and away, Mallory imagined how this deal might play out with a little tweaking. If she played this right, Roberto Castillo could very well help her prove to the world that she wasn't a sweet little girl any longer.

REQUEST YOUR FREE BOOKS!
2 FREE NOVELS PLUS 2 FREE GIFTS!

SPECIAL EDITION®
Life, Love and Family!

YES! Please send me 2 FREE Silhouette Special Edition® novels and my 2 FREE gifts (gifts are worth about $10). After receiving them, if I don't wish to receive any more books, I can return the shipping statement marked "cancel." If I don't cancel, I will receive 6 brand-new novels every month and be billed just $4.24 per book in the U.S. or $4.99 per book in Canada. That's a savings of at least 15% off the cover price! It's quite a bargain! Shipping and handling is just 25¢ per book*. I understand that accepting the 2 free books and gifts places me under no obligation to buy anything. I can always return a shipment and cancel at any time. Even if I never buy another book from Silhouette, the two free books and gifts are mine to keep forever.

235 SDN EEYU   335 SDN EEY6

Name	(PLEASE PRINT)

Address		Apt. #

City	State/Prov.	Zip/Postal Code

Signature (if under 18, a parent or guardian must sign)

Mail to the **Silhouette Reader Service:**
IN U.S.A.: P.O. Box 1867, Buffalo, NY 14240-1867
IN CANADA: P.O. Box 609, Fort Erie, Ontario L2A 5X3

Not valid to current subscribers of Silhouette Special Edition books.

Want to try two free books from another line?
Call 1-800-873-8635 or visit www.morefreebooks.com.

* Terms and prices subject to change without notice. Prices do not include applicable taxes. Sales tax applicable in N.Y. Canadian residents will be charged applicable provincial taxes and GST. Offer not valid in Quebec. This offer is limited to one order per household. All orders subject to approval. Credit or debit balances in a customer's account(s) may be offset by any other outstanding balance owed by or to the customer. Please allow 4 to 6 weeks for delivery. Offer available while quantities last.

Your Privacy: Silhouette is committed to protecting your privacy. Our Privacy Policy is available online at www.eHarlequin.com or upon request from the Reader Service. From time to time we make our lists of customers available to reputable third parties who may have a product or service of interest to you. If you would prefer we not share your name and address, please check here. ☐

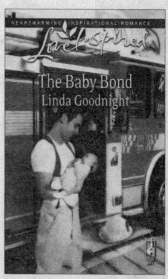